M. W Macdowall, August Becker

Tempted of the Devil Passages in the Life of a Kabbalist

A Story Retold From the German of August Becker by M.W. Macdowall

M. W Macdowall, August Becker

Tempted of the Devil Passages in the Life of a Kabbalist
A Story Retold From the German of August Becker by M.W. Macdowall

ISBN/EAN: 9783337021207

Printed in Europe, USA, Canada, Australia, Japan

Cover: Foto ©Andreas Hilbeck / pixelio.de

More available books at **www.hansebooks.com**

TEMPTED OF THE DEVIL

Passages in the Life of a Kabbalist

A STORY RETOLD FROM THE GERMAN

OF

AUGUST BECKER

BY

M. W. MACDOWALL

TRANSLATOR OF FRITZ REUTER'S 'AN OLD STORY OF MY FARMING DAYS,
AND K. E. FRANZOS' 'JEWS OF BARNOW'

ALEXANDER GARDNER

Publisher to Her Majesty the Queen

PAISLEY; AND PATERNOSTER ROW, LONDON

1888

CONTENTS.

———

PREFACE.

I N these days when mystical theosophy so much prevails amongst a certain set of people—whether under the name of Esoteric Buddhism or any other—it is interesting to consider what was the tendency of the same sort of teaching at the end of last century. The minds of men were then more or less divided between transcendentalism and the doctrines of Voltaire. Magicians and astrologers astonished the multitude with their marvellous deeds, and some of them were even recognised as adepts by several of the greatest *savants* of the time.

The two forms of theosophy which then excited the most attention, and attracted the largest number of earnest students, were Zoroastrianism, and the occult teaching of the Jews as contained in the Kabbalah or Qabalah.

It is with this latter that we are now concerned, for in " Des Rabbi Vermächtnis"—the novel from which our story of "Tempted of the Devil" is taken—Dr. Becker describes the effect which the study of the *Practical* Kabbalah had on the lives and characters of the initiated, and those who came in contact with them.

The Kabbalah has not only exercised a marvellous influence on Jewish mysticism, of which it is also an outcome ; but has likewise been regarded as a study of immense interest by some of the most profound scholars of the 16th and 17th centuries.

According to tradition, the doctrines of the Kabbalah were taught by God Himself to certain of the angels, and were by them communicated to Adam after his expulsion from the garden of Eden. By Abraham they were partially introduced into Egypt, and there it was that Moses was first initiated in their mysteries, which he afterwards taught the seventy Elders. And thus, from generation to generation, the Kabbalistic doctrines were handed down in unbroken succession until the days of Rabbi Simeon ben Jochai, who, as we learn from the Talmud, lived at the time of the Destruction of the Second Temple. Having fallen under the ban of Titus, this Rabbi was forced to hide away in a cave for twelve or thirteen years, lest he should fall into the hands of the Romans and be put to death. The Kabbalah had never hitherto been written down ; but had—as the name Kabbalah, *Received*, signifies—been handed on from age to age by oral teaching alone.

Kabbalistic tradition informs us that during his confinement in the cave Rabbi Simeon devoted himself to meditating on the 'Sublime Kabbalah,' and teaching its doctrines to his son, and to those of his disciples who continued to visit him secretly for instruction. After his death, the Book Sohar —*i.e.*, Splendour—was compiled by his son and Rabbi Abba, his secretary, as an epitome of his teaching. This book may be called the heart, or kernel of Kabbalism.*

The cardinal doctrines of the Kabbalah are these :

The Supreme Being, His nature and attributes.
The Cosmogony.
The creation of angels and men.
The nature of angels, demons, and elementals.
The import of the Revealed Law.
The transcendental symbolism of numbers.
The peculiar mysteries contained in the Hebrew
    letters.
The equilibrium of contraries.†

The Kabbalah may be divided into four heads, viz : 1. The Literal Kabbalah. 2. The Unwritten Kabbalah. 3. The Dogmatic Kabbalah. 4. The Practical Kabbalah.

---

* See Beer's 'Geschichte der jüdischen Secten,' and Dr. Ginsburg's 'Kabbalah.'

† See 'The Kabbalah Unveiled,' p. 15, translated by S. L. MacGregor Mathers.

The Literal Kabbalah falls into three parts : The Gematria, Notarikon, and Temurah.

The Gematria contains the mystical teaching of Biblical interpretation by the numerical value of the letters forming the word or sentence under consideration.   For instance, from the words (Gen. xviii., 2) : 'And lo, three men stood by him,' it is deduced that the three angels, Michael, Gabriel, and Raphael, were meant, because the Hebrew letters forming the words : 'And lo, three men,' and those making : 'these are Michael, Gabriel, and Raphael,' have the same numerical value.

It must be remembered that there are no separate figures for numerals in Hebrew or Chaldæ, so that each letter has a fixed value.

The Notarikon has two forms.

1st. It teaches how every letter of a word may also be taken as an initial or abbreviation of another word, thus making new words or sentences.

2nd. In this case, 'the initials or finals, or both, or the medials, of a sentence are taken to form a word or words.'*

Temurah (or Temura) is Permution.   It contains fixed rules by means of which one letter may be substituted for another, and through it we are also taught the hidden meanings that belong to the shape of each letter in the Hebrew alphabet.

The Unwritten Kabbalah is the name given to

---

* See 'The Kabbalah Unveiled,' p. 9.

that Kabbalistic knowledge which is never put upon paper, and the possession of which may not be confessed by the initiated.†

The Dogmatic Kabbalah contains the doctrinal part of this esoteric teaching, and may be divided into four heads, the last of which is known to very few people :

 I. The Book of Creation (or Formation).
 II. The Sohar (or Zohar), with its developments, &c.
 III. The Commentary on the Ten Sephiroth.
 IV. The Purifying Fire.

Mr. MacGregor Mathers says that the Book Jetzira (or Yetzira), which he translates Book of Formation, ‘treats of the Cosmogony as symbolized by the ten numbers, and twenty-two letters of the alphabet, which it calls the thirty-two paths.’ It is regarded by Kabbalists as very ancient, and is ascribed to the Patriarch Abraham. Dr. Ginsburg, however, and many other critics, are of opinion that it really dates from the 9th century of the Christian era, and he says that ‘its fabrication was evidently suggested by the fact that the Talmud mentions some *treatises on the creation.*’ These were, however, magical in character, as we learn from the stories told about them in the Talmud, and were by no means identical with the Book Jetzira. In

course of time they were lost, and it is supposed by
Dr. Ginsburg that the Jetzira was written to take
their place.

* In the Sohar, we read of the Supreme Being,
who is hidden behind the three Kabbalistic veils:
† 1st, Ain = Negativity; 2nd, Ain Soph = the Limitless; and 3rd, Ain Soph Aur = the Limitless Light.
This Being is 'boundless in His nature,' possessing
neither 'will, intention, desire, thought, language,
nor action.' From Him proceed the Sephiroth, or
ten Emanations, which are 'begotten, not made,'
which are at once 'infinite and finite,' and which,
although separate, are yet united in perfect balance
by the Ruach, or Holy Spirit. The doctrine of
Trinity in Unity as shown in the Sephiroth can
only be mentioned here, as any notice of so difficult
a subject would make the introduction too long.
It is through the Sephiroth, which in their united
whole represent the Archetypal Man (the Adam
Kadmon), that the creation gradually evolved, and
it is to them, says Ginsburg, that the 'Anthropo-
morphisms of Scripture and the Haggada refer.'

The Book Sohar is composed of several treatises,
which tradition teaches us were collated from the
words of Rabbi Simeon ben Jochai by his son
Rabbi Eleazar, and his secretary Rabbi Abba; but

---

* 'The Kabbalah Unveiled,' and Dr. Ginsburg's 'Kabbalah.'
† 'THE CLOUD - VEILS OF THE AIN FORMULATING THE
HIDDEN SEPHIROTH, AND CONCENTRATING IN KETHER, THE
FIRST SEPHIRA.'

since then various amplifications and commentaries have been added to it. Many Jewish historians and theologians, on the contrary, hold that it was composed by Moses de Leon, who first introduced, and sold it in Europe, alleging that he had found the MS. in the possession of some Arabian Jews, who venerated it for its occult teaching and antiquity. Those who regard him as its author look upon the Sohar as a pseudograph of the 13th century.

Dr. Ginsburg is of opinion that the distinctive tenets of the Kabbalah are founded on Neo-Platonism, and gives several examples in proof of this assumption. It cannot, however, be denied that the Jews had been possessed of an esoteric Theosophy, that embraced magic and its attendant occultism, long before the Kabbalah was finally written down. This Theosophy probably had its rise in the ancient home of the Jewish race, was strengthened by the Egyptian mysticism learnt during the sojourn of the children of Israel in the Land of Goshen, and was no doubt further developed at the time of the Babylonish Captivity.

Moreover, regarding the connection between Neo-Platonism and the Kabbalah, we learn from Dr. Edersheim* that:

‘If . . . we have noticed a remarkable

---

* ‘The Life and Times of Jesus the Messiah,’ by the Rev. A. Edersheim, D.D.

similarity between Philo and the Rabbis, there is a still more curious analogy between his teaching and that of Jewish Mysticism as ultimately fully developed in the "Kabbalah." The very term *Kabbalah* (from Kabal, to hand down) seems to point out not only its *de*scent by oral tradition, but also its *a*scent to ancient sources.* Its existence is presupposed, and its leading ideas are sketched iu the Mishnah. The Targums bear at least one remarkable trace of it. May it not be that as Philo frequently refers to ancient tradition, so both Eastern and Western Judaism may here have drawn from one and the same source—we will not venture to suggest how high up—while each made use of it as suited their distinctive wants? At any rate, the Kabbalah also, likening Scripture to a person, compares those who study merely the letter to them who attend only to the dress ; those who consider the moral of a fact to those who attend to the body ; while the initiated alone, who regard the hidden meaning, are those who attend to the soul.' Again, the 'Makom' of Philo, like the 'Ain Soph' of the Kabbalah, being unconditioned, can only be comprehended through His manifestations.

As the Kabbalah solved this difficulty by the doctrine of the Sephiroth, or Emanations from the

---

* For further information see Edersheim's ' History of the Jewish Nation.'

Unknowable, so Philo taught that there were 'Potencies' and 'Words' which proceeded from God. '"Potencies," we imagine, when viewed Godwards ; "Words," as viewed creationwards. They were not emanations, but resembled Plato's 'archetypal ideas,' on the model of which all that exists was formed."*

Other likenesses might be pointed out, but to do so would be to enter too much into detail.

Whether Neo-Platonism learnt from the Kabbalah, or the Kabbalah from it, is a question for scholars to decide.

As time went on, Kabbalistic students began to devote themselves to the study of the Sohar to the exclusion of the other books of the Kabbalah, and therefore became known by the distinctive title of Soharites.

The Practical Kabbalah, or the wonder-working Kabbalah, the defence of which was so zealously taken up by Kircher, a learned Jesuit, is the power of divination gained by transposing the letters that spell the sundry Divine Names, and making a computation according to the numerical value of each by certain fixed rules only known to the initiated.   It is a further occult development of the science of numbers, and is used for magical, instead of metaphysical enquiry, to the intense horror of pious Kabbalists.   It is not the *use*, but the *misuse*

---

* See Edersheim's ' Life and Times of Jesus the Messiah.'

of their system. Last century, however, it gained a great influence over the imagination of many learned men, whether Jewish or Christian, and led to very strange, and often melancholy results. Beer, in his 'History of Jewish Sects,' gives many extraordinary instances of the aberations of the so-called adepts of the Practical Kabbalah, some of which are referred to in 'The Mystic Numbers.'

M. W. MACDOWALL.

TEMPTED OF THE DEVIL.

CHAPTER I.

An old clergyman's tale.—*Bracebridge Hall.*

Gewichtiger, mein Sohn, als du es meinst
Ist disser dünne Flor—für deine Hand
Zvar leicht, doch zentnerschwer für dein gewissen.
            —*Schiller.*

IT is for your sake, my son, that I am about to
relate the story of my past life, and especially
of certain incidents that are burnt into my memory
with letters of fire.

I begin my self-appointed task in fear and
trembling.

My heart is full of a holy awe when I consider
the unfathomable nature of God, and the inscrutable
mysteries that surround Him. I reverence His
infinite wisdom in setting a limit beyond which the
human intellect may not soar, and His loving-
kindness in hiding a knowledge of the future from
us, seeing that we are too weak to bear the fulness
of such light. Yet in our ignorant folly we are

often tempted to knock at the door whose opening would bring swift destruction upon us, and grow childishly angry with our Heavenly Father for refusing to grant the desire of our silly hearts. We have all much need to pray for enlightenment, that we may be enabled to recognise the wisdom and mercy of God's dealing with us, in hiding from us those things we ought not to know, and in keeping us from playing with His Light, which in our weak hands would become a consuming fire, the world's bane.

Alas! it is only too easy to stretch out a rash, sacrilegious hand to grasp the veil behind which the Divine is hidden from our eyes. And to do so is not impossible. But no mortal can endure to look upon the brightness of the glory of God; such power was withheld even from the disciple at Sais. Hence it is that a noble-minded friend of our family, wise David Benasse, always says : 'To be arrogant is to tempt God—knowledge comes last of all—to see God is to die!' And for this same reason, the occult teaching, that has come down to us from antiquity, warns us in no ambiguous terms to beware lest we misuse the power it places in our hands. And yet, one terrible night, I, sinful man that I am, dared to commit this sacrilege. I was tempted to use the holy and awful legacy entrusted to me by the old Rabbi for a wicked and foolhardy purpose. I desired to look behind the veil.

How great is the long-suffering of God! He had mercy upon me, and did not slay me in my madness; but preserved me then and afterwards, giving me a life of much quiet happiness.

I was not unlike you as a young man, my son; for I was eager, enthusiastic, and impatient in the pursuit of knowledge. Nothing was more hateful to me than intellectual laziness, and want of sympathy with, or interest in, whatever raises men above the comfortable and commonplace level of ordinary existence.

My father was a clergyman in Thuringia, and was rather better off than many others of his cloth. When I left school he determined to send me to the university of Halle to study divinity, that I might afterwards take Holy Orders. He spared no expense on my education, for his ambition, the dearest wish of his heart, was to make me a trained theologian, strong in the triple armour of doctrinal theology, polemics, and homiletics. He little regarded any other sort of knowledge, but consented to my attending the *physica sacra* lectures as the utmost latitude I could possibly desire. Such were the views held by orthodox people when he was young, and they still clung to them by choice, though not of necessity.

But the dawn of a new day had already begun to glimmer in the gloomy, narrow, pious old town on the Saale, in the stronghold of Lutheranism.

Semler, the father of modern theology, had taken

up his residence there several years before the time
of which I write, and, after having himself escaped
from the bonds of Pietism, had lighted the Rationalistic torch in the very midst of the orthodox camp.
A new generation had grown up since his coming,
who had taken firm foothold on the ground, which,
ever since the days of Spener and Franke, had
been left in the undisputed possession of the
'Stillen im Lande.' Another spirit had been
awakened in men's minds, one directly opposed
to that which ruled in Franke's celebrated institu-
tion, the Halle Orphanage—a place built and
endowed to provide for the due training of divinity
students who were too poor to pay for their own
education.

I had been very carefully brought up in a pious
household ; but when I went to the University my
father was so kind as to let me lead an independent
life, free from outward control. I took lodgings in
the house of a good, religious couple, stocking-
weavers by trade. They were kindly souls ; but I
was a great puzzle to them. They could not
understand how, being a divinity student, I was
able to live without pecuniary assistance from
Franke's Orphanage.

One of the most curious chapters in the world's
history is that containing the simple annals of
German poverty, and the most touching examples
of it are to be found in Saxony and Thuringia. It
was always so in those parts. The road to learning

was long and weary to many a poor student. The young patrician and the sons of well-to-do parents led a merry or studious life at the University, untroubled by sordid cares; while many of the other undergraduates glided through the streets, their faces pale and haggard, and bearing in their whole appearance the unmistakable stamp of indigence. Those of them who came from the Orphanage often walked down to the University in long lines, totally unobservant of what was going on around them, wrapped in their own thoughts, and wearing an expression of exaggerated humility, or of religious exaltation on their worn faces. It is a sad thing to be a poor dependant; but to have to raise your eyes to heaven for the sake of gaining your daily bread, to be obliged to fold your hands and play the hypocrite before God, that you may eat and be satisfied, is the saddest thing I know. My disposition was too cheerful and frank to allow me to bear patiently with a religiosity of this sort. I looked upon it as canting humbug, and saw no excuse for the poor fellows in their absolute penury, for many of the other students were apparently as needy as they, and yet did not become either sycophants or hypocrites.

Amongst the ascetic pariahs of the place, my attention was especially drawn to a red-haired youth, whose freckled countenance was peculiar enough to have attracted the notice of a stranger, even if his look of exaggerated humility had failed to do so, surrounded as he was by so many others of the same type. Calm astuteness and calculating sagacity were to be seen in the lines about his mouth, while his eyes betrayed a mixture of cunning and watchful ferocity that ill-accorded with the dove-like gentleness and humility which he strove to impress upon the world as his most prominent characteristics. He was like nothing so much as a wolf in sheep's clothing. So *I* thought at least. But my landlord, the stocking-weaver, informed me that Ephraim Lebrecht was a true Christian, and that he was held in great reverence at all the prayer-meetings in the town, because of his eloquence and the consistency of his walk and conversation. To which I answered that no one had a greater respect for really good people than I, but that such persons seldom made so much ado about religious phrases as Lebrecht and his fellows, who by their spiritual pride often caused the enemy to blaspheme. My landlord looked at me with silent compassion, and went away.

Two brothers had taken rooms in Märker Street. They were twins, and came of a noble family in the North Country. As my lodgings were not far from theirs, I often used to see them ride past, their caps displaying the distinguishing colours of the corps to which they belonged. They were very wild, like most of the other students of their rank, especially those who came from the Baltic Provinces, and were continually at war with the

Council, or the Proctors. This was particularly the case with Count Leo, who was always engaged in some piece of wild mischief or adventure, and who thereby gained great *kudos* from his companions. Otherwise he was not so great a favourite as his brother Hermann, for he was not so frank, kind-hearted, and chivalrous as the latter, whose only real fault was a very quick temper.

One day I was much astonished by seeing Ephraim Lebrecht's red head at the window of the brothers' sitting room. What they could possibly have in common with sanctimonious Ephraim was more than I could imagine. And yet, strange as it seemed, the matter was perfectly simple of explanation.

The relatives of the two young scapegraces had heard somehow or other of the manner in which they had begun their academical career, so they sent the authorities full power to place the lads under the charge of some trustworthy mentor, and Ephraim Lebrecht was the person chosen to act in that capacity.

I often saw him in the window after that first day, and it seemed to me that his office suited him, that he was growing fatter and more consequential looking. I was undoubtedly interested in the man; probably because of the disagreeable impression he made upon me.

I had not been long at Halle, however, and was too conscious of my inexperience to have much

confidence in my own powers of observation or
instinct with regard to character. My landlord
and his family were of one mind in praising
Ephraim for his consistent life and real goodness,
so that at last I began to blame myself for my pre-
judice and injustice, and to take myself to task for
disliking any man because of the colour of his hair,
and of something I had perhaps misread in his
expression. Then came stories of the extraordinary
influence he exercised over his pupils. And in
truth, both young men seemed to have sobered
down in the most marvellous way, and to have
given up the wild and reckless behaviour that had
before characterised them. Count Hermann did
not therefore abandon his old friends; but Count
Leo, the younger of the brothers, who had formerly
been the ringleader in all their pranks, was changed
in every respect. He began to frequent prayer
meetings in company with his tutor, and also to
attend any of the University lectures that had the
slightest bearing on religious subjects.

As was only natural, every one in Halle was
filled with astonishment at the sudden conversion
of such an unmitigated scapegrace. It was more
than a nine days' wonder.

Count Hermann's actions were also a subject of
interest to the gossips of the place. People noticed
that he had grown much less wild than in the old
days when Leo had been his constant companion
and instigator in mischief, for he now either re-

mained quietly at home, or else rode out to call at a certain country-house in the neighbourhood of the town, where a poor but beautiful girl of his own rank was living with her parents.

Soon afterwards another rumour got abroad to the effect that the two brothers, formerly so inseparable, were no longer on good terms. One day, loud and angry voices were heard in their rooms, and a few minutes later the neighbours saw Ephraim Lebrecht's red head come crashing through the window, like a glowing shell from a mortar. It stuck fast in the window-frame, wedged in by the broken glass ; but was at last drawn back by a pair of strong arms.

The story was soon in every mouth. Some people were of opinion that Dr. Faustus, instigated by the Prince of Darkness, had suddenly arrived on the scene, had seized Ephraim by the collar, and had tried to fling him out into the street ; but that the young man's goodness had given him such supernatural strength that his assailant had been obliged to beat a hasty retreat. The rest of the world, however, maintained that Count Hermann had himself been the aggressor. I was afterwards told that when the latter was questioned by some of his comrades as to the truth of the story, he had looked so stern and unapproachable that no one had ventured to pursue the subject.

This event took place shortly before the end of the term, when the Seerieds and their tutor left

Halle for the North, and I saw no more of any of them for a long time ; one, I never met again.

CHAPTER II.

' I do not deny that most [of the Alchemists] were imposters;
but we should have to cast aside all belief in historical evidences
were we to deny that there have been men at various times who
possessed the secret of making gold.'

—*Justi's Chemistry.*

THE times of which I write were strange and
exciting. The last quarter of the eighteenth
century had begun. All things were in a state of
transition, and great strides were being made in
every sphere of intellectual activity. Klopstock's
poems had an immense influence on everyone; his
odes set the spirits of men on fire. Many eager
students of nature threw themselves heart and soul
into the search after the great secret, the corner-
stone of knowledge, the 'Philosopher's Stone.'
Light, was the watch-word that resounded on
every side, and yet men wandered dim-eyed
through the mist, thinking they saw, and blessed
in that belief. They steeped themselves in Ossian,
whose writings had come to them from the other
side of the North Sea. Him, they specially wor-
shipped.

In spite of all this, Freethinking had never been
possessed of sharper lances, nor had better known

how to use them.   It was an age of contrasts.
While soft-heartedness and sensibility, qualities
inherited from the Pietism of their immediate predecessors, held sway over the educated classes
throughout the land, and found practical expression in the 'Werther' published by young
Goethe, Lessing had given a sharp point to his
critical pen, had called attention to the works of
Shakespeare, and had written 'Emilia Galotti.'
Then 'Goetz von Berlichingen' appeared upon the
stage with the clang and clash of armour, and
stirred the minds of the nation.   The 'storm and
stress' period was rapidly approaching, and Bur-
ger's 'Leonore' was taking her ghostly ride over
the length and breadth of Germany.   Every one,
whether in town or country, wept over the sorrows
of Werther.   Country squires and nobles sympa-
thised with Goetz.   Clergymen's daughters in rural
districts read and re-read Hölty's tender spring
songs, wandered with the creatures of his imagination in the moonlight to where the weeping willows
grew, and shivered with terror at the thought of
ghostly church-yards, and the fate of Bürger's
Lenore.   The greater part of Saxony regarded the
'magician' Schröpfer with superstitious awe—he
it was who afterwards shot himself at Rosenthal,
near Leipzig, after a spiritual séance of great
notoriety.   Strange rumours were everywhere
afloat concerning mysterious brotherhoods, the
revival of the esoteric teaching of the Rosicrucians,

and the doings of certain Illuminati. And all this in the days when Lessing was writing against the errors of superstition!

We, in Halle, were, so to speak, at the central point of the movement, and, as may readily be supposed, we were not, and could not remain, uninfluenced by the general excitement of public opinion.

Professor Semler was then at the height of his fame, and was undoubtedly the greatest man at the University. It was not without a long and bitter struggle against adverse fortune that he had risen to such a position, for he had first come to Halle as a poor student maintained by the help given him at Franke's Orphanage. Pietism had therefore of necessity wrapped him for years in its folds. But at length he set himself free. As a teacher, he followed in the footsteps of his former benefactor, Baumgarten, lectured on Church History, dogmatic Theology, and Hermeneutics. In addition to his professorship, he was afterwards appointed Director of the Theological Schools. Hundreds crowded to hear him—his lively, pleasant lectures, together with the novelty and boldness of his views, which were utterly opposed to sentimental religion and cant of every sort, were very attractive to us young men. In addition to this, our admiration was awakened by his spotless character, and by the unfeigned piety that was the motive power of his life. We also loved him for

his personal amiability.   Rationalism found in him
one of its staunchest supporters.   Yet he was not
without a strong natural bent towards mysticism,
and a love of dabbling with the inexplicable was
such a marked feature in the man as to have
roused a feeling of astonishment, had he not been
so entirely a child of his times as to be one of its
fittest representatives.   But as years went on, the
century changed faster than he, so that this apparent contradiction in his character afterwards
brought him into conflict with it, and embittered
his latter days.

His was no unusual case.   Other men, who in
their youth had fought in the forefront of the
battle of enlightenment, fell in their old age into a
superstitious faith in magic and alchemy, while
others, again, who for long years had devoted
themselves to the study of the occult sciences, and
had wandered far into the realm of mystical super-
naturalism, ended by falling into a state of gross
unbelief.

Professor Semler was kind enough to take a
fancy to me, and I was one of the highly favoured
few whom he admitted freely to his house.   The
encouragement we received on such occasions to
talk to him as openly as to one of ourselves, had
an elevating influence upon us young people.   He
had even then begun to devote many of his leisure
hours to chemical investigations.   I was sometimes permitted to accompany him on his expedi-

tions in search of minerals across the Giebichstein to the Petersberg, or up the river through the beautiful valley of the Saale. Words of strange import would drop from his lips at such times, betraying his intense interest in the mysteries of nature, an interest which was much increased by his large acquaintance with the writings of the Middle Ages. Such studies had always had a great charm for me, and the glamour they cast over me only became the more potent when I heard them expatiated on by the great *savant* at my side. Another circumstance that increased the pleasure of those walks was that we often met a man who was held in high esteem as a writer on scientific subjects, and as a teacher at the University. This was Dr. von Leysser, Director of mines and saline works in the district of the Saale, and President of the Natural Science Association at Halle. He was equally famous as a chemist and mineralogist, and his 'Flora Hallensis' was so good as to win great praise from Linnæus. Moreover, he was as kind as he was learned, and I soon began to seek his company by myself.

It was about this time that an anonymous publication appeared in Halle, entitled 'Beiträge zur Beförderung der Naturkunde.' I read it eagerly in my leisure hours, and was encouraged to do so by Professor Semler's approbation. One statement made by the author astonished me not a little. It was to the effect that the alchemistic transmutions,

denied by all the younger chemists of the day,
were not only possible, but were indisputably
proved by certain incidents which had taken place
at Halle in 1750 at the Apothecary's Hall attached to the Orphanage.

I will now try to relate the story as shortly as
possible.

One of the assistants in the shop referred to,
who was much interested in reading everything he
could lay hands upon that had any connection
with chemistry, noticed that a stranger began to
haunt the shop when he was alone in charge, and
wondered why he did so. The man would buy
this or that as a sort of excuse for coming ; but he
seemed to go there chiefly that he might enjoy the
conversation of the young chemist, for on going
out into the street he would, as often as not, throw
away the things he had bought, and the packet
would be brought back to the shop by one of the
boys belonging to the Orphanage. One Sunday,
when all was quiet without and within, and the
chemist's assistant was seated alone in his usual
place behind the counter, reading intently, the
door opened, and the stranger came in unnoticed.
He asked the young man what book it was that
had so rivetted his attention. It was a treatise
upon Alchemy, was the reply, but was so ob-
scurely written in some places as to be incomprehensible, and should therefore never have been
published. The stranger said he thought such

books often contained more truth than people were willing to allow, and that some of the propositions put forth in them were unanswerable. He then went away, inviting the young apothecary to visit him in order that they might have some further talk together. The latter did as he was requested, and went to call on the stranger at his lodgings in Claus Street. He found him in his study surrounded by numerous phials and matrasses, many of which contained a blood-red fluid. An ivory box was lying on one of the tables. The young man tried to lift it, and was so much astonished at its weight that he uttered an exclamation of surprise. Upon which his host opened the box, and with a golden spoon took out a small quantity of the grey powder with which it was filled, offered it to the youth, and desired him to try it in the apparatus for refining metals in the laboratory at the Orphanage. On being told that the quantity of powder he had given was much too small to admit of the success of any such experiment, the stranger became angry, and declared that he was giving far more than was necessary. He then shook the greater part back into the box, leaving only a few grains in the spoon. These he carefully removed with cotton wool, wrapped in a bit of paper, and handed to his guest, desiring him to throw it on molten silver. The young man went home thinking deeply of all that he had heard and seen. Late that night he lighted the furnace,

smelted the silver, threw in the powder, and
watched for what should happen next, with a smile
of incredulity. The metal foamed and seethed,
nearly boiling over the edge of the crucible, blood-
red bubbles forming on the surface. The very
flames that surrounded the vessel took the colours
of the rainbow. A quarter of an hour later the
foam cleared away, the metal presented a bright
surface like a mirror, and when it was poured out,
it showed yellow in the light of the lamp. Early
next morning the young chemist returned to the
laboratory to inspect the result of his last night's
work, and there he found—a lump of pure gold,
somewhat heavier in weight than the silver he had
smelted, and strewed, as it were, with tiny crimson
grains. Unable to trust the evidence of his own
eyes, he took his treasure to a goldsmith in Claus
Street, who was reckoned the best craftsman of his
guild in the town. The latter tested the quality of
the metal, and pronounced it to be the purest gold
he had ever seen. He gave the young man thirty-
six rix-dollars for the lump, and begged him to
come back again soon.

I felt strangely excited by reading this story in
a grave scientific document. I questioned Professor
Semler as to whether he thought it could possibly
be true, and he answered that he had no hesitation
in believing it, so many other cases of the kind had
undoubtedly taken place. When I asked who
was supposed to be the unknown author of the

'Beiträge,' I learnt to my astonishment that it was no other than the famous Dr. von Leysser—the great authority on all subjects connected with mineralogy. Semler even gave me to understand that his friend could tell me a great deal more about it, if he chose to do so.

I hastened to call on the worthy Doctor, whose acquaintance, as I have already said, I had made some time before. I succeeded in inducing him to confess the fact of his authorship. When I afterwards ventured to express my doubts as to the truth of the alchemistic story, he said very gravely:

'Do you think that I should ever publish anything as a fact, for the truth of which I have insufficient proof?'

'From what source did you obtain the story, sir?' I enquired.

'From the best possible—the man to whom it all happened. I can trust him as myself, and he has told me the story a hundred times. I speak of my father-in-law, Herr Reussing, who is now apothecary at Lobegrün.'

I was rendered speechless by this information, for old Reussing was well known to be a quiet, honest, and most respectable person.

Herr von Leysser now proceeded to give me some further particulars regarding the affair. He told me the name of the jeweller who had tested the gold; but when I asked if nothing more had been heard of the stranger, he said that no one

knew anything for certain. As soon as Reussing
had convinced himself that the metal he had taken
out of the crucible was really gold, he had hastened
to the stranger's lodging to tell him what had happened. But the man had disappeared. His rooms
were empty. Broken phials were scattered about
the floor, and a little heap of money was lying on
a table; exactly enough to pay his host's reckoning.

I asked whether no one had any suspicion as to
who the stranger could have been. Herr von
Leysser answered that the kind of tincture Reussing had seen in his bottles led to the belief that
he was the Adept Sehfeld, who, in 1745, had for
some time taken up his abode at Rodaun, near
Vienna, in the house of one Friedrich, superin-
tendent of the baths. While there, he had
employed himself in making gold, until at last
public attention was drawn to his mode of life.
Maria Theresa had him arrested and thrown into
prison, where he met with much harsh treatment;
but nothing would induce him to tell his secret,
which he said he would rather die than disclose.
After a time he had been removed to Temesvar.
The Emperor Francis, however, who took a great
interest in alchemy, had managed to have him
released from jail; but had arranged that all his
actions should be watched by two faithful
Lorrainers, and reported to him. This, as it
turned out, was a useless precaution, for Sehfeld
had soon managed to elude the vigilance of the

honest soldiers, and make his escape. Every attempt to find him had proved abortive.

Herr von Leysser then went on to give me many interesting details which I need not repeat here, as they have nothing to do with my story. I shall, therefore, only tell you that Sehfeld had never shown himself openly since his flight from Austria, and that vague traces of his existence were alone to be found here and there, such as his mysterious appearance at Halle. For, as Herr von Leysser said, alchemy brought but little good fortune to its disciples. Kings and Princes, one and all endeavoured to capture these makers of gold, and confine them in cages for their own behoof. Setonius, Wagnereck, and many others had died of torture and imprisonment, and only those who were wise enough to shun publicity, and clever enough to evade it by hiding themselves away like Philalethes* and Laskaris, escaped the snares that were set for them. It might, he said, be taken as proved that these men were really adepts, although it could not be denied that alchemy was a science whose name was often misused by adventurers, and taken as a cloak under which to conceal their charlatanry, and deceive the multitude. He did not, for instance, recognise Hofrath Beireis of Helmstedt

---

* Thomas Vaughan.—*M. W. M.*

as an Adept, although he was generally regarded as such.

If I have dwelt longer on this subject than seems necessary, it is because it furnishes the best explanation of the mode of thought that prevailed at Halle during my university career, and shows what influences surrounded me, and contributed to the development of my intellect and character.

The information given me by so famous a scientist as Herr von Leysser could not fail to make a profound impression upon me. His words had borne the stamp of truth. 'I know perfectly well,' he had said in conclusion, 'that the facts I have stated will be vehemently questioned ; but I will never justify myself by a single word.' And it was so. Fiery as were the attacks made against the statement contained in his book, he maintained an obstinate silence as long as he lived.

I often used to go and see Professor Semler in the evening when he had taken off his company coat, and had shaken his wig free of the professorial dust that clung to it on public occasions. Clad in a loose dressing-gown he would then give himself up to the chemical studies and experiments which were the only recreation he cared for. Little did he guess what bitter grief they would one day cause him, a grief that should sap the well-springs of his life, and bring him to the grave. When I asked him whether he held the transmu-

tation of metals to be possible, he assured me
he had no doubt that it was. Again, when I
asked him whether he believed that there really
were people who possessed the secret, he put on a
significant mien, and said that the Rosicrucians,
who were once more becoming objects of public
interest, were generally supposed to be in
possession of it; but with what truth he did not
know with any certainty. Still, it was an
undeniable fact that some persons did exist who
knew how to make gold.

In one of our confidential talks he told me that
a Jew in Halle had one day brought a co-
religionist to see him. The stranger wished to
consult him as a scholar about a matter which
puzzled him, to wit, a paper inscribed with
Hebrew characters, two words of which he could
not make out. The man had sighed deeply as he
made this confession, for, he said, his ignorance of
the signification of these words was a great
distress to him, and he was everywhere seeking
some learned man who should be able to tell him
what they meant. He went on to say that the
Jews of Fez, Tunis, and Tripoli—places where he
had once resided—had inherited the secret of
making gold from their forefathers, and that they
were in the habit of turning their knowledge to
account privily, so as not to arouse the coveteous-
ness of the natives. Now, he said, while he was
living in that country he had often helped his

master in his alchemistic labours, and had then carefully followed the directions given in the paper he had brought with him ; but unfortunately he had forgotten the meaning of the two words, without which nothing could be done. Professor Semler told me that he had not only striven his best to find out the meaning of the words, but had even consulted various Orientalists of his acquaintance on the subject—all in vain. When the Jew learnt on his return the non-success of his application, he had loudly bewailed his hard fate, and had said that he must needs go back to Africa to learn the secret. Semler had never heard of him again.

This, and other stories of the kind, made such an impression on my imagination that I one day told the Professor how deeply I regretted not having been educated as a physicist, for as matters now stood I was unable to devote myself to the solution of so weighty a problem ; one that would perforce lead to the discovery of how to prepare the Elixir of Life.

To which the worthy man replied :

'It is very doubtful, my young friend, whether in that case you would have cared to discover the Philosopher's Stone. The physicists and chemists of the present day pursue a very different course. They consider themselves above all such " childish dreams," as they call them. If you, as a theological student were to throw yourself ardently into the

study of Oriental languages, you would, in all like-
lihood, attain your end much sooner.'

' How ?' I asked.

And he answered by enquiring :

' Have you never heard of the esoteric doctrines
of Judaism, of the Kabbalah ?'

' Yes, I have often heard the word mentioned of
late, and always as though it were something
mysterious, and connected with magic arts. I
never thought there could be much sense in it.

' There it is,' Semler went on in his usual impul-
sive fashion. ' There it is ! Let me tell you that
the two incomprehensible words in the paper
brought me by the African Jew were Kabbalistic
signs, a mysterious Chaldæan cypher, the key to
which is unknown to us, as we do not happen to
have any considerable Kabbalist at Halle just now.
A knowledge of the Kabbalistic alphabet would
have been of no small service to us under the circumstances ; but it is questionable whether one of
the initiated would have cared to give himself any
trouble about so small a matter.'

I could not quite make out if the zealous teacher
of Rationalism were in jest or earnest. But nothing
could have been more serious than his manner
when he went on to speak of the strange events
that were then taking place in Eastern Europe. In
Poland, for instance, a great Thaumaturgus had
arisen ; a Rabbi, who by means of the Kabbalah
worked such marvels that our wizard, Schröpfer,

was not worthy to be mentioned in comparison
with him. And besides this man, another, as great
as he, was now on his way to Germany accompanied by a large following. This latter magician
was generally supposed to possess the secret of
making gold, as all travellers who had met with
him were much struck by the enormous wealth he
appeared to have at his disposal. Semler was al-
luding to the great Betsch or Baalschem, who
reformed the Jewish Sect of Chasidim, and to the
Patriarch Frank, who had lately been set free from
the fortress of Czenstochau, and was now making
his way to Germany through Moravia and Bohemia.
The Professor then went on to relate that he had
once seen that Rabbi Eibenschützer, about whose
Kabbalistic amulet a vehement controversy had
raged amongst Jewish *savants* in 175—, and that
he had often heard in his boyhood of Rabbi Löw,
who, by the help of the Kabbalah, was able to foretell future events. He added that there were many
clergymen, even in country parishes, who had devoted much study to this mystical lore, and that
many did so still.

He was only stating a fact in saying this.

When a boy I had often heard covert allusions
made to this or that clergyman, who had been
secretly instructed in the mysteries of the Kabbalah
by some of the wandering Rabbis, who had
travelled through Germany during the first half of
the century, and many floating legends had

gathered round the dwelling-places of all who were suspected of indulging in such studies. But I was very much astonished when the preacher of enlightenment, the upholder of freedom of thought in religion, the learned head of the university of Halle, corroborated these dark rumours. I believed whatever fell from the lips of him who permitted himself to doubt everything of which he thought he had insufficient proof.

It was with strangely mixed feelings that I now remembered having seen an old Bachur* in my boyhood, of whom the neighbours said that he understood the Black Art, that he spent the night in reading books of magic which taught him how to call up spirits at his will, and that he could heal diseases by means of Hebrew words and amulets, discover secrets, and conjure ghosts by the use of magic quadrates; and that by the observance of certain Chaldaic rules as to the magic combination of figures, he could foretell future events with perfect success. He must, therefore, have been a Kabbalist. I had also heard in those times of magic crystals, on which were inscribed strange Hebrew characters and the mystic names of God; but people oftenest spoke of Kabbalistic tables, by means of which it was possible to reckon what should befall anyone in times to come, and they said that if he whose future was thus foretold

---

* Student of the Talmud.—*M. IV. M.*

happened to forget the fate that had been assigned
him, the prophecy came true in every particular;
while for him who set resolutely to work to stem
the tide of adverse fortune victory was certain.

The conversations I had on these subjects with
the scientist, Leysser, and the freethinker, Semler,
had a great influence upon me. With eager
impulsiveness I threw myself on the track of the
mysteries that had been shown me, and diligently
pursued my Hebrew studies. I embarked on
Knorr von Rosenroth's ' Kabbalah Denudata;'*
on the Sohar itself, and was filled with amazement
at the richness of a literature, and the marvels of a
teaching, of whose very existence I had formerly
had so vague and imperfect an idea. I at once
came to the conclusion that I had stumbled on the
original source from which Gnosticism had sprung,
for studying Church History had in some measure
made me acquainted with the tenets of that sect.

But astounding as the teaching of the Kabbalah
appeared to me, I was yet far from penetrating
below its surface : its essence remained a sealed
book. I drifted like a rudderless ship. I wandered
through a dark labyrinth without a torch to guide
me on my way.

I was to find the torch I needed in Ephraim
Lebrecht, the red-haired pietistical student of
divinity, who had left Halle several terms before

---

* Now translated into English by Mr. Macgregor Mather.—*M. W. M.*

with his pupils, the young lords of Seeried. He had now, however, returned to the university to complete his education. On renewing my acquaintance with him, I found him changed in every respect. No one would have taken him to be the same person. Instead of being a narrow-minded sectarian prig, he had become a clear-headed, not to say hard-headed, sort of person, and one of the most interested auditors at Professor Semler's lectures.

Semler had always recognised Ephraim's great abilities, and was very much flattered by his having embraced more liberal opinions, for he, naturally enough, considered that the change was in a great measure due to the convincing arguments contained in his lectures, and he could not forget how he himself, as a youth, had been freed from the bonds of the same narrow-hearted sectarianism by the late Professor Baumgarten. These things all combined to make it easy for Ephraim Lebrecht to win the good man's trust and liking ; the more so, that the zealous student and persistent seeker after light had very much improved in his personal appearance. His manners had become easy and pleasant, and he had a wonderful power of making his immense reading of use in heightening the interest of his conversation, instead of making it ponderous.

I felt very mistrustful of him for a long time after he came back, but at length the extent of his information, the keenness of his intellectual grasp, and the acuteness with which he interpreted theological difficulties, began to have a certain attraction for me. I gradually got over my secret dislike to him, and a sort of intimacy sprang up between us. One day he gave me the following account of the causes that had brought about his change of opinion, and, as he did so, his expression was one of awe and mystery.

It was, he said, as a Chilicast that he had left Halle, and arrived at the old Castle of Seeried with his pupils. He then believed firmly in the approaching fulfilment of the prophecies contained in the Revelation of St. John, in the nearness of the millennium, and in many other doctrines that were held by the Gnostics of early Christian times. Soon after his arrival at Seeried he had discovered a library full of curious books situated in an ancient tower belonging to the building. These books were treatises on the esoteric teaching of the Kabbalah. He began to read them forthwith, and was soon engrossed in the surpassing interest of his new study. It was a revelation to him. He saw those things clearly expressed, of which the 'Quietists,' and the Mystics of the school of Jacob Böhme had only had a dim foreboding, and he perceived that what they had sought to express in ecstatic language was very often taken from the philosophical teaching of the Kabbalah ; but undigested and misunderstood. For instance,

how sublimely was the fall of Satan there treated
in the spirit of Zoroaster, and how strangely
grotesque were the misconceptions which the
Mystics had deduced from the account.

Ephraim then went on to speak of the occult
powers to which the initiated might attain by means
of the Kabbalah—even to the foreseeing of future
events. My curiosity was much aroused by this
last announcement.

He told me in a whisper that he had found a
little book containing all the great mysteries in the
Red Tower of Castle Seeried. Its existence was
obviously unknown to the family, and he had therefore taken it away with him amongst some other
ordinary books, that he might have an opportunity
of studying it at leisure. He would afterwards put
it back in the library when he returned to his
pupils.

My head was so carried by all that I had heard,
that I could think of nothing else. Even my
favourite poet, Klopstock, ceased to content me
with his ecstatic endeavours to approach more
nearly to the Divine. I looked upon his efforts
as mere poetical dreams. The Kabbalah alone
awakened my enthusiasm. Lebrecht encouraged
me to study the book, and took pains to feed my
thirst for that kind of knowledge, until it became
even more intense. He told me that the Kabbalistic
Tree was the real Tree of Life, the Tree of Knowledge, and that the command not to eat of it was

only intended for the multitude, who were too weak
to bear such a revelation, and who naturally shrank
from venturing beyond the common track.   He
then proceeded to lead me gradually onwards towards an understanding of the hidden meaning of
the words as explained by the Kabbalistic method.
His system was peculiar to himself.   And it soon
came to pass that I began to doubt many things
which I had formerly believed ; but of the truth
and power of the esoteric teaching to which I had
opened my mind, I had no doubt, in spite of my
imperfect knowledge, and the confusion of my
ideas and views respecting it.

I sought the light, and imagined that I was on
the road to find it, when I began to grasp the
doctrines of Christianity from a sceptical point of
view.

I ceased to take part in the amusements of my
fellow-students, and spent the night bending over
obscure documents ; over the Sohar, whose in-
most meaning I struggled to reach, forgetting that
the Kabbalists themselves maintain that it will
never be fully understood until the end of days.
How happy I esteemed myself that I had found
the one and only road that led to true wisdom,
while all the time I was yet wandering in the
paths of error.   For the Kabbalah no longer
served me as a well-spring from which to draw
ever more convincing proofs of the truth of
Christianity.   I sought it now in the desire to

attain that dangerous wisdom, against which
many a solemn warning may be read in its pages.
Its philosophic teaching no longer seemed its
essence in my eyes; but its magic power alone.
It was the *Practical* Kabbalah that aroused all my
interest and enthusiasm. The art of foreseeing
what the future held in store, was to me the
highest and noblest object at which it aimed.

Ephraim Lebrecht one day brought me the ' En
Rogel ' of Rabbi Löw, a book which treats of this
matter. But it was in vain that I strove to gain a
clear conception of the signification of its dark
hints. All of these writings agreed in pointing
out the necessity of holding intercourse with the
initiated, who alone possess the key to the
wisdom for which I thirsted. What wonder that,
thrown back upon myself as I was, success was
unattainable. What wonder that the joy, with
which I had at first pursued my search into the
hidden mysteries, should have been turned into
sadness, or that the discouragement which
weighed upon me should have so physically un-
nerved me as to change a naturally cheerful youth
into a fretful hypochondriac. The curse already
rested upon me, which comes to all who disobey
the command of Scripture, and strive to discover
those things which the Providence of God has
concealed from us. For I neglected the proper
subjects of study to spend myself upon problems
I was not fitted to solve, and so I laboured in vain.

c

No one saw the uselessness of my efforts more clearly than I did myself. My mind lost its vigour, and my body was consumed by the fruitless striving of the jaded intellect. I sought the light, and yet the brightness of my day was darkened. My life seemed useless, and of no account. I longed for the grave—for eternal Death, or eternal Life ; for eternal Darkness, or eternal Light. Anything that would put an end to this terrible uncertainty.

My body could bear no more. I fell seriously ill, and my anxious father came, and took me home.

CHAPTER III.

' Wenn sie den Stein der Weisen hätten ;
Der Weise mangelte dem Stein.

Thr Täppischen ! Ein bunter Schein
Soll gleich die plumpe Wahrheit sein.

Ich suchte nach verborgnen goldenen Schätzen,
Und schauerliche Kohlen trug ich fort.'
                                    —*Faust.*

YOU must remember, Reinhardt, that I was a true child of the times, and that will explain many things otherwise incomprehensible.

Count St. Germain was then the object of general curiosity throughout central Europe ; Cagliostro was making ready to appear in his great rôle ; the Rosicrucians were the theme of constant wonderment, and were accredited with the possession of the secret of the Practical Kabbalah—a knowledge to which other societies and orders, such as the mystical brotherhood of Free Ma ons, and illuminati of various sorts could only aspire. It was an adventurous age, full of adventurous thoughts and men. Whilst Catherine the Second was doing extraordinary things in the East, and leading the most eccentric of lives, a very singular and wonderful person had arisen in Germany—the wizard

Schröpfer.　He had done marvellous things close
by, and so how was it possible for me to have
escaped the excitement that was in the air I
breathed, even apart from the other influences more
directly at work.

Once removed from Halle, my mother's tender
care and nursing soon restored my bodily health.
But my father shook his head when he enquired
into the progress I was making in my studies.　He
was dissatisfied with my work and its results, which
he ascribed to the ill-regulated ideas of modern
times that prevailed even in theological lecture
rooms.

As soon as I got stronger, I began to wander
about my father's parish, both in the little town
where we lived, and its neighbourhood, recalling
past scenes of my boyhood.　How distinctly I remembered the way in which my comrades and I
used to persecute the Jew boys of the place, and
force them to pronounce the name of 'Jesus,' whilst
we slipped softly and half affrightedly past the
threshold of the grey-bearded Bachur, who was
believed to be a student of the Kabbalah *maschiith*,
and therefore a magician.　With what a shiver of
awe had we not watched him assemble his little
flock in the evenings, at the time of the New Moon,
that they might worship the Creator of the firma-
ment under the free vault of heaven!　With what
curiosity had we not waited close by the low
windows of the Jewish houses on Saturday even-

ings, as the Sabbath was drawing to a close, until the moment when all the lights were blown out with strange ceremonies, while old Bachur Benasse gazed at his nails and finger-tips—a custom that I now knew rested on a passage in the Sohar. How we had trembled when we saw the Bachur's family drinking red wine on Easter-Eve, believeing, as we did, the ghastly old legend, which cost hundreds of Jewish lives during the middle ages—that it was Christian blood. And once, when we had watched old Benasse go to the public well on New Year's Day, and throw crumbs of bread into the water, murmuring the while those words of the Prophet Micah : 'Cast all their sins into the depths of the sea,' we had thought in our ignorance that he was trying to bewitch the water, whereupon we had made such an uproar that the populace had risen against the poor Jews with the same cry that had so often been raised of yore, and accused them of having poisoned the well. My father had had great difficulty in calming the mad wrath of the people, and saving the innocent old man and his co-religionists out of their hands.

I recollected every incident of that time as clearly as if it had only taken place a week before. Bachur Benasse was long since dead, and his son had succeeded him in his ill-paid office of assistant minister. During the stay I was now making with my parents, a Chief Rabbi of my father's acquaintance came to our little town to hold some religious function. I had a short talk with him. He was a learned Talmudist and Orientalist, and expressed himself pleased to learn that I had taken with such eagerness to the study of Hebrew. But when I led the conversation to the Jewish secret teaching, the Kabbalah, his face darkened, and he told me, with great solemnity, to beware of a science that was either too holy or too unholy to be a beneficial subject for human research ; for it took upon itself to explain the hidden mysteries of God, and was only too apt to lead to sectarianism, unbelief, arrogance, woe, and destruction. I had forgotten that as an orthodox Talmudist, he was necessarily a violent opponent of Rabbi Eibenschützen. Soon afterwards I learned from a young Jew in the town, whom I had known for years, that the son of the late Bachur Benasse, who had succeeded his father as assistant minister, was secretly a Kabbalist, and that he was in the habit of reading a little book immediately after prayers. He always hid it away again carefully ; but the young Jew had discovered it on one occasion. He was, however, accounted a good man and worthy of all respect. He was no longer young.

One evening after the lamps were all lit in the houses, I set out to call on the Bachur. He lived in a small house built of wood and stucco, the beams and shutters of which were painted red. It was situated close to the gate of the town. I found him at home reading, while his wife and daughters sat at work round the table. The room was hot, and he had taken off his coat, so that the 'Tephilin' or 'Phylacteries,' and the so-called 'Ten Commandments,' were exposed to view. On seeing me, he hastily put on his coat, after which he turned to welcome me, a slight flush of embarrassment upon his face. The wife and daughters left the room shyly. I asked the Bachur about his family, and he did not hide from me the fact that he sorrowed because he had no son—a matter of bitter grief to every Jew—but he spoke with resignation, bending meekly to the will of God.

When I gradually brought the conversation round to the Kabbalah, he became visibly embarrassed, and it was not until he perceived that I was not altogether unversed in its teaching that his mistrust vanished. He told me how astonished he was to find that I should have embarked on the study of so great and difficult a subject—one that hardly any man was capable of comprehending before he had reached middle age.

As our conversation went on he became more confidential, and showed such a gentle, humane, loving spirit, that I was filled with amazement, and could not forbear asking him from what source he had gained the pure, high tenets he held ; his principles were so much in accordance with those of Christianity. He smilingly answered that they were the fruits of the tree which he helped to

foster. He then proceeded, in somewhat mysterious fashion, to speak of one who should come to
reap the harvest and feed the poor with its sweet
fruit, who, indeed, was already approaching from
the East.

The Bachur was even then a Soharite, and one
of the earliest followers of the Patriarch Jacob
Frank in Germany ; while the ' Saintly Master,' as
he was called, who had a short time before been
set free from imprisonment, was then journeying
through the Slavonic Lands on his way to the
West. But I knew nothing of this at the time,
and so did not understand the allusion. My mind
was full of one idea and one only : to gain instruction in the Practical Kabbalah ; to learn how to
use the magic tables and quadrates so as to be
able to foretell future events.

I had fallen so deeply into error, that it was in
this alone that I saw the triumph of Kabbalistic
wisdom, and the main object of its teaching. The
phantasy had taken complete possession of me,
that the prophetic science which enables its Adepts
to take a clear, untroubled view into the distant
future, is the light that should enlighten us, make
everything comprehensible to us, and uphold us.
I talked long and confidentially with good Bachur
Benasse. He had acknowledged that the Kabbalah worked miracles. So I thought the right
moment had come to tell him frankly and openly
the object of my visit, that I desired to be

instructed in the Kabbalah *maschiith*, not so much
for the sake of its theurgy, as to be taught the
secret of the Kabbalistic mode of reckoning, to the
end that I might learn to foresee the future.

Before I had finished speaking, the man sprang
to his feet, and stood facing me, with every sign of
horror and pious indignation depicted on his pale
countenance and trembling form. His very lips
had grown ashen-white. He stretched out his
shaking hand in mute entreaty. But when I
persisted in speaking, he raised his arm solemnly,
and said with a grave impressiveness that I shall
never forget :

' Forbear ! keep silence, lest your tongue be
paralysed for uttering such awful words ? Hush,
hush, or tear it out, rather than let it continue to
speak so foolishly. It were better for you to have
no tongue than that you should allow it to express
such a sinful desire. Did not the angel Jophiel
say unto the great Rabbi Ishmael, called the
" High Priest ": "Thou worm, wherefore dost thou
dare ?" And do *you* not fear to draw down upon
yourself the wrath of Heaven by cherishing this
mad folly ? '

I was very much surprised by the vehemence of
his indignation, but was not therefore to be turned
from my purpose. I told him that I should not
fail either in perseverance or courage in enduring
the discipline necessary to the attaining of such
knowledge, upon which the Bachur's face took a

look of contemptuous scorn of which I should
never have imagined it capable.

'And who art thou?' he exclaimed, in high,
strident tones. 'Who art *thou*? The foot of an
elephant is sufficient to crush thee, and yet thou
deemest thyself strong enough to bear the burden
of the infinite on thy weak shoulders! Thou
wouldst look behind the veil that God himself has
placed. What foolhardy wickedness may not the
mind of man conceive!—Go—Depart from my
house lest the walls fall upon you—go, without
delay.'

With that he left me to myself.

I was so much taken by surprise, that at first I
could only stare stupidly at the door through which
the Jew had disappeared. Then I went out into
the night, and wandered beyond the town seeking
coolness and calmness in the fresh country air.

At length the excitement passed away, and I
began to think quietly over what had occurred.
The Bachur really believes, I said to myself, that
God does not suffer any one to enquire too far into
His mysteries. If this is the case, what is the good
of this esoteric teaching which promises so much?

But before long I returned to the subject from
another point of view. Why did God, I demanded,
permit this science to exist, if man might not make
use of it?

In this state of mind I returned to the university.

My father had had a serious talk with me before I started, and after my arrival at Halle, I tried, for his sake, to devote my attention to the special studies that had reference to my future calling ; but my mind and thoughts were still fixed on the same object as before, and in this I only showed how much I was in sympathy with the current ideas of the time.

The deeper spirits of that day possessed nothing of the cold, clear judgment of modern philosophy ; the dry unfruitful doctrines of Voltaire did not satisfy them. They demanded something different as a stimulous to thought, therefore gave themselves up to a sort of visionary mysticism. And it was only one of the many strange contradictions of the time, that Semler, the Rationalistic theologian, the sceptical enquirer into the truth of received opinion, the bold searcher after light, should have stilled his thirst for knowledge at the same miraculous fountain, and have gained the proofs of his assertions from the same source as the visionaries, magicians and members of those secret brotherhoods, new examples of which seemed to spring into life like mushrooms in the course of a single night.

This was the consequence of a stronger combination of circumstances.

Whilst the Kabbalistic movement, which had been set afloat by Sabbatai Zewy in the Levant, was quietly permeating Judaism, a Frenchman had

come home from India, bringing with him the
Zend-Avesta, the most sacred book that contains
the teaching of Zoroaster, the Persian Reformer of
the ancient Chaldæ-Babylonian religion.   This he
had translated and made known in Europe.   But
a few years had elapsed since that time, and already
the light of Zoroastrianism was casting its magic
rays in the lodges of those secret brotherhoods
who had devoted themselves to seeking after light.
Freemasons, Philaleths, Rosicrucians, and finally
the Illuminati, all united in worshipping it as the
good principle after the fashion enjoined by
Zoroaster and his faithful Parsi followers.   As a
natural consequence of embracing the religion of
the Magi, magic—that is to say, the art of Maja,
goddess of prophecy and poetry—grew to be
accepted as the highest wisdom., and magician,
Kabbalist, Chaldæan were the names given to the
men who demanded the greatest reverence, and
gained it too, as I   know   very well.   Like
Sabbatai and others of the same pretensions, they
sought as far as possible to imitate the great
Persian teacher in their personal appearance.   The
cultus of these secret orders was often of much
Oriental pomp in its outward expression, and
appears to have been a good deal modelled on an
obscure conception of the ancient Egyptian Isis
worship.   Even Mozart's opera, the ' Zauberflöte,'
is an example of the prevalence of these ideas, for
he brings the Parsi Zoroaster upon the stage under

the very similar name of ' Sarastro,' the high-priest of Isis.

One evening, soon after my return to Halle, Ephraim Lebrecht, who had welcomed me back with great effusion, took me to one of these lodges. I do not intend to describe everything that I saw there, and only mention the circumstance because it led to the following conversation with Lebrecht, which will give you a better notion than anything else of the point I had reached in my dogmatico-philosophic training. After that I shall proceed as rapidly as I can to relate the history of the catastrophe of my life, which is sure to be a warning to you, Reinhardt.

Well, then, I went to the Lodge one evening, as I told you before. So far as I could make out, a good deal of solemn foolery was going on, arising more or less from self-deception, and public opinion was much mistaken in believing that this Lodge was in possession of the secret after which I still craved. I soon perceived that the knowledge these people had of the Kabbalah, or of Zoroastrianism, was of a most superficial description, and that the wise men and Adepts, before whom they bowed, were only acquainted with a few fragmentary scraps of the Kabbalah and of the wisdom of the Chaldæans.

I did not attempt to hide my disapprobation from my companion, when we were walking home together.

'What do these people mean,' I said, 'by deceiving themselves and others after this fashion.'

'They worship the light as much as anybody else,' replied Ephraim, shrugging his shoulders. 'They desire to have it, and therefore seek it in the writings of the prophet, who proclaims the eternal supremacy of Ormuzd, the God of Light, over Ahriman, the God of Darkness, and who plainly foretells the millennium.'

'But,' I objected, 'what practical aims have they in view?'

'A nearer approach to God, love of their neighbour, and the improvement of mankind, all of which are as much part of the teaching of the Kabbalah as of early Christianity, and besides this, they desire to discover the Philosopher's Stone as ardently as any of the other worshippers of light.'

The look of scorn on Ephraim's face was not necessary to show me at whom his ironical words were pointed. Everyone in those days believed that the secret of the ' Philosopher's Stone ' was to be found in the ' Zend-Avesta ; ' hence the sensation caused by the French translation of the book, and many and curious were the strivings after the marvellous arising from a study of its pages. These principally emanated from French Lodges, and spread amongst the Freemasons, and even amongst German *savants*.

I took no notice of Lebrecht's intended satire, and went on, after a pause :

'But this horrible amalgamation of superficial, half-comprehended ideas! These people would Zoroastrianize the Kabbalah and Christianity without a moment's hesitation.'

'And why not?' he answered. 'They are only walking on the path that others are unconsciously following. You, yourself, Bergmann, know enough of the Kabbalah, to understand the method it teaches of gaining the meaning that underlies the outward sense of Biblical phrases. Have you never thought of this when you were listening to the famous scriptural commentator of our university?'

An awkward silence ensued.

It was the custom at that time for Rationalistic theologians, who opposed the literal interpretation of the Bible as enforced by the orthodox school, to explain the meaning of Holy Writ by a sort of Kabbalistic process. Professor Semler did so with special boldness, and often with subtle discrimination ; but I could not help feeling that his method was so unsystematic, uncritical, and inconsequent, that I sometimes wondered whether he fully understood it himself. These reflections had struck me more persistently of late than ever before.

Nothing was better fitted to shake my confidence in the man, who had done more than anyone else to sap my faith in authority, than the pointed, but veiled sallies contained in the general remarks Lebrecht went on to make concerning the shallowness of the acquaintance of learned divines with the Kabbalah.   They sought for the well-spring of knowledge in Gnosticism, he said, while true wisdom was only to be found in the Kabbalah, a wisdom to which none could have access save with the help of the initiated amongst the Jewish *savants ;* vain especially was the assistance offered by the semi-ignorance of the orators of the lecture-room.   Once in possession of the secret knowledge, one could listen with calm disdain to the rationalising vagaries of modern exegisists.

In the course of our conversation, Lebrecht continually repeated the well-known axiom, that the Kabbalah was the key to all knowledge.   For him who busied himself with its teaching, he said, all other learning was superfluous.   It was the book with the seven seals; the Tree of Knowledge, whose coveted fruit would at length fall into the hands of every earnest student of its wisdom.   It embraced the fundamental religious doctrines of all nations, was the basis of Gnostic and Christian dogma and the first Christians, even the Founder of Christianity had known no other philosophy.   The teaching of the Nazarites, of the Disciples, of St. John the Baptist, and of the Sabæans*, who date as far back as the birth of Christ, came from the Kabbalah. And in the spirit of this holy esoteric science, known to the wisest men amongst the children of Israel, the Books of Jesus Sirach and of the

---

* Star worshippers. — *M. W. M.*

Wisdom of Solomon were composed. Even going further back in the history of the 'Peculiar People,' its influence might be clearly traced in the Book of Job, as also in the writings of the Prophets belonging to the time of the Babylonian captivity ; an instance of this might be seen in the 'chariot' of Ezekiel, and in the 'Ancient of Days' mentioned by Daniel. Daniel especially, he asserted, must have been a great Kabbalist, hence the Scriptures say of him, that ' in all matters of wisdom and understanding' that the king (Nebuchadnezzar) enquired of him, he found him ' ten times better than all the engravers of hieroglyphics and magicians that were in all his kingdom.' He must, to a certain extent, have been one of the Fathers of the Holy Jewish mysteries, and the Kabbalah itself was either the Spirit of Judaism purified in the fire of the Zoroastrian faith, or else it was Zoroastrianism sanctified in the sacred fountain of Jewish wisdom.

' Then our modern visionaries are led by a true instinct when they strive to amalgamate the two systems ?' I asked of my companion, as we walked slowly back to our lodgings in the quiet night.

' A dim foreboding, or instinct, if you like to call it so,' he answered. ' Not more than that. The teaching of Zoroaster had quite as great an influence on the religions of modern nations as Judaism ; the doctrines of the Last Judgment and

D

of the Resurrection are peculiar to it, and
Christian Gnosticism and Neo-Platonism are
deeply tinctured with its influence. The Kabbalah formed the connecting link between the two.
For just at the time when the Hebrews were
living as strangers and foreigners in the land from
which their forefathers had originally wandered ;
while they were sitting sadly by Babel's streams,
thinking of Zion, Zoroaster arose.* To the old
traditions of the Chaldæan Magi, he added his
doctrines regarding Ormuzd, the God of Light,
and Ahriman, the God of Darkness and of matter,
and showed how Darkness is finally conquered by
the power of Light. On their return to Jerusalem
the Jews brought these ideas home with them,
and those who remained behind helped them to
work them out after their own fashion. A great
number of the customs and observances that
obtain amongst the Jews at the present day have
their origin in Zoroastrianism, as, for instance, the
washing of hands, and the ablutions at the time of
the New Moon. The prayer-books in general use
amongst the ignorant are more or less imbued
with it ; even the 'letter of divorcement,' and the
'certificate of gift,' presented by the husband on
the morning after his marriage, are still made out

---

* The exact date of Zoroaster's birth is a disputed point. Some
of the Parsis hold it to have been much earlier than this.
—*M. W. M.*

after the old Chaldæan model. The ceremonial customs of the Parsis are similar to theirs in many respects, and all of the Jewish writings since the captivity betray the influence of the Zoroastrian faith.'

'But the Kabbalah,' continued Lebrecht after a pause, 'the Kabbalah is the font in which Zoroaster's holiest mysteries were purified from the dross that clung to them. Only the wisest amongst the people were permitted to approach it and drink of its waters ; it resembled the Image at Sais, behind whose veil Truth was concealed. The Kabbalah is the clearest mirror in which it can be reflected. In it we see spiritualised the most ancient wisdom of the nations that dwelt by the Ganges and Euphrates, the Jordan and the Nile—and great Zoroaster's sublime teaching. It is no longer an equal battle between the Good Principle and the Bad that is there described. The victory of Light is made manifest, and Darkness becomes its shadow—the Spirit created and still labours ; matter stands beneath. Dualism becomes Monotheism, or, to be quite frank, Pantheism.* For the essence of the allegorical and symbolical teaching of the Kabbalah may be summed up in this : The

---

* According to the Kabbalah, the Universe is a manifestation of God. It is, as it were, the 'garment of God.' 'He not only contains all, but is Himself all, and exists in all.' See ' The Kabbalah Unveiled,' by G. L. Macgregor Mathers, p. 44.

Universe is the Revelation of the Divine Being. Read Spinoza, and you will find the figurative language of the Kabbalah translated into the sober phrases of philosophy.'

'What?' I asked. 'Does the Kabbalah contain the principles of Spinoza?'

'You will be able to judge when you have read his works.'

'This, then, is the reason that orthodox Rabbis have such a horror of the secret science, which, they say, leads to unbelief.'

'Not only for that reason, I think. Perhaps it may also be because the study of the Kabbalah has driven so many of its disciples into the bosom of Christianity,' answered my companion. 'Again, some of the Jews doubt the eternal salvation of those men who have made their esoteric doctrines known to the world by means of the press ; while many others forbid their study on the ground that the Kabbalah is the veritable Tabernacle, the Holy of Holies, and may only be approached by the wisest of men. That it should be so, is very comprehensible to me. But all the same, you and I will, therefore, keep the *firmer grasp of the key to this wisdom.*'

So said my red-haired counsellor. We had meantime reached the door of my lodging, and as I stopped to say good-night, he seized my hand, and continued :

'Yes, my friend, let us cling to the key which

will admit us into the garden, containing the tree
of life and knowledge, the fruit of which can make
us like gods able to see the future as clearly as the
present.   Good night !'

With that he took his departure, well knowing
the burden he had cast upon my soul.

I had subjects for meditation, enough and to
spare.

I once read in the works of a Kabbalistic
author, that evil can only be hurtful when it is
accompanied by something good.   Give the liar
understanding, and the wicked man wisdom, and
then, and then only, will they become dangerous.
Set about a malicious story with a few grains of
truth, and it will not fail to attain the end for
which it was invented.   Let Lebrecht's object be
what it would, he would have had far less chance
of influencing me, had it not been for the con-
straining power of the truth that was contained in
his words.   What he had said of the development
of the Kabbalah, and of the superficial knowledge
people had concerning it was true as far as I knew,
and the rest was evident.   His remarks regarding
Semler did not fail in their effect.   I grew indifferent to all the University lectures, and sat
brooding over the Sohar.   Then I began to study
Spinoza's ' Ethics,' after which I went on to
Descartes and Locke.   I armed myself with
doubt as with a garment, and when the voice of
God spoke softly to my stubborn heart, I refused

to listen, and said blasphemously :
  ' I should believe, if I could see Thee.'

    .   .   .   .

And so I wandered — a little Faust — even
further on the road that leads to destruction.

My philosophical reading was too superficial,
my taste for the pernicious too uncritical, for my
mind not to have been confused by the immense
number of books that I consumed. Theology
sickened me, as was only natural. I had to go
through the phase upon which I had entered, like
so many of my contemporaries. I had set out
with a strong belief in the marvellous, and ended
by reaching the portal of Atheism.

But this was not all. I soon perceived that
Lebrecht did not consider the views he pro-
pounded as by any means true. And finally
when books were given me to read, which
subjected the Kabbalah to merciless criticism, and
made out that the Sohar was composed by a
fraudulent Spanish Jew in the fourteenth century.
I accepted the dictum at once—so strangely
credulous had unbelief made me—and thus lost
the last authority to which I had clung. Everything that existed seemed nothing more than a
delusion or a deception in my eyes.

It was not without much agony of mind that I
reached this stage. But at length I succeeded in
putting on—outwardly, at least—a light *débonnaire*

manner, an indifference to all religious subjects, and a frivolity, which was as characteristic of the time as mystical rhapsody. Nothing was sacred to me, and, strangely enough, my red-haired mentor seemed to agree with me in every respect. I had fallen a prey to scepticism, and belonged, body and soul, to that suicidal system, which, in consequence of its refinement in doubt, even doubts the certainty of doubt. Books had no longer any interest for me, and the Professors shook their heads over my backsliding, for I ceased to attend the university lectures, and lived a careless, idle life. like so many other students. I even gave up my visits to Professor Semler. For what good would seeing him have done me? To the fencing-room and ale-house alone did I care to go, and in these I appeared oftener and oftener as time went on.

What can I tell you of that part of my life? There is nothing to say about it, for it had only momentary worth and interest. It was full of noise and bustle, and was yet utterly devoid of happiness.

The conflict was by no means over, and the remembrance of my father still stood in the background of my thoughts after I had said farewell to Theology. For these reasons, I was almost always in an irritable frame of mind, and ready to prove my skill with the rapier on the smallest occasion, thereby gaining for myself the reputation of fire-eater. As was only natural, I did not care to

guard the wretched life that had fallen so low.   I
laughed at all who troubled themselves with study
—threshing straw, as I called it.   I laughed as I
looked Death in the face every time I stood sword
in hand awaiting the commencement of a duel.
How I could best enjoy myself and kill time were
the chief questions of existence to me in those
days.

Lebrecht had at first accompanied me regularly
to the fencing-room, but latterly had seemed to
avoid me.   Soon afterwards I heard that he had
become tutor to a young count belonging to the
same family as the twin brothers he had formerly
taught.   Professor Semler had warmly recommended him for the situation.   It mattered little
to me what he did or where he went; other
anxieties pressed upon me, and I did not even
care to try to recollect the name of the people in
whose employment he was.   I often saw him
going about with a handsome young fellow whom
I took to be his pupil; but I asked no questions
about him.   The careful tutor took his charge to
another fencing-room, where the Pomeranian,
Mecklenburg, and old Prussian nobility encoun-
tered their equals in rank, who came from Kurland
and Livonia.   So we met no more.

The news of my father's serious illness came
upon me, in the midst of my mad career, with the
suddenness of a thunder-clap.   My mother
summoned me home, and received me weeping.

I was not so hardened as to be untouched by grief when I saw that my father was dying. More especially did my pain increase when I found that he knew all about my rebellion against law and order, and that he had received an anonymous letter which bluntly informed him of my decided antipathy to taking Holy Orders. A circumstance that filled him with bitter sorrow.

I stood by his death-bed, and saw how his child-like faith enabled him to await the coming of the King of Terrors without fear. The dying Christian fixed his eyes upon me with tender affection, while addressing to me words of exhortation unmingled with reproach. What he said had all the greater effect upon me for that reason. I felt that I was a despicable wretch when, taking my mother's hand and mine, he blessed me, and continued in a broken voice :

' Serve God humbly and faithfully, honour your parents, and all will be well with you.'

My name was the last upon his lips.

The tears shed by my mother and by the whole parish for him, who had been so long their faithful guide, burnt into my conscience, and the bitter pain I felt sowed the seeds of repentance and despairing hope in my heart. A good man—my father—had passed away, and he had not lived in vain. Could it be because of his firm and unshaken trust in God ?

I heard my sorrowing mother pray for me—and

it came to pass that she led me back to God like a little child. I found much comfort in seeing my way clear before me through the mists of the unbelief I had formerly encouraged, and resolutely determined to learn the lesson of self-control. My studies must and should be completed, now that my mother was to a great extent dependent on me in her old age.

I went back to Halle, and threw myself energetically into my work. The effort did me good and brought me strength. My understanding developed, my judgment grew riper ; the old superficiality no longer contented me, for I now saw clearly the difference between really knowing, and only thinking one knew. I found moderation a truer guide than enthusiasm. I learned to understand Semler better than before, and the worthy man rejoiced in the goodness of his heart when I returned to him.

Lebrecht had gone away with his pupil. I heard many stories of the lad's proficiency in fencing, and was told that he had even come off victor in one or two duels, both there and at Jena. But I no longer cared about these things—any more than for the necromancy that occupied the public mind even more than ever. I did not even like to hear the latter spoken about, as it reminded me too distinctly of my former interest in the subject.

As soon as I had passed my examination, I

returned to my mother's house in the little
Thuringian town, where I began to act as curate to
the old gentleman who had succeeded my father
as clergyman of the parish.

I had been rather inclined to melancholy since
my father's death, and longed to get away from the
old place, and have an independent position, a
parish of my own—in the country, if possible.
And this wish was fulfilled.

One day I received a letter from Professor
Semler, in which he told me that if I wanted to
have a country parish, a very good living was to be
had.   Count Arthur von Seeried-Strandow, head
of the richest and noblest family on the shores of
the Baltic, had applied to him—as he had already
done on other occasions—for a suitable person to
present to the family living, and had said that a
pupil of his, Semler's, would be much preferred to
any other.

Seeried-Strandow?   Was not that the surname
of the twin-brothers that had formerly lodged in
Märker Street, and also of the youth who was now
travelling under the tutelage of red-haired Ephraim
Lebrecht.   A journey to Halle convinced me that
I was right in this supposition.

Professor Semler received me with great kindness, and encouraged me to accept the offer of the
living.   For, he said, the Count already knew all
about me, as he, Semler, had proposed me as tutor
for the son and heir.   But the Count had decided

to engage Ephraim Lebrecht for the office, for he had been much pleased with the effect he believed his opinions to have had on the young man, in giving him broader and more liberal views on religious subjects than he had had when he first arrived at Castle Seeried with his pupils, the owner's twin-brothers.   The Count now wished to have an enlightened and pious clergyman as parish priest, and did not think that the position would be suitable for Lebrecht.   Professor Semler thought that I was the kind of person wanted.

When I heard all the particulars, I declared myself satisfied.   Shortly afterwards I was presented to the living of Seeried.   And with this change in my outward circumstances, a new epoch in my life began that had nothing dogmatic about it.

CHAPTER IV.

' Wer geht im fernen Thale
Den müden Pilgergang,
Im heissen Sonnenstrahle
Die flache Heid' entlang?
Sie wallen froh im Glanben
Als blüthen ihnen Lauben
Der fremden Erde zu.
Und als der Tag verflossen,
So beut, im wald verschlossen,
Ein gastlich Dach dem Häuflein Ruh.'

SCHMIDT VON LUBECK.

THE journey from Thuringia to my new home
was so long and troublesome in those old
days, that many and various preparations had to
be made before it could be undertaken. My dear
mother's arrangements kept her busy for several
weeks. As the only sort of post-chaise that could
be got in country places was most uncomfortable,
being built rather for the transport of luggage
than for the accommodation of human beings
endowed with the sense of feeling, we gratefully
accepted the carriage, which an admirer of my late
father presented to us as a parting gift.

Much as I longed, in my somewhat morbid
condition, for quiet and solitude, it was yet with

deep pain that I took leave of the well-remembered scenes of my boyhood, of the place where my father had lived and worked, and of the friendly faces I had known so long, and set out for the distant parish where my lot was now cast. It was a bold step to take, for it was a sort of expatriation, and I wondered how it would answer. A sudden wish flashed into my mind that I could see what it would be like. And then I smiled at myself, for I had never felt so strongly as at that moment how great was the gulf that separated me from the eager-hearted boy, who had passionately desired to unriddle the mysteries of the art by which the seers of old had gazed into the future. I had become a grave, sad-hearted man, and desired above all things to hold myself aloof from all ill-regulated enthusiasms, that I might the better devote my life to the duties of my calling, and thus become an active and useful parish priest. The Bible henceforth should be my only oracle. On the evening before leaving my old home, I opened it at hazard, in accordance with ancient custom, and the thumb of my right hand pointed to these words of the Prophet Jeremiah :

'The heart is deceitful above all things, and desperately wicked : who can know it ?'

It was a great truth ; but what bearing had the words on my future life, I wondered ? I marked the text, however, and its meaning was revealed

to me in after days, so that I have never forgotten it.

At length the moment came when we had to
take leave of my father's grave, and set out on our
journey, recommending ourselves to the protection
of the Most High.

It was in the early Spring.

As we drove out of the little town, and into the
blossoming country beyond, we could hear the
chime of the morning-bells. My mother bore up
wonderfully ; but when the steeple of the principal
church finally disappeared from view on turning
the corner of a wood, her tears began to fall softly,
and my heart grew heavy within me. Thus we
set out on our journey through the wide world to
make a new home amongst strangers.

A few days later, we had left the hilly and
varied scenery of Thuringia behind us, and had
entered a flat country, where the horses had
literally to wade through sandy roads from one
posting-station to another. Dark fir trees grew
on the wretched moorland soil, the villages were
few and far between, and the inns were little
better than pot-houses. At long intervals a small
market town might be seen in the wide expanse
of plain, and, here and there, a few cultivated
patches of ground, forming oases in the desert ; or
perhaps long stretches of meadow-land on which
flocks of geese were driven out to pasture. Such

was the character of the country through which
we had now to wend our way.

Where no inns were to be found, we often met
with a kind reception at the parsonage.

The nature of the scenery through which we
were passing did not make a disagreeable impression upon me.   Its monotony and gloom were so
much in accordance with my state of mind at the
time as to soothe, instead of depressing me ; and
then it was so different from the beautiful and
varied country to which I was accustomed in
Thuringia that I felt as though it were a new
world.   Gradually, however, my pleasure in it died
away, and I would get out of the carriage and
trudge through the sand for a change.   My mother
would meanwhile remain where she was, her hands
clasped in her lap, and her thoughts busied with
the past and future.   It went to my heart to see
how anxiously she looked at me sometimes.   Could
she have had a foreboding that all was not well
with me, that I had not yet attained that certainty
of faith which was necessary before I could
properly fulfil the duties of my high calling ?

We had left Berlin behind us, and yet we drove
on and on through a sandy country.   It sometimes
appeared to me as if our journey would never end.
The weather was hot, and I gazed longingly over
the heath to see whether I could not discover the
church tower of the next village rising above the
low fir trees.   I tramped along the road up to my

ankles in sand, keeping pace with the tired horses, round whose heads swarms of flies were buzzing noisily.

The air in the fir-wood through which we were passing was so close and breathless that we were glad to reach the freer space beyond. After proceeding a little further, we saw a thick cloud of dust rising on the edge of the wood we had left behind us, and so lighted up by the vertical rays of the sun, that it shone like a pillar of fire. I gazed at it fascinated, and saw that it seemed to approach us more and more nearly. A strange expectancy came over me. I was reminded of the pillar of cloud mentioned in the Old Testament, by means of which the children of Israel were led through the wilderness,—and this land of sand and sunshine looked very like a wilderness to me. I was ready to regard anything as an angel that would lead me quickly through it.

While I yet gazed, the shining cloud parted, and I saw a carriage come out from the midst of it, and rapidly approach us. It was much lighter than ours, and was drawn by six powerful horses. When it came nearer, I perceived that it was a well-appointed equipage, with a coat of arms on the panel. Two ladies were seated in the carriage—one of them a woman of some forty years of age, and of a very high-bred and attractive appearance; the other, a young and beautiful girl, who so strikingly resembled the elder lady as to make it impossible to mistake their relationship.

I had time enough to make these observations, for when the liveried postillion, who rode and guided the leaders, cracked his long whip loudly, and shouted to our driver to 'get out of the way in the devil's name,' his mistress desired that her carriage should be drawn up, and then driven slowly past us.

I was standing on the grass by the road-side. I had no eyes for the splendid greys, the carriage or its accessories, and saw, almost without seeing, the herons on the coat of arms surmounted by a coronet. But I could not refrain from looking after the two ladies, who had returned my bow with smiling courtesy. The elder lady had greeted my mother also as she passed.

As I stood gazing after the carriage, the young girl looked back, turning her lovely child face once more on the poor clergyman, and his old mother, who were following slowly over the dismal heath.

At that moment the monotonous landscape gained a charm in my eyes. The sunshine was pouring full upon the wide moor, whose level expanse was broken here and there by single fir trees, or little clumps of spruces, or, perhaps, of juniper bushes. The carriage was rapidly disappearing round a sharp turn in the road, and would soon be lost to sight behind the wood by the side of which the road appeared to run. The cracking of the postillion's whip might still be heard in the distance. And again a cloud of sand arose, and floated for some time in mid-air.

Our carriage proceeded slowly on its way over the heath, now in sunshine and now in shade.

I know not how it came that my thoughts dwelt so persistently on the people who had just passed us. What had I to do with them, or they with me?

That they were 'great folk' on their way home from Berlin we learnt at the next posting-house from the very laconic postmaster. They had been there, and were gone again.

How strange it seemed, that meeting on the desolate heath, where their mere presence had lent the landscape a charm that was not its own; and now they were gone, and nothing was more unlikely than that we should ever again cross each other's path!

Once more we set out on our journey, going further and further into the great North-German levels. Our road ran past quiet pools bordered with alder bushes, and tiny hovels and farm-houses with thatched roofs. We also saw many a peaceful church and parsonage standing side by side, the latter often placed in the midst of an orchard. But not yet had we reached our destination. At length we left the sandy flats behind, and came into a more fruitful country, where the arable land was so good as richly to repay cultivation; where

great meadows were to be seen interspersed with
corn fields, and numerous flocks of geese were
grazing on village greens. There were gentlemen's
seats also, with straight avenues of trees, whose
branches interlaced, leading up to their doors, and
huge watch-dogs patrolling all round the house.
The country was not thickly populated; but it
yielded bountiful harvests. We could easily see
that the poverty of the sandy flats was unknown
there. But still, it too was a level country. The
air was strong and bracing, refreshing as sea
breezes. And no wonder, for the sea was really
nigh at hand. We were at last drawing near the
district in which our new home should lie.

My heart beat quickly at the thought. The
melancholy habit of mind into which I had fallen,
especially since my father's death, had often caused
me to long to get away from the beautiful and
smiling landscapes of Thuringia, and take up my
abode amid sterner scenery. The Baltic coasts
had then seemed the very acme of my desires. To
have for my parishioners, simple country folk, or
fishermen, fulfilled the dearest wish of my heart.
These were the reasons that had induced me to
accept the living offered me through Semler with
so little hesitation.

I fell into a sort of waking dream as we drove
slowly through a cool, shady wood, that seemed as
though it would never come to an end. I tried to
picture my new mode of life, and to imagine what

kind of man Count Arthur von Seeried-Strandow
might be. It was obvious that he was a freethinker in religious matters, or he would never have
chosen as tutor for his son, a man who had begun
life as a Pietist ; but who had afterwards become a
Sceptic, always, as he thought, to remain so. He
wished his son to be a man of the world, but considered religion necessary for the people, from a
political point of view. A good many men
amongst the higher classes held the same opinions
as he did ; men who tried to form themselves after
the model of their great contemporary, 'old Fritz'
of Prussia. What Semler had told me of the
Count confirmed this idea. But I might, at least,
hope to find him a cultivated man, who was not
indifferent to the acquisition of knowledge, either
for himself or his family, for had he not sent his
step-brothers to Halle, and afterwards his own son
to that and other Universities.

I was much puzzled to account for the confidence shown in Ephraim Lebrecht, to whom the
Count had confided the charge of his only son—
turncoat though he knew him to be. Added to
this was a feeling of astonishment at the fortuitous
course of events by which I was called to exercise
the priestly office amongst the same people who
had already given employment of another sort to
my former acquaintance. I cannot say that this
thought was a particularly pleasant one. For I
could never recall the influence Ephraim had

managed to exert over me without shame. And
something seemed to tell me, that in teaching me
to apprehend the Kabbalah after such a fashion
that I must needs come to esteem this 'Key of all
wisdom' as an imposture, he had been working to
attain some secret end as yet unknown to me.
Whilst carefully undermining my regard for the
worthy Semler by his satirical criticisms, he had
taken care to gain the good man's whole trust and
confidence for himself. In our talks about the
Kabbalah he had endeavoured to induce me either
to embrace Mysticism, or to lead me down the
devious paths of Atheism, and that he had for a
time succeeded in depriving me of all spiritual
stay, I have already told you. Since then I had
made deeper research into theological subjects,
and had been led to believe in a steady evolution
of the idea of the Godhead amongst the nations of
antiquity until it reached its highest point in
Christianity ; the Kabbalah, therefore, appeared to
me now as neither more nor less than one of the
many considerable factors in this process of
development. What object could Lebrecht have
had, I wondered, in treating me as he had done?

While I was yet puzzling over this question we
reached the end of the forest, and came out on a
wide green plain, shut in by woods on every side.
For in this district woods form the usual horizon
line. The corn seemed as though about to come
into ear, and the rape was already in flower. On

the other side of some broad meadows, intersected by a narrow sluggish stream flowing down to the sea, was a white-washed church with a grey pointed roof, a square tower, and a shining weather-cock, rising high above the dark alder bushes and silver-grey willows beside it.

I asked the man who had driven us from the last posting-house what was the name of the village we were approaching.

'That's Seeried, your Reverence,' replied the man in the Low German dialect of those parts.

Seeried! The long journey was over at last.

Much as we had desired to see the place for which we were bound, the sight of it surprised us a little. It was so much prettier than we had expected, the broad meadows were full of spring flowers, the sun was shining through the clouds that now and then overcast it for a moment, and the church-tower showed above the tops of the blossoming trees, giving the scene a pleasant home-like look. A cool sea-breeze was blowing, rather freshly perhaps. A wooded park lay on our right, stretching down as far as the banks of a small lake, formed by the waters of the sluggish stream I mentioned before, and beyond the trees rose a rugged old tower, which we thought probably marked the position of the Castle. A little further on, we came in sight of a large and stately building, standing at the end of a wide avenue.

My mother several times uttered a long sigh, and

I looked about me with mingled feelings, or returned the friendly greetings of the country men we met, many of whom stood cap in hand gazing after us meditatively.

It was an encouraging sight.

Children also came out into the road and stared at us curiously; even the stork that chanced to be in the meadow stretched out its long neck, and gazed at us for a full minute, after which it flapped its wings, and tried to fly away quickly. Seeing this the children began to sing:

> ‘ Stork, stork, hear our cry,
> Long legs cannot fly ! ’

It almost seemed as though the bird wanted to announce our arrival in the village, for it crossed our road twice on its flight to the church-tower, where it finally disappeared amongst the trees. My mother, who had watched its movements with great attention, drew a long breath of relief, and said:

‘ That is a good sign, and if the stork clangs with its bill as we drive into the village, it will be an excellent omen for you, my son. It would be too much to hope that it should have built its nest on the roof of the Parsonage.’

I smiled inwardly at this innocent superstition; but would not have said anything to disturb it for the world, it made the dear woman so happy.

The horses now began to go a little quicker, and the first houses of Seeried soon came in sight. We

turned down the wide road—street it could not be
called—that ran between the village hedge-rows.
Geese and poultry were pecking amongst the
grass at the road-side, and now and then dogs ran
barking out of the farm-yards to see who was
passing ; but no human face was visible anywhere.

The church stood on a slight eminence. It was
evidently a very old building, but had been white-
washed. Great lime trees stood about it, their
branches rising as high as the roof, and shading
the grassy *plateau* that surrounded it on every
side.

Close to the burying-ground stood a pleasant
one-storied dwelling, built of stone, and set in the
midst of a garden. At either side of the entrance
gate was a lilac bush in full flower, filling the air
with fragrance. The stork was on its nest on the
roof of the house, and when the driver stopped the
carriage at the gate, telling us that this was the
Parsonage, it began to clang loudly with its bill,
just as my mother had wished.

I must confess that the whole scene made a very
agreeable impression on both my mother and
myself ; everything looked so peaceful and bright.

The driver now proceeded to unharness his
horses, and lead them away, leaving the carriage
with its pile of luggage standing at the garden
gate. This I opened and went up to the house.

The door was unlocked so I opened it and went
into the entrance hall, which was strewed with

juniper needles, while garlands of green leaves were
hanging on the walls.   No one was there, however.
I opened another door and went into what was
evidently meant to be the parlour.   Its deal floor
was sanded.   Some stands beside the wall were
covered with little bits of juniper, which made the
room smell sweet and fresh.   Vases filled with
early roses and wall-flower were placed on the
table and on the broad window seats.   My mother,
who had followed me to the house, made her
way into the kitchen, and stood still in breathless
astonishment when she discovered some beautiful
cups and saucers in the cupboard, and a new tin
coffee-pot on the dresser.

Were these preparations made for us, I
wondered, or had we come to the wrong house?

I heard a sound in the next room, which looked
into the back yard, and desiring to find out
whether there was any mistake, I opened the door,
and saw two young girls so busily at work weaving
a garland that they did not hear me.   I could
only see the face of one of them.   She was a
pretty child, whose pale yellow hair hung down in
thick plaits.   The other, who was better dressed
and more slenderly made than her companion, had
her face turned to the window.   Startled by the
sound of my footsteps, the yellow-haired girl
suddenly looked up and saw me.   She uttered an
exclamation of dismay, and rushed out at the back
door.   Her companion turned and looked at me,

hesitated a moment, and then ran away lightly after the other.

Was it possible, or did my eyes deceive me? Was it really the same young girl who had passed us with her mother on the heath? It could not be—my eyes must have played me false. What was so easy as to make a mistake as to the identity of a person you had only seen for an instant.

Still wondering was she, or was she not the same, I went back to my mother. We took counsel together as to whether we ought to remain in a house which, although empty, was yet swept and garnished as though for expected guests. While we were thus deliberating, a horseman rode up to the gate, where he drew rein, and apparently began to examine our well-laden carriage at leisure.

We could see him through the window. He was a man of some fifty years of age, of a strong, well knit figure, and sat his horse as though forming part of it. His face had a somewhat harsh expression. In another moment he sprang lightly from the saddle, and tapping his foot impatiently on the ground, looked about as if in search of some one. At length he signed in the direction of one of the nearest houses, and a man hastened out. He threw the reins to him without a word, and turned towards the garden gate.

Judging from his dress that he was either the land-steward, or the private-secretary of the lord of

Seeried, I went out to meet him.   I could now see
more distinctly what he was like.   He was of
middle height.   His bearing, which was upright,
without being stiff, made him look taller than he
really was as he walked up the path leading to the
house flipping his right leg with the thong of his
whip.   His riding breeches were of an English cut,
and he wore a low crowned English hat instead of
the cocked hat that was then in general use.

English dress and customs, together with English literature, were beginning to make their way in
Germany.   The dress was more comfortable and
manly than the French, and was adopted, more
especially when travelling, riding, or shooting, even
by those who most abhored the prevailing Anglo-
mania.

I went forward to meet the stranger with a bow;
he returned my greeting slightly, stood still, and
asked :

'I have the honour of speaking to our new parson,
have I not ?'

'Your servant, sir,' I answered.

'Then you have upset all our calculations, and
have taken us by surprise ! Have you entered into
possession of the house yet ?' he enquired.

'I ventured to go in as I was told it was the
Parsonage.'

'I hope,' he continued, 'that you found some one
there to receive you ?'

'I was not so fortunate,' I replied.

'*Parbleu !* Where has old Peter hidden himself? We have a sufficient excuse for our seeming inhospitality in the fact that we did not expect you so soon, although we did send a carriage to meet you at the beech wood, because of a vague idea that you were coming ; but you must have missed it. We had also hoped that we should have had a few lines from you to let us know the day of your arrival. Well, as you *have* come, I can introduce you to your new home as well as anyone else.'

The stranger's manner was dry, not to say slightly dictatorial, which made his words sound coldly courteous, nothing more.

He preceded me into the house, where my mother, who was waiting for us, received him with a curtsey.

'Your aunt, I suppose ? ' said the stranger.

'My mother,' I answered.

'And your father ? '

'Died several years ago,' I replied, inwardly angered by these curt questions.

'Was he a clergyman too ? '

'Yes, at—in Thuringia.'

'Ah indeed ! Allow me to welcome you to Seeried, madam,' he said more gently, as he turned to my mother. 'I hope that you and your son will keep house happily together, until you get a daughter-in-law to help you. How do you like the place ? '

My mother answered that she thought the house seemed very nice.

The stranger then looked round the room, and said :

‘I see that some sort of preparation has been made for your reception. The children have not been altogether idle. But where can they be? Is there no one in the house?’

At this moment we heard footsteps rapidly approaching across the entrance hall, and immediately afterwards a thin, grey-haired little man came in, whose dark grey coat, brown waist-coat, white cravat, black stockings and buckled shoes, plainly marked his condition in life. He was bareheaded, and had two enormous keys in his hand— the church keys evidently. When he saw us in the room, he stood respectfully in the doorway, while our visitor exclaimed :

‘Master Peter, Master Peter, where had you hidden yourself with the keys instead of being here to welcome the new clergyman? You were in the church, were you? Well, then, no doubt you have put it in fit order to be seen for the first time. Pastor Bergmann,’ he continued, turning to me, ‘this is your sacristan, old Peter, a faithful keeper of the keys, who, in the fifty years during which he has held that office, has seen many a clergyman enter on his duties here, but never one so young as you—or perhaps so learned. Be kind to him, and patient with him—he deserves it.’

I went up to old Peter, who shyly bowed his head, and, when I held out my hand, would have kissed it.

'No, no,' I said, 'don't do that ; but promise to help me as well as you can, and to show me how to win the hearts of my parishioners.'

I shook him heartily by the hand, and the old man shaded his eyes as he answered :

'Your Reverence is very kind. Make allowance for your old servant.'

The gentleman with the riding-whip smiled, and said :

'That's all right. But now, old keeper of the keys, tell me where the girls are ? '

'They are either in the orchard or in the church-yard ; they called me out of the church.'

'Well then, Pastor, would you not like to come and make the acquaintance of two of the lambs of your flock ? '

So saying, he left the room, his spurs clinking at every step. I followed him, my mother remaining to speak to the old sacristan. We went out at the back door, through the yard, and into the large orchard behind, which was separated by a horn-beam hedge from the burying ground, while the latter was bordered by hazels. 'God's Acre' was a pleasant sight with its hazel bushes, snowballs, roses, lilacs and elders, and the green leaves of the great lime trees surrounding the church looked particularly fresh against the white-wash of the building.

There was a well in the yard at the back of the Parsonage, and plenty of ducks, geese, and chickens were pecking about.

' Look there, Herr Pastor,' said my guide, ' these creatures will be as glad as the rest of the world that you have come, for your mother will see that they do not starve. But where in the name of wonder have those girls hidden themselves ? '

A low laugh drew our attention to one part of the hedge, and on approaching it, the two girls, I had formerly seen in the back room, rose from behind it.

' There you are,' cried my companion, shaking his riding-whip at them laughingly, ' there you are, you rogues ; shake hands with the Pastor, and bid him welcome. My daughter Helen, and the sacristan's grand-daughter Christina.

They immediately held out their hands over the low hedge. Yellow-haired Christina's, strong sun-burnt fingers gave me welcome, and then the tiny hand of my strange companion's lovely little daughter was laid in mine, and so slender and delicate was it, that it reminded me of an apple-blossom.

Helen was little more than a child. She wore a simple white frock without any trimming. It fitted her to perfection, and was in perfect keeping with the country life she was leading. As she stood there looking at me over the hedge with a strange mixture of child-like trust, maidenly reserve, and respect for my priestly office, I thought she much resembled the young lady who had driven past us on the heath with her mother. If it were not she, the likeness was marvellous.

'And now,' said Helen's father, drily, 'the Pastor is properly introduced to the Parsonage, you will be glad to be left alone for a little, I am sure, Herr Bergmann. Christina, will you be so kind as to go to the Castle with Helen, and tell the Countess that she was not mistaken—Pastor Bergmann has arrived, and there is no fire in the kitchen; do you understand? Good bye,' he continued, addressing me, 'I shall ride on, leaving you to the charge of old Peter. We shall soon meet again.'

The two girls hastened away, keeping close to the hedge, their white straw hats glinting in the sun. We returned to the house. My curiosity was much excited as to who my companion might be. As he did not tell me his name, I thought I might ask him what it was. So as we went down the steps into the garden together, I ventured to say :

'And pray, sir, may I ask who it is I have the honour of counting as my first acquaintance in Seeried? To whom am I indebted for the kindness of welcoming me to my new home?'

He looked at me enquiringly, and then said :

'Did you ever read Lavater's "Physionomy?"

But who is there now-a-days that has not done so?
Well, and for what do you take me?'

I felt rather awkward, for the stranger, fixing his
eyes upon me interrogatively, slowly drew his
snuff-box out of his pocket, opened it, and awaited
my answer.

As I was obliged to reply to a question put after
this fashion, I said:

'I do not thoroughly understand Lavater's
theories.   But if I am to answer you, I think that
you must be either the agent or the private-
secretary of Count von Seeried-Strandow.'

'Agent—secretary!   Not so bad!   I am something of the kind,' he said, with a curious smile on
his harsh face.   Then taking a pinch of snuff, he
gave old Peter some directions that I did not hear.
After which he added: 'Good bye, Pastor, we shall
meet again soon, and shall get to know each other
better.'

With that, he walked rapidly down the garden
path, mounted his impatient horse, threw a piece
of money to the man who had held it, and rode
away at a gallop.

CHAPTER V.

'Think you it is a pleasant thing to have to do with ghosts?'
                                DER GROSSKOPHTA.

'Ganz einsam liegt auf dem Kirchhof
Das stille Pfarrerhaus.

.   .   .   .   .

'Der tote Vater steht draussen
Im schwarzen Pred'gergewand.'
                                HEINE.

PETER now went to call some of the men who
had come in from their work in the fields,
to carry our boxes into the house and dispose them
as my mother thought good. When this was
done I changed my dusty clothes, and then made
enquiries about our driver, whom I wished to pay
and dismiss; but Peter informed me that this was
already done, and that all the expenses I had
incurred during the journey would be repaid by
the Count.

When I asked the old man who my unknown
visitor had been, he simply enquired whether he
had not told me himself. And on my assuring
him that he had left me to guess what office he
held, the sacristan replied that he would tell me
himself the next time we met, which would most

probably be on the following day, when I should
of course go up to the castle to call upon the
Count and Countess.

I asked no further questions on the subject, but
desired Peter to show me the church, leaving my
mother to arrange a little feast out of the remains
of the provisions we had in our luncheon-basket.

We went across the burying-ground towards the
table-land on which the church stood. The graves,
and even the vaults, where many of my predecessors in office were buried, were covered with
turf.

Their names and the date of their death were
engraved on the headstones. I stood still involuntarily, and began to read the inscriptions, wondering whether my grave would ever lie side by side
with these. Old Peter could not resist the
temptation of enlarging on the meagre records,
thus making me better acquainted with the history
of the family at the Castle, which was the central
point of all his revelations.

'Look, sir,' said he, pointing almost reverentially
at a grey and mossy tombstone, 'that stone covers
the dust of as good a man as ever lived, Pastor
Gildemeister, God rest his soul. He was clergyman here nearly fifty years ago. Ah, how well I
remember that time! I was sacristan even in
those days, although I was but young. It was
then that we married Count Frederick of blessed
memory to his first wife, Countess Julia von der

Schulenburg, and a year later we christened Count
Arthur, the present lord of Seeried-Strandow.
Then Countess Julia died, and was buried in the
family vault at Strandow. Oh but she was proud
and stately, as you will see from her portrait in the
picture-gallery at the castle. Her son grew up
and went abroad. When he was away on the
grand tour the old gentleman found it dull work
living alone, so he married again, that the family
might be in no danger of dying out, for you see it
was a risky thing to have only one life to depend
upon. His second wife was a Baroness von
Bohlen, who died the following year in giving
birth to the twins, whom we christened in the
church here. Pastor Schimmelmann, who lies
under the square stone yonder, was my master
then, and he was a very good man. After that *he*
came,' continued Peter, pointing, with what was
almost a look of disgust, at an upright tablet.
'He was a different sort altogether. When he
described the terrors of hell, and thumped the
reading-desk on the pulpit, one could almost have
believed that the end of the world had come, and
that one could both hear and see the thunderings
and lightnings of the day of judgment. He was a
harsh, stern man, and yet he could go softly at the
castle. But I must not speak evil of the dead;
he has found his judge, and I will not say more to
increase his suffering.'

'What was his name?' I asked, bending over the stone in order to read the inscription.

What I saw there startled me not a little.

'How can this be?' I cried. 'Lebrecht? Gothold Samuel Lebrecht?'

'You seem to know the name, sir?' said the sacristan.

'The young Count's tutor is called Lebrecht,' I answered. 'Is he a son of that man?'

'Not a son,' was the reply, 'but some sort of relation he must be, he resembles him so much in mind.'

Here he interrupted himself as though fearing he had said too much.

'Ah well, sir,' he went on after a pause, 'it is no business of mine, is it, to criticise the Count's choice of a tutor for his only son. He is learned and wise, and ought to know what is best. Besides that, I've been chattering a great deal too much.'

'Not at all, Peter, you interest me with your old stories, I answered. 'So Pastor Lebrecht was not a good parish priest?'

'Did I say that, sir?' enquired the sacristan. 'But there is no use denying it. The truth remains the truth, whether I said it or not.—Pray, sir, let us come away from his grave. I don't want to disturb his rest—he doesn't have too much of it.'

As he said this, he turned away, and led me up from the burying-ground to the green *plateau* on which the church was built, and on which the lime trees grew. He invited me to sit down on a bench, which was placed in such a position as to command an extensive view of the village and the surrounding country, including the river, wood and meadowlands.

'You see,' said old Peter returning to his former theme, 'I am not afraid of him, for my conscience is clear. When he was alive, I often told him boldly what I thought, and it needed a good deal of courage to do that. Now that he is dead, I could meet him without fear, and that is no idle boast. For you must know, sir, that he has no rest in the grave, he *walks*'—with that the old man's voice sank to a whisper—'do not laugh. I am telling you no mere tale.'

'Then you believe in ghosts?' I asked.

'It is no question of belief,' he said. 'On certain nights he gets into the pulpit, thumps the reading-desk there, and preaches his ghostly sermon to the empty benches. Once, when I had heard a good deal of these strange occurrences, I determined to go and see for myself what went on, so, committing my soul to God, I opened the church-door and went in. A dark figure was in the pulpit, waving its arms and speaking. I stood and listened to the ghost's sermon.'

The old man stopped short. Some lines of Hölty's song, 'Be true and just in all thy dealings,' flashed into my mind—

' At midnight by the altar stands
    A figure dark and wavy,
A priest it is whose unclean hands
    On other's faults were heavy.

' The doom of such is sad and dire ;
    They haunt their former churches,
Preach against sin in words of fire,
    And *search* the money boxes.'

I could not help smiling when I remembered
having heard a story of the same kind in Thuringia
when I was a child, and recalled the shiver with
which I had drunk in all the details. My smile
did not escape old Peter's observation.

' Sir,' he said, with earnest solemnity, ' I know
that educated people do not believe in such things
now-a-days. And yet there are matters that all
the wisdom of the world cannot explain. Even
you, reverend sir, may come to a time in your life
when you will feel that your knowledge is inade-
quate, and that your intellect cannot aid you.
Pardon me for saying this. I do so as a warning,
that you may be on your guard, and may not be
too much taken by surprise by what you will perhaps one day see. You might otherwise die of
fright, like your predecessor in office. It is true
that the Count laughs at the whole thing, and says
that the poor man died a victim to a lively imagination, and to the indulgence of a superstitious
belief. But I do not see why a forefather of Count
Arthur may haunt the castle, and walk down the

long corridor leading to the Red Tower, where he used to live as a wizard and student of the black art, and it should yet be held impossible for a clergyman to haunt the church and parsonage. Can *you* see any sense in that, sir?'

' I quite agree with you,' I said, inwardly amused at the zeal old Peter displayed in behalf of the ghostly rights of the clergy. 'But tell me, how did my predecessor die?'

' This was the way of it,' answered the sacristan. When Pastor Lebrecht died, he was succeeded by a clergyman of the name of Engelreich. His grave is the last in the row, the one with the white head-stone. When he heard the story of how Pastor Lebrecht haunted the church, and even preached there at night, he laughed at me for be-lieving such cock-and-a-bull tales, and then scolded me. But one day when he was going to a funeral, he went into the back room at the parsonage to get his surplice out of the cup-board, and there he saw his dead predecessor, whom he had known personally, and who was now trying to get before him. Pastor Engelreich quickly made up his mind what to do ; he snatched the surplice from the peg, leaning over the ghost's shoulder to do so. A few days later he told me, very gravely, what had chanced. Nothing further happened for nearly six months, when Pastor Engelreich went one Sun-day to get his surplice on his way to church, but to his horror and amazement, he found Pastor Leb-

recht standing behind the surplice, holding out his
hand to him. He called to the ghost—this he told
me himself as we were walking up the path to
church, and I noticed that his face was as white as
a sheet—" Thou shalt not keep me from doing my
duty, happen what may? "   After that he went
bravely into the church, and ascended the pulpit
steps.   He was still deadly pale ; but his address
to the people was most touching—the Countess
and her daughter will tell you the same.   At the
end of the sermon, he suddenly staggered and fell,
and on rushing up the pulpit stairs to help him, we
found that he was dead.'

Old Peter told me this strange tale in a low awe-
struck voice, as he sat beside me on the bench
under the lime trees in front of the church.   I
remembered having heard a somewhat similar story
related of Pastor Philippi, court-preacher at Merse-
burg, who had died in the year 1736, under much
the same circumstances.   The event had caused
great excitement at the time.   But when the
sacristan told me his story in the full light of day,
it did not make much impression on me, for I did
not believe in ghosts.

' Tell me,' I asked, ' what did Pastor Lebrecht do
that such evil things should be said of him, now
that he is dead ? '

' Said of him?—What had he done?   Well, I
will not add to the evil that is said of him ; but he
is accused of many sins—avarice is not the worst.

They say that it was he who persuaded Count
Frederick to take a third wife to himself in his old
age. She survived him, and now lives at Strandow
with her son Charles. And there it is that Count
Leo, one of the twin brothers born of the second
marriage, has also taken up his abode.'

'What harm was there in that?' I asked.

The old man looked at me enquiringly, as
though doubtful whether to say more.

'Speak openly, Peter,' I said. 'I shall be grateful for your confidence.'

'Very well,' he answered. 'In the first place,
Count Arthur, our present lord, was married and
had two fine children, and, as was only natural, he
did not care to have his old father go a-wooing for
the third time. In the next place, they say that
Pastor Lebrecht persuaded Count Frederick to
marry on purpose to anger the heir, who had never
thought much of his Reverence. Thirdly, the
young lady who was brought to reign at the Castle,
came of a very pious stock, so that the marriage
was bound to increase the Pastor's influence in the
parish. Fourthly, the Pastor managed so to bring
matters about that it was arranged that Herr
Ephraim Lebrecht should be appointed tutor to
the two young counts, Hermann and Leo, and he
soon made dispeace between the twin brothers,
who had formerly been all in all to each other.
Fifthly, after the old Count's death, mischief was
made between Count Arthur, who was now head of

the family, and his step-brother Hermann ; but in this they all took part : the two Lebrechts, the widow and Count Leo, who had become what they call pious—God save the mark.   Ah, sir, he was such a brave, noble-hearted, young gentleman, my heart feels like to break when I think of him.'

'You mean Count Hermann?' I asked after a pause, during which the old man had been struggling to repress his emotion.   'I knew him a little, and would gladly hear that things were going well with him.'

'You knew him?   Ah, then, there is no need to tell you how good, and honest, and true he was, although he was hot-tempered and thoughtless. Our master is hard and stern, so it was easy for those who lighted the fire, to fan the flame.   But, you don't take it ill of me for speaking in this way, sir?'

'Certainly not.   I shall be grateful to you for telling me the rights of the matter.'

'Well, you see, Count Arthur had always been devoted to his step-brother, Hermann, until the twins came back from Halle with their tutor.   He then plainly showed his disapproval of Count Hermann's conduct at the university, which had been described to him as exceptionally wild, and told him that he must at once turn over a new leaf, and marry a great lady who lived in the neighbourhood.   He insisted on this as head of the family, for, failing his own son, Hermann was the next heir to the estates, being, as he was, an hour or two older than Leo. But Count Hermann declared that he had quite made up his mind whom he intended to marry, and then he took to wife a penniless girl of good birth, whose acquaintance he had made at Halle. So the quarrel began, and was much embittered by those others of whom I told you. At last Count Arthur received a letter from his brother Hermann, in which the latter announced his intention of leaving home and country, and taking service in a foreign army. He was sure to make his own way in the world, he said, and all that he would now ask of the Head of the family was, that the younger son's portion he had refused for himself, should be made over to his wife and new-born son. And our master did as he was asked, for he has a good heart, much as he tries to hide it. I believe he still sorrows for his brother, although he has never mentioned his name from that day to this, and the poor young wife has never come to Seeried with her child.'

'What has become of Count Hermann?'

'No one knows for certain. We learnt that he had gone to Holland, had entered the Dutch army, and had been sent out to the Colonies with his regiment. He probably died of the climate. They say that many do. Poor young fellow.'

Old Peter struggled hard against his emotion, and complained of the glare of the setting sun which was shining full on his face as he sat beside

me on the bench, for he did not wish me to notice
that it was to brush away his tears that he passed
his coat-sleeve across his eyes.   He now rose, and
asked me if I should like to see the inside of the
church.   So jingling his great keys, he preceded
me across the green turf that clothed the *plateau*
on which the church was built.

The church was white-washed within and without, so that it was impossible to recognise any of
the ancient ornamentation it concealed.   It had
been freshly done in honour of my arrival, and
some birch boughs were arranged against the walls
for the same purpose.   The pulpit alone, where
Pastor Gotthold Samuel Lebrecht was supposed to
preach his ghostly sermons, and the Count's family
pew, still showed the beautiful old carving that used
to adorn the whole building.

When I proposed to ascend the tower in order
to gain a view of the surrounding country, Peter
advised me to climb the oldest lime tree in the yard
instead, saying that I should find a sort of stair-
way leading to the top of the tree, that it was much
safer than the tower, and that the view was better.

We did so, and a splendid view we had ; as we
gazed through the green leaves of our natural
observatory.   The parsonage was immediately
below us, beside the church-yard, and I could see
the stork keeping watch upon the roof.   All was
quiet in the village ; but the labourers were already
beginning to troop home from their work in the

fields. Little fishing-smacks were crossing the lake at the edge of the wood, and directing their course towards the village. Then through an opening in the wood, I saw a green plain spreading out as far as the eye could reach. How astonished I was when old Peter said, pointing to it :

'That is the sea, your reverence—the Baltic.'

It was the first time that I had seen it. I feasted my eyes upon it, and rejoiced that my lot was cast within sight of the waters of the great deep.

From this point all that I could see of the Castle was an ancient red-brown tower, whose massive walls stood out against the dark-green foliage of the trees in the park. It did not seem to be more than a quarter of an hour's walk from the Parsonage. I know not how it was that the sight of the Castle instantly recalled the image of the young girl with whom I had shaken hands over the low hedge that afternoon ; perhaps it was because my unknown visitor had sent her there to announce my arrival.

I turned the conversation to the girl, and asked who she was, hoping thus to arrive at some idea of her father's position ; but the sacristan looked at me calmly, and enquired whether my visitor had told me nothing about her.

'Yes,' I answered, 'he said that she was his daughter.'

'Well, he told you the truth ; she is his daughter,' said the old man dryly, and then he drew my attention to the fishing-boats that were returning

from the sea, by way of the river and lake; adding
that the people would soon be at home, and would
be sure to wish to see me.

So we came down from the lofty wooden plat-
form that was built round the stem of the lime
tree, near the top, crossed the turf, and went round
the other side of the church. As we were passing
the chancel, I noticed a new building attached to
it. It was of marble, and built in the style of the
day. Old Peter informed me that it was the
mausoleum Count Arthur had erected for himself.

'But is not the family vault in the old church at
Strandow,' I asked, and the sacristan answered:

'Yes, the one they have used for many years;
but they were buried here in the old time, as may
be seen from the armorial bearings on the walls.
And Count Arthur wants to be buried at Seeried.
They say he has good reasons for it.'

'A secret reason, I suppose, Peter?'

'A mystery at least, sir,' replied the old man
with a look of great importance. 'And a secret,
too, if you come to that, for it is not a thing that
ought to be told to many people.'

He evidently desired that I should regard him
as a person who was treated with great and merited
confidence, and I felt that to hurt his vanity by
showing my inward amusement at his airs of
superior knowledge, would effectually prevent his
satisfying my curiosity as to what he thought were

Count Arthur's reasons for wishing to be buried at Seeried.

'Then,' I said, 'the Count told you all about it.'

'Oh no ; Count Arthur is not the kind of man to confide in one of us. You see, sir, he is a just and upright man, a true nobleman, and one who does his best for all his people. He permits none of his stewards to oppress their subordinates, and sees to it himself that his estates are properly managed. He neither screws his people, nor yet allows them to neglect their duty any more than he does his own. He has an eye to everything. I believe that he must have learnt this mode of governing from old Fritz, with whom he served for a long time. God be thanked for that, for the ways I speak of are good ways, and have brought about much needful reform. But—but—they say that old Fritz was not often to be seen inside a church, and that his thoughts about our holy religion were not such as it would do for us to share, for if we did the world would get on a wrong tack, and be altogether shipwrecked. And then, you see, the Count is a philosopher too, he confesses it himself, and gets French books that I should not care to look into. Whoever agrees with him on such subjects wins his heart at once. That red-haired fox of a tutor, who accompanied the twins from Halle after Count Frederick's death, was not long in finding it out; for that he was as sharp as a needle and as cunning as a fox no one can deny.

G

When he first came, Count Arthur questioned him
about the learned Professors at the university,
laughed at him, and argued with him, until the
clever rascal saw that it was time to give way, and
own himself beaten. He said that the Count had
awakened his doubts on such and such a subject,
greatly to the delight of the latter, who was often
heard to say that young Lebrecht had plenty of
sense, and so many good qualities, that it was quite
worth while trying to cure him of his narrow-minded
folly. He was indeed a very different sort of
person from his name-sake and cousin at the
parsonage. So the Count said and believed, but I
would take any odds that they were really
partners, and were playing a secret game. I never
trusted them. Time passed on, and at last the
tutor was converted to all of Count Arthur's
opinions, soon after which he went back to Halle
to complete his education, taking with him a large
sum of money, which he had been given to help
him on in the world. The Count was much
pleased to hear a few months later from a celebrated Professor that Ephraim Lebrecht was
considered one of the most enlightened and able
young men at the university. Then it came about
that our master had so much confidence in him as
to entrust him with the charge of his only son, the
heir of Seeried-Strandow, with whom he is now
making the grand tour. I only wish that the
young gentleman were safe home again. How

happy his mother would be. She never trusted that tutor.'

It was quite impossible to interrupt the garrulous old man, so when he stopped here for an instant to take breath, I hastened to ask—

'But the mausoleum? What had it to do with Ephraim, or he with it?'

'Ah, yes,' cried the sacristan. 'Although Count Arthur has given up all religious faith, still—there is something—but he would never confess it, that he does believe. It is,' and the old man came very close to me that he might whisper in my ear, 'It is a prophecy that was made him by a Jew in Amsterdam when he was in Holland some years ago.'

'A Jew,' I enquired with interest.

'Yes, the Count repeated it laughingly to Pastor Schimmelmann after his return, and he told me. I have never spoken of it again from that day to this.'

'What did the Jew prophesy?'

'Prophesy isn't the right word. He reckoned up the Count's life by means of the Chaldæan and Hebrew Algebra,' was the reply, in low mysterious tones.

'By the magic tables? He was a Kabbalist then?' I asked, hoarsely.

'Yes, yes, you are right,' whispered my companion.

'And what was the result of the computation?'

'The result?' cried the old man, in a voice that was sharp with terror. 'No, sir, no; I cannot tell you now. Question me no more until—until New Year's day. One thing alone I may say, and it is this: the Jew foretold that Count Arthur should die eight days before he did, and that the shadow of the Count's mausoleum should fall upon his grave.'

'That was a strange prediction, but one about which Count Arthur would hardly trouble himself,' I answered lightly, knowing the superstitious and credulous character of the old man.

To which he made reply:

'And yet the Count has built himself a mausoleum here, instead of contenting himself with the old one at Strandow.'

'What advantage did he gain by that?'

'If you had ever been at Strandow, you would know how high the church in which the Seerieds are buried stands above the surrounding country, and that its shadow really falls in the evening upon the Jewish cemetery. Nothing of the sort is to be feared here.'

Such was the answer I received.

I have written down the whole conversation as well as I can from memory, because the sacristan gave me so much information regarding the family under whose protection I was to begin my career as a country clergyman, and because this information will make my story easier for you to follow.

I have now made you acquainted with the scene in which the drama of my life was to be played, and have mentioned nearly all the persons who took part in it. Perhaps you may recognise in them some of the people you know here at Hainbuchen. Old Peter, the sacristan at Seeried, was the grandfather of our present sacristan of the same name, and our faithful old servant Christina, was the golden-haired girl, who was standing behind the hornbeam hedge with the other girl called Helen, when I was introduced to them both on the afternoon of my arrival. Who Helen was and is, you shall soon learn, if you have not already guessed.

I shall add but little more to the history of that day. When I went into the house I found a sumptuous repast awaiting me. The Countess had sent it down to my mother by the sacristan's little grand-daughter Christina, with a message to say that she was sure we must be too tired to lay in any stores that evening. Then the villagers trooped up to the Parsonage to see me, and welcome me to Seeried with a hearty shake of the hand. After which I went to bed quite tired out, and slept very comfortably, untroubled by any visit from the ghost, or by dreams of the family chronicle old Peter had unfolded.

CHAPTER VI.

'In this short time that I've been present here,
What new, unheard-of things have I not seen!
And yet they all must give place to the wonder
Which this mysterious castle guards.'

The Piccolomini. (Coleridge's Trans.)

NEXT morning I set out to pay my respects at the Castle, accompanied by the old sacristan. As we passed through the village, the men all touched their caps in friendly greeting, and the women brought their children to speak to me. I was much pleased with the kindness of my reception, and the beauty of the day further increased my cheerfulness.

My thoughts were very busy as I pursued my way. I was going to see the Count, the man who was lord paramount in the parish to which I had been appointed clergyman. I hoped to make a favourable impression upon him, for much of my usefulness depended upon it. Then the image of the lovely girl I had seen on the previous day rose up before me, and while I was yet calling to mind every incident of our introduction, we came to a part of the road overlooking the graves of the former clergy of the parish. The sight of their tomb-stones reminded me how closely their lives had been connected with those of the lords of Seeried, and I wondered whether some garrulous old sacristan would ever stand beside the green hillock beneath which I was laid, and discourse of my doings. The allusion old Peter had made to the Kabbalistic prophecy now flashed into my mind, and turned my thoughts for a moment to the old longing for power to look into the future, and learn what it should bring forth. But the novelty of my surroundings, and the loveliness of the day soon dispersed all such gloomy thoughts. I feasted my eyes on the sparkling waters of the lake, and on the deep shadows of the trees in the park, where a cuckoo was shouting his glad cry in the green twilight, and a deer might now and then be seen crossing a glade in the wood. I was much delighted with the beauty of the landscape, and when I remembered that the sea was close at hand, my whole soul was filled with joy, and with deep gratitude to the kind providence that had cast my lines in such a pleasant place.

We had not walked very far through the thick woodland when we came to an open space surrounded by great gnarled beech trees. Their roots protruded from the ground like petrified snakes, while the ground itself was, in some places, firm and turfy, and in others, a morass. In the centre was a round pool, black and gloomy beyond description.

Far in the background, to one side of it, was a large castellated building, whose turrets and gables rose higher than the tops of the trees ; more especially was this the case with an old and gigantic round tower attached to one end of it, from which the outer coating of lime had fallen away sufficiently to display the red-brown colour of the bare walls. A few more steps, and the Castle was lost to sight behind the trees. The marsh, beside which we were walking, seemed all the more gloomy and forlorn because of this. It was a wild, melancholy, and dreary scene.

'Let us walk a little quicker, your reverence,' suggested the sacristan.

'Why, Master Peter?' I asked.

'I do not like this place.'

I was growing accustomed to his strange ways, and thought his dislike to the marsh probably had its origin in some curious old family tradition. Being interested in such things, I went on to say :

'It is not a particularly cheerful spot, I grant you ; but what is the matter with the bog, that you should have such a horror of it?'

Peter looked at me askance.

'There is no harm in the place itself,' he answered, 'but a foul deed was committed here, which makes it an unpleasant spot to linger in. It did not get the name of the Slough of Blood for nothing.'

'What do you mean? How did it get such a ghastly name?'

'You may well say "ghastly,"' answered the old man. 'With the exception of the Red Tower, or Count Ruttger's Tower, as it is also called, this spot is more dreaded than any other for miles around—for—a—curse—was—laid—upon—it.'

Peter whispered the last words very low and impressively. Then he continued:

'Long ago, when the lords of Seeried-Strandow were the wildest chieftains in the whole North Country, having at their command large bands of armed retainers, their vassals determined to make an earnest appeal to their master's justice and generosity. Certain of their number were deputed to go to him accompanied by the old clergyman of the parish. But when they reached this spot, they were met by their lord and his brothers, who, having received warning of their intention, came out to meet them at the head of their armed force, fell upon them here, and slew them all. Their blood dyed the waters of the pool, and their stiffening corpses bore silent witness to the tyranny of their oppressors. It is said that one of the young lords stabbed the clergyman with his own hand, at the same time crying, "Bend thy proud neck, haughty priest, thy lord and master is here!" And then it was that the old man cursed the place with his dying breath. He prophesied that the day should come when the pool should be stained

with the blood of one of the noble house of Seeried-
Strandow, and that the guilt of that day's work
should not even then pass from the family, but
should rest upon it, until certain of its daughters
should become the wives of country clergymen,
and a pastor's daughter lady of the castle.'

'And has the prophecy been fulfilled?' I asked,
as we picked our way amongst the roots of the
trees on the borders of the pool.

'Not yet—or only in part,' replied the sacristan.
'One of the young gentlemen was killed somewhere hereabouts by a woodman whom he had
horsewhipped. And later on, Count Ruttger, he
who died in the Red Tower, you know, was
wounded here by a stag, and the story goes that
this very Count Ruttger would have married a
clergyman's daughter had his father not forced
him to wed another woman. The different members of the family are never very friendly with
each other now, and that comes from the curse the
old clergyman laid upon them. Besides that, the
wood is a very awful place to walk through at
night—the spirits of those who were slain here rise
out of the marsh, and flit through the wood at certain seasons. I have seen them with my own eyes,
and can give you the names of many others who
have witnessed the same sight. But I saw something even worse than that on the night of the
first Sunday in Advent, when I was going home
from the castle, where I had been to offer my re-

spectful congratulations to the Count and Countess
on the twenty-second anniversary of their wedding-
day.'

'And what did you see, Master Peter?' I enquired.

He stood still and gazed fixedly at the pool for
a few moments. Then shaking his head slowly
and mysteriously, he went on :

'Look, sir, it was just there—no, I cannot tell
you—let us hasten away.'

'If you ought not to tell me,' I said, 'you are
quite right to keep silence.'

I then proceeded along the broad path without
another word. The sacristan looked at me several
times as though hoping to be questioned. Finding
that his expectations were vain he could restrain
himself no longer, and said :

'Well, sir, as you want to know what I saw on
the night of Advent Sunday, I will tell you. The
weather was rather cold, so the butler gave me a
glass of wine before I left the castle, after which I
set out on my walk through the wood thinking no
evil. The moon was shining through the clouds,
and its light fell full upon the pool over yonder.
All at once I saw something white in the water
and thought it was the reflection of the moon, but
when I looked more carefully I saw that it was—
I cannot bear to think of it—it was the Count
himself, and his face looked as pale and wan as
that of the moon.'

'What? Do you mean to say that Count
Arthur had fallen into the pool?'

'No. Count Arthur was sitting in the drawing-
room of the castle with his wife and daughter. I
had seen him as I passed the window. But
whether what I saw was his double, his wraith, or
what else it might be, I cannot tell.'

'And then, Master Peter,' I asked.

'Nothing has happened as yet, but it is not a
year since I saw it,' sighed the old man. Then
stopping short, he stretched out his arm to draw
my attention to the scene before me.

We had come out of the wood, and had reached
an open space in the midst of which stood the
Castle, and close to it was a small lake, on the blue
waters of which several swans were to be seen.

'Here we are. That is Castle Seeried, sir,' said
the sacristan, openly delighted at the impression
made upon me by the building.

Immediately in front of it was a fountain, whose
waters fell into the basin below with a sort of
cadenced murmur. The central part of the Castle
rose to a height of three stories, and was supported
on either side by great wings two stories high. It
was built after the fashion of the palaces of the
Netherlands or Brabant, in the *Renaissance* style
as it is now called. This comparatively modern
building was attached to an old tower by a variety
of curious pinacles and twisted gables of irregular
form, which were placed at unequal distances, and

towered one above the other with their weather-cocks or chimneys. This was the remains of the old Castle, whose architecture was a pain and grief to the eyes of all the *connoisseurs* of that time.

Old Peter told me that the modern building had been begun by the father of Count Ruttger, and had been completed by the latter according to his own plans, in spite of the hermit life he led in the Red Tower, where he devoted himself to the study of alchemy and the magic arts.

This same Red Tower was enormous in girth and height. The ancient lime trees in the court-yard only reached half way up its massive walls. There it stood, gloomy, dark, impenetrable, ghost-like, towering far above its surroundings.

A broad avenue over-arched by trees led up to the Castle. The grassy lawn, intersected by a stream, was alive with swans and other water fowls, which might be seen enjoying themselves now on land, and now in the water. On the other side of the lawn was a sort of garden or pleasance, laid out after the French fashion, with curves and spirals, beech borders and dwarf trees, amongst which were introduced a number of mythological and allegorical figures carved out of stone. Beyond that again, the wood was so disposed as to form one of those parks that were so much admired last century. In it might be seen rockeries, grottoes, hermitages, and labyrinths, with some epigramatic sentence carved or written on rock or stone within the maze. There were water-works of every description, and artificial mounds forty feet high, from one of which, as I afterwards found, there was a splendid view of the sea.

Several smaller buildings adjoined the Castle for the use of the land-steward, secretary, and other officials employed on the estate. These houses were not visible from the avenue, but we could see them distinctly as we came up the narrow path leading to the Red Tower. At length we reached the broad fosse surrounding the Castle. Beyond it were flower-beds and bosquets of sweet smelling shrubs.

Old Peter now began to discourse of Count Ruttger's ghostly doings in the Red Tower, and of his nocturnal pacing of the long corridor leading to it. No one, he assured me, would trust himself within the walls of the Tower for fear of the ghost, which had been seen by many people, and by himself amongst the number. It was late one evening that he had met it in the corridor, and he had at once recognised it from its black velvet doublet and pale brow. You could not mistake them, for you could see the same any day in the picture hanging in the portrait gallery, or in the one in the Red Tower. Count Arthur, he confessed, would listen to none of these stories, refusing to believe them; but his incredulity did not prevent their being true; and then, it must not be forgotten that the young heir and his sister had once seen their ancestor's ghost when they were children, and were playing in the corridor connecting the new building with the Red Tower.

The old man talked of these things so long, and with such conviction, that my imagination was kindled, and I gazed at the Tower with even more interest than at first.

Suddenly it flashed into my mind that I had heard of it before, and that, somehow, in connection with my Kabbalistic studies.

'Master Peter,' I asked, interrupting him in his long and garrulous tale, 'is there not a library, or, at any rate, a collection of books in Count Ruttger's Tower.'

The sacristan looked at me again with one of his strange questioning glances before answering.

'Yes,' he said at length, 'there is a cabinet in the laboratory with curious Chaldaic symbols painted on it. No one knows the meaning of them. It is said that the cabinet is full of books of magic and other devilry of the sort. No honest Christian would trouble his head with such things, for if any man opens one of these books there is no hope for him either here or hereafter ; he falls a prey to the Evil One, because having once tasted of that forbidden knowledge, he cannot refrain from it. The end of Count Ruttger is an awful warning to all foolhardy persons who desire to meddle with the magic art. He was one day found in his laboratory in the Red Tower with his neck twisted, his glasses

and retorts all scattered around him. The doors
of the cabinet were standing wide open, and a
Hebrew book of incantations was lying half-torn
upon the floor. The window was open, and yet
there was a strong smell of sulphur in the room,
which plainly shewed that something devilish had
been there. It is no jesting matter to have dealings with the red-haired fiend, reverend sir, he is
not one to stand any nonsense. He gives nothing
for nothing.'

'He does not seem to have interfered with the
young Count's tutor,' I answered, 'and yet he read
that book, as he told me himself.'

'Do you think that he got off because of his red
hair or his wickedness?' enquired the old man in
a tone of deep consideration. '"Like will to like,"
as the proverb says, and no doubt they had many
a friendly meeting up there in the Tower room.
But they had no good object in view, you may be
sure of that. The red-haired fiend would never
have taken the trouble to enter into an alliance
with that other of whom you spoke, unless it had
been to further some evil design. I never thought
that good would come of it when I saw how Herr
Ephraim Lebrecht flattered Count Arthur, and
whispered calumnies against poor Count Hermann.
And afterwards, when I heard that my lord intended to trust his only son to the guidance of
that hypocrite, I could no longer hold my peace ;
but Count Arthur would not listen to a word I had

to say. He bade me be silent for a silly old fool.
Since then I have never alluded to the subject ;
but, mark my words, reverend sir, mischief will
come of it.'

'What do you mean, Master Peter ?'

'What do I mean ? Can I say more than this.
Seeried-Strandow is a magnificent estate, and one
which even *saintly* Count Leo would have no
objection to possess. But now, sir, please follow
me, you will find it pleasanter in the shade.'

We then crossed the fosse by means of a rustic
bridge and entered the garden, which extended as
far as the Castle walls, and was planted with all
kinds of flowering shrubs, bird-cherries, fruit trees,
and flower-beds, the whole intersected by grassy
walks.

I glanced up at the windows of the Castle with
an involuntary hope of seeing the sweet girlish face
that so persistently haunted my thoughts. But no
one was visible anywhere, except a maid-servant,
to whom old Peter smilingly touched his hat.

All at once, when we turned the corner of the
path, we perceived a young lady seated on a
wicker chair under a blossoming apple tree at a
little distance from us. I could not at first see her
face distinctly for it was bent over her book. Her
yellow hair was untouched by powder, and her
dress was perfectly simple.

As we approached more nearly, she became
aware of our presence, and looked up to see who

was there. Laying down her book she rose to greet us, and I saw that it was Helen. How sweet and innocent she looked as she stood there under the apple tree, whose blossoms were put to shame by the delicate pink and white of her complexion.

I was young in those days, and hitherto no woman had made any impression upon me. Helen was little more than a child, but my heart beat quickly as I approached her. The shy dignity of her manner gave her a wondrous charm. Conquering the timidity I felt at addressing her, I said :

'Pardon me for disturbing you, however unintentionally, but I cannot let this opportunity pass without thanking you in my mother's name, and my own, for your kind thought in decorating the Parsonage——.'

'Ah, pray do not say so much about it,' interrupted the girl. 'It is not worth talking of, and to tell the truth, my help was nothing better than a hindrance to the sacristan's grand-daughter. Chrissy really worked, and we shall both be glad if you and your mother were pleased.'

'So kind a reception could not be otherwise than pleasant,' I answered.

'And have you got everything comfortably settled now at the Parsonage?' she enquired.

'As much so as is possible in so short a time,' I replied ; 'and I like the place so much, that I am determined to do all in my power to gain the good will of those with whom it rests whether I go or stay.—But do not let me keep you longer from your studies.'

Helen blushed when she saw me glance at the two books she had left lying on the garden seat. Picking them up, she said :

' I wonder whether you will think less well of me, Herr Pastor, if I confess that my studies were of a very simple kind ?   Look, these are the books I was reading.'

I would not take them at first ; but she insisted, alleging that unless we were frank with each other we could never become friends. So I looked at the books.   Greatly to my astonishment, I found that one of them was ' The Vicar of Wakefield ' in the original.   I had not expected to find that the young girl was so highly educated as to be able to read the language of Shakespeare, Milton, Sterne, and Goldsmith, and I could not help expressing my amazement.

' Ah,' interposed the old sacristan, ' that will be the story of the clergyman's family which the young lady here translated into German for my Christina. There is no harm in it, is there, your Reverence ? '

' Certainly not.   I only wish there were more stories like it for girls to read,' I answered rather pedantically. 'And these,' I continued, opening the other book, ' are Hölty's poems. I did not know that they had been collected yet. Which is your favourite, Miss Helen ? '

She hesitated a moment.   Then she said :

'What I like so much in Hölty is the simplicity of his language, the depth and purity of his feeling, the *naïveté* of his thoughts, and the swing and music of his verse.   I know several of his poems by heart.   When I took up the volume to-day, I found one or two little pieces that were new to me ; amongst others, a very pretty one which I was induced to read by finding a description of an apple orchard in it.'

I turned over the pages slowly, and found the alcaic lines to 'The future queen of my heart,' and those addressed 'To the apple trees under which I first saw Julia.'

Old Peter was growing impatient, and I suddenly became aware that I was lingering longer than good manners warranted, so I returned the books without further remark.   Meanwhile the girl had turned shyly to the sacristan.

'Why did you not bring Chrissy with you, father Peter ?' she asked.

'I could not ; you see his Reverence is going to wait upon—upon the Count and Countess,' answered the old man, tapping the ground impatiently with his foot.

'I will go in and let them know,' cried the young girl, running down the gravelled path without further leave-taking.   In another moment she had vanished through a side door.

While we continued on our way to the principal

entrance, I could not help remarking that Miss Helen seemed to be particularly well educated, to which old Peter made answer:

'And no wonder, considering the amount of money that has been spent on her education.'

'Then her father must be not only a very enlightened man, but a rich one to boot?' I said.

The old man nodded, and answered dryly:

'His affairs are in good order. But now, reverend sir, look, there are the door-steps before you. You cannot miss your way, so I will wish you good-bye for the present.'

He then left me, and went to see his friends amongst the servants of the Castle.

Left to myself, I at first thought more of Helen than of the visit I was about to make. Sweet visions passed before me of a happy, peaceful home, and of a wife in whose bright eyes I should always be able to read sympathy and encouragement. But—I was drawing near the steps that led to the front door, and had to turn my thoughts to other things. Surrounded by the modern building was a quadrangle which was partially paved, and was set about with orange trees in tubs. This I crossed, and so reached the steps that led to a glass door. It opened from within. On my enquiry, the porter informed me that the Count and the Countess were at home.

Another servant in livery led me to a long corridor, which was carpetted from end to end,

He told me that my visit was expected, and that
the Count had given orders that I should be shown
into the morning-room on my arrival, as he had
seen me before. I was much surprised to hear
this, but had no time to wonder where and when it
could have been, for immediately afterwards the
servant opened the door of a sort of ante-room,
and begged me to enter. As far as I could judge
from merely passing through it, the room was
handsomely furnished ; but I was hardly capable
at the moment of taking in a distinct impression
of such things. My guide now opened the folding-
doors beyond, and ushered me into a large and
lofty apartment.

While I stood shyly on the threshold, a gentleman came forward to welcome me. He wore an
embroidered velvet coat of a reddish-brown colour ;
his waistcoat was also embroidered. Two ladies,
who were seated at the far end of the room, rose
and advanced a few steps towards me.

' How do you do, Pastor,' said the gentleman, in
a voice that I had surely heard before, ' I am happy
to see you.'

I looked at him enquiringly, and recognised the
stern face of the stranger who had welcomed me
to the Parsonage on the preceding day, though its
expression was now softened by a smile. It was
Count Arthur himself.

' And,' he continued, with an easy courteous
manner that was extremely attractive, ' allow me

to make you acquainted with my wife and daughter. The latter, however, you have met before—— '

He went on speaking for a few moments, but I either did not hear, or did not understand what he said. For there stood the beautiful lady whose carriage had passed us on the heath, and in her daughter, I at once recognised—Helen!

CHAPTER VII.

'" Die Wunder, die er thut?"
'" Märchen !"
'"So viele haben doch gesehen—"
'" Blinde !"
'"So viele glauben—"
'" Tröpfe !"
'"Es ist zu allgemein ! Die ganze Welt ist davon überzeugt."
'"Weil sie albern ist."'

DER GROSSKOPTA.

I WAS utterly confounded, and not a little ashamed of the absurdity of my position. I turned red and pale as I stammered out a few incomprehensible words of excuse, and my shyness increased every moment when I recollected all that had passed in my interviews with the Count and his daughter.

The Countess came to my relief by saying pleasantly :

'I wish I had known that you and your mother were on your way here, Herr Bergmann, for I should then have been sure that it was you when I met you on the heath, and should have introduced myself. You would have made the rest of your journey so much more quickly and comfortably by coming with us, and leaving your luggage to follow.'

She asked me to be seated, and led the conversation to other matters, so that I was at length able to master my confusion to a considerable extent, and answer the Count's questions about Professor Semler, for whom he expressed the highest esteem. I avoided looking at the young lady, and if ever I did so by accident, my eyes immediately sought the carpet.

Helen sat quietly beside her mother, taking no part in the conversation, which, it must be confessed, would have come to an untimely end had it not been for the gallant efforts made by the elder lady. Her husband's enquiries about some of the learned men in Halle, enabled her to turn our attention to general literature, and I must say that I had never yet heard any woman discourse on the literature of her time with so delicate a criticism, and justness of thought. I was particularly struck by what she said of Richardson's novels, which were then extremely admired in Germany. She pointed out how slightly sketched were the characters of Pamela, Clarissa, and Sir Charles Grandison, and showed that the heroes and heroines of these books were rather incorporated virtues and vices than typical men and women. Her opinion of the German tales of Dusch and Starke was also clear and to the point. The Count smiled, and said, sarcastically :

'What is all this? my opponent has come round
to my way of thinking, and acknowledges that I
am right.   You confess now, Cornelia, that neither
English nor German writers can hold a candle to
the French.   In which of their works can you find
such perfection of style, and refinement of expression, as in the writings of Diderot and d'Alembert,
or such wit and variety as in those of Voltaire.
His novels——'

'You are jumping rather too quickly to a con-
clusion, Arthur,' answered the Countess. 'In
Sterne, Goldsmith, and one or two others, the
English have authors, with whose greatness no
Frenchman of the present day can hope to vie, for
French literature is thin and carping, not broadly
human like the other.'

'Bah!' cried the Count, snapping his fingers
lightly. 'Not one of them is worthy to be compared with Voltaire, for they are all sentimentalists
more or less!   And the world is with them there,
hence the favour in which Ossian's poems are held!
"The times are all awry," and the present generation is incapable of appreciating Voltaire as he deserves.   As for our German poet, he is perhaps
great enough to tie Wieland's shoe-strings. These
young poetical upstarts are all jealous of Wieland,
he stands so high above them.'

'Their opposition is perhaps founded on better
grounds,' replied the Countess. 'It may be that
they are actuated by the same reasons as those

which induced the author of "Emilia Galotti" to
enter the lists against the best French dramatists.'

'And these reasons, Cornelia?' asked the Count.

'That the German can beat the Frenchman, and
does not need to import the dry leaves of French
literature that he may adorn himself therewith.
Where is the Frenchman who has attained the sublime heights of Klopstock, or has shown the taste
of Lessing? The literary genius of France may
be characterised as: effect in perfection of form!'

'That is a daring proposition, Cornelia,' said the
Count.

'But it is true, for all that,' answered the Countess.
'Look, here is a copy of Lessing's "Nathan," which
was published the other day. It is a case in point.
How much more nobly does he treat the subject
of ecclesiastical intolerance than Voltaire and his
followers, and how much more convincing are his
arguments than their frivolous tirades against what
is holy?'

'I thoroughly agree with you in your apprecia-
tion of Lessing,' replied the Count, 'but "one
swallow does not make a summer." We began by
talking of novelists, my dear; what German can
you mention?'

'There is only one,' she said, smiling, 'who is
capable of forcing your Frenchmen, one and all, to
retire before him. In which of their books will
you find such wonderful delineation of character,
such depth of feeling—Rousseau alone shows some

slight capacity for it—and such power of expression
as in " Werther " ! '

'Ah, there we are at last,' cried the Count laughing heartily, and springing from his chair. 'It is a
mad book, and was written by a madman, who by
means of it has driven everyone in the Empire,
both gentle and simple, as mad as himself.'

I had hitherto listened in silence to the conversation between the Count and his wife, but the former
now turned to me with a quick movement and
said :

'And what do you think, Pastor Bergmann, of
the mad pranks literature is now playing in Germany ?   I hear that all the great geniuses are trying their best to outdo each other, and that the
storm and stress of spirit they endure makes them
leap over all the old barriers of decorum with the
agility of human grasshoppers.   You are a
Thuringian, and can tell me whether it is true
about the wild life that they say is led at the Court
of Weimar, and whether the son of the town-coun-
cillor of Frankfort really makes the princes and
princesses there dance to his piping? I have heard
so many incredible stories that I hardly know what
to believe.'

'The state of matters there is rather eccentric,' I
answered ; 'but things are not so bad when you
look at them closely as they appear to be at a distance.   The muse of poetry sees to that. And
then, my lord, you must remember the condition

of the Court of Weimar is only one of the signs of
the times, and that they are wild and troubled, and
leavened with the yeast of change.'

'You are right, Pastor,' said the Count. 'The
times are wild, and portend great changes. Young
men must learn betimes how to venture out into
the troubled waters, that they may not be overwhelmed. My son will learn to do this. A wise
hand is guiding him. Thus taught, he will breast
the waves, and ride safely through the storm.'

An irrepressible sigh broke from the lips of the
Countess, her husband glanced at her, and then
went on :

'Yes, indeed, the world was never madder than
it is just now. At many Courts it is the fashion to
wear the blue Werther coat with brass buttons,
yellow waistcoat, white trousers and top boots—the
'genietracht,' as they call it. And why should that
astonish me? Is it not the thing in Berlin to wear
red waistcoats, because it is said that Jesus wore
one when he went to Jerusalem? Madness! They
are all symptoms of the same disease.'

Count Arthur's manner showed how keenly he
felt on the subject. It was strange to me to notice
with what vehemence of dislike he spoke of the
silly, but not worse than silly manifestations of the
social and æsthetic spirit of the times in Germany,
while he felt nothing but admiration for the French
philosophers, who acknowledged no authority but
their own poignant wit, and who heedlessly shook

the foundations of Church and State, until at last both fell with a mighty crash during the great French Revolution. Count Arthur's mental attitude towards the Encyclopædists was shared by almost everyone who belonged to the *haute societé* of the day. They greeted the destructive tendencies in the works of these men with acclamation, only to shrink back aghast before the *results* of this teaching, as before an unnatural, inexplicable phenomenon.

The Countess, who had sighed at the mention of her son's tutor, and who probably guessed what turn the conversation would now take, got up to leave the room with her daughter. She bade me farewell very kindly, saying that she hoped soon to have the pleasure of making my mother's acquaintance.

When the two ladies had left the room, it seemed to me as if they had taken all the sunshine with them, it felt both colder and darker. Although my shyness grew less, my comfort did not increase. Had I been alone my thoughts would have turned sadly to the consideration of the melancholy fact that pretty little Helen was no simple maiden to be wooed by me, but a high-born lady, a daughter of the noble house of Seeried-Strandow. I had no time, however, to indulge in such reflections, for the Count began to speak to me at once.

' I am very glad to see you alone,' he said, ' for we can now discuss several matters in peace without being disturbed by feminine terrors. As you have already seen, he continued with a slight smile, it is better to let women think they have the victory in an argument, it makes them so much happier. They must be allowed to go on believing many a thing that a man's fuller knowledge forbids his accepting. No woman can appreciate Voltaire, or his opinions.'

'Thank God!' I ejaculated in my heart. I had nearly said it aloud.

The Count seemed to read my thoughts—perhaps my manner may have betrayed them—for he went on to say:

'If you are the kind of man Professor Semler described you to be, you will find helpful friends in my wife, and in our daughter, whose education I have always left her mother to direct. As for myself, I will not hinder you in any way, but rather assist you when I can. Then, with regard to the religious education of the people, I think that every thing should be done decently and in order. No exaggeration anywhere. I will have no Methodists about the place; "Quietists," as they are called, are extremely obnoxious to me. But mind, I do not want a philosophising peasantry either. No, no; let every man on my property go to heaven his own way—I hold with Frederick the Great in that. So now, Herr Bergmann, you understand; no Methodists and no Atheists; let the people believe all that is reasonable in the

Christian religion, and even a little more, for it is necessary that they should ; the common people need something of that kind to keep them straight. We do not.   Voltaire has raised the veil, and let us see ; but we must take care to keep it over the eyes of the masses.   You understand me, Pastor ? '

I understood him perfectly, and bowed in silence ; for had I allowed myself to speak, I could not have helped protesting against what he had just said.   My thoughts, moreover, were much occupied with other things.

The Count continued to talk in the same strain for some minutes, after which he returned to the curious signs of the times.   He thought it very extraordinary, he said, that after Voltaire and his followers had set Reason on her throne in the face of the whole world, a wizard like Schröpfer should still be able to fool people of the highest rank in enlightened Saxony, and mystic folly make people mad enough to believe that a Cagliostro possessed the Philosopher's Stone and the Elixir of Life.

I might have told him that these things were only the necessary reaction from the unfruitful doctrine of negation preached by the French philosophers, for the human soul can never be satisfied without a foreboding of its high origin, and of the communion of spirits.

' The world,' he cried, ' has gone mad.   It seems as though Europe were being Zoroastrianised, and regarded this as a sign of progress.   At such times

each man is thrown back upon himself, and has to
see to it that he is not drawn away into the whirl-
pool. We must do our duty, Pastor, and make a
firm stand, not only for our own sakes, but in order
that our children may learn from our example.
Look you, Herr Bergmann, chance, or as you
would probably say Providence, was kind, in
forcing me, though sorely against my will, to make
the acquaintance of the man who, of all others, was
best fiitted to preserve my son from the dangers of
the age. A clear head was needed for that, and
he has it. My son shall learn to stand on his own
feet, and Ephraim Lebrecht is the man to teach
him to do so. Only think, he came here a sour-
faced Methodist, hanging his head almost to his
knees ; but at length he was converted, thanks to
Voltaire, for no weak words of mine could have
worked so radical a cure.'

The Count spoke with that kind of modesty
which seems unconsciously desirous of awakening
the hearer's belief that the effect produced was
really due to the eloquence of the speaker. I contented myself with listening to him, as he evidently
did not care to have my opinion on the subject.
So he went on to tell me how necessary he thought
it, that other and more enlightened views should
be held by the members of his family, for it seemed
to him that his house had been oppressed for
generations by a gloomy and superstitious faith in
tradition.

He then rose, and going to one of the windows, drew the heavy crimson damask curtain a little aside, and looked out. He beckoned me to join him. The window overlooked that part of the garden which lay close to the old part of the castle, whose walls were masked to a considerable height by trees and shrubs. The Red Tower was at the further end of it, and the Count's eyes were fixed on its massive proportions in gloomy reverie.

' Look at the Tower yonder,' he said at length. ' There it stands, a monument of the past, seeming to presage evil, so much is it out of keeping with its surroundings. Were it able to speak, it could tell us many a strange and barbarous tale, and even as it is, the legends attached to it are not a few. One of my ancestors, Count Ruttger, the alchemist, used to shut himself up there, and devote his life to the study of a science which was the madness of his time, and in the pursuit of which he came by his death. He must have been a man of great talent, although somewhat phantastic in his ideas. It was while he was in Brussels that he began to interest himself in alchemy and other occult sciences, and after his return home he devoted all his time to these studies, of which certain relics yet remain. Tell me, Herr Pastor, what do you think of the Kabbalah ? '

So saying, he turned suddenly and looked me full in the face. There was a curious strained ex- pectancy in his expression, and his grey eyes seemed as though they desired to look into my very soul.

I was too much taken by surprise to be able to answer at once, and he went on in the quick way that was habitual to him.

'Do you think that there is really anything in this so-called occult teaching of the Jews, of which we hear so much in these latter days?'

'That it must be so,' I answered, 'is proved, I think, by the antiquity and richness of its literature.'

'That is insufficient proof,' he said. 'The belief in witches is also very old, and much paper and ink have been wasted on the subject. The same may be said of alchemy—as the Tower over there will show, for Count Ruttger's library contains as many alchemistic as Kabbalistic tomes. I looked into them once, and can easily understand how impossible it is to find the light when one turns down dark paths in search of it. I should have put my question thus. Do you believe there is a science, the knowledge of which endows its disciples with supernatural powers?'

'Pray explain your meaning a little more clearly, my lord,' I said with eager anxiety.

'Well,' he replied in a tone of assumed indifference, 'such as being able to call up the spirits of the dead, to heal the sick, to see that which is hidden, in short, to—to gain a foreknowledge of future events.'

'The Kabbalah tells us that its highest priest-
hood may have this power if they choose to use it ;
but it strongly condemns anything that, however
remotely, approaches what it calls the *Practical
Kabbalah.*'

'What do you mean?' cried the Count impatiently. 'I want to know if it is possible to
predict any man's future by means of the Kabbalistic numerals—whether the Kabbalah approves or
disapproves of such conduct is a matter of
indifference to me.'

I was silent for a moment, and could not help
remembering what old Peter had told me of the
Kabbalistic reckoning that had been made for the
Count by the Amsterdam Rabbi. Count Arthur
was evidently thinking of it too—his questions
seemed to confirm the truth of the old man's
statement. All this made it difficult for me to
answer at once, and I began to consider how I
should express what I had to say ; but the question
put to me was too distinctly worded to permit me
to do aught else than reply, that from all I had
heard and read on the subject, I could not disbelieve in the existence of such occult powers.

Thereupon the Count looked at me strangely,
and moving away from the window, began to walk
up and down the floor, his harsh features subdued
to a deep gravity. Whilst I was yet regretting
the answer that had been, as it were, forced from
me, he came up and stood before me, his gold

snuff-box with the portrait of Voltaire in his hand.
He slowly and sardonically took a pinch of snuff,
regarding me the while. Then he laughed softly,
but it was not a pleasant laugh to hear.

He put down the snuff-box and came to me
again, patted me on the shoulder, and said :

'Never mind, Pastor, there cannot be much in
an art which is so contrary to nature and reason.
If one of these prophecies ever chances to come
true it is by accident, and who can count upon
that? Suppose, for example, that a Kabbalist,
knowing somehow that our family burying-place
was situated near a Jewish cemetery, were to prophesy that the shadow of our vault should fall
upon his grave, and that, in consequence of this, I
had had a new vault built in a place that is far
removed from any Jewish cemetery, do you think
the prophecy would be fulfilled?'

I did not say what I thought. In the first place
I was rather shy, and in the second, our acquaintance was too short to admit of my speaking
frankly, and saying that his own conduct was proof
positive that he, at least, was inwardly convinced
of the soothsayer's power of divination.

The Count was not dissatisfied with my silence.
He made no further allusion to the matter, but
after a few contemptuous references to the
Kabbalah, he promised to introduce me to the
library in the Red Tower if I cared for such

nonsense, for I should there find a number of books dealing with the subject.

I thanked him, and said that I should like to see them.

Count Arthur now began to speak of business matters. In these I found him sensible, large-minded, kind and generous in everything he said ; he justified all that the sacristan had told me of his love of justice, his capacity, and his active interest in his estate and the people belonging to it. Nothing was done without his knowledge. He kept his stewards and over-seers under strict control, and required that the peasantry should do their duty by him, as thoroughly as he did his by them. He was an of the best stamp. The enlight-ened absolutism, of which Frederick the Great and Joseph II. were such admirable representatives at the end of last century, was a ruling principle of Count Arthur's life, and when I left him, I felt that I had just made the acquaintance of a man, who was manly in the true sense of the word, and whose only weak point was his acceptance of the shallow free-thinking tenets which were so commonly held at that time. On reaching the quadrangle, I found old Peter waiting to conduct me to the village by another path through the wood.

At the other side of the wood we came to an un-dulating plain that stretched out from thence to the sea. The wind was sighing dismally amongst the reeds that grew sparcely in the sand, the great sails of the wind-mill on a hillock at some little distance creaked and groaned as they turned, and even the whistling of the miller's man, who was standing in his shirt-sleeves within the upper door-way, sounded melancholy, he had chosen so sad an air.

Or was it the faint sinking of my own heart, that made the whole world seem less bright than when I set out for the Castle.

I went into the garden as soon as I got home, for I longed to be quite alone with my own thoughts, and the first thing my eyes rested on was the part of the hedge across which the two girls had shaken hands with me. I saw Christina in the little garden surrounding the sacristan's cottage, which lay next to the grave-yard. She had just finished watering her flowers, and was now carrying a pail of water from the brook to sprinkle the linen she was bleaching in the meadow close by. Several other girls were busily employed in the same way. Perhaps it was a cheerful scene to contemplate, but it made me feel so depressed, that when I went in to dinner my mother asked whether I had met with an ungracious reception at the castle.

It seemed to me as if I must needs bury a secret hope that was very dear to me, and yet I had not known before that I had been cherishing any such hope.

The ghost did not appear to me on the following

Sunday, and seek to prevent me entering the pulpit, as it had done to my predecessor in office. The Countess and her daughter were, however, in church, and I was afterwards told that I looked pale and nervous when conducting the service. This was not caused by any of the ordinary terrors of a young preacher, I can answer for that.

My sermon had been carefully prepared, and seemed to have given general satisfaction, judging from the hearty greetings I received on leaving the church. My fingers ached after the vehement grasp given them by the elders, and others of the congregation who considered that they had a right to mark their approval in this manner. I paid very little attention to the pleasures and pains of this bucolic method of testifying satisfaction with my conduct, for I was too much taken up watching the slender figure walking down the path beside the Countess. Their carriage was waiting in the village street, close to the church gate; but instead of at once going to it, the two ladies turned their steps to the Parsonage garden, where they found my mother, and surprised and pleased her with their account of the success of my first sermon. Helen had a small bunch of wall-flowers and carnations in her hand as well as her hymn-book, and she had pinned a rose in her dress. It chanced to be my favourite flower, and I—was glad that she wore it.

I remained standing under the lime trees talking

to different members of the congregation, for I
could not have faced her at that moment. The
elders accompanied me down the green slope to
the burying-ground. When I at last moved away,
and on reaching the graves of the former clergymen of the parish, they began to tell me what sort
of men they had been. I let them speak on without interruption, although old Peter had already
told me the same stories, but after a more long-
winded fashion. And it seemed to me that the
time would come when these men's children would
say: Ah, yes, Pastor Bergmann; it was he who
married Count Arthur's son Frank to so and so,
and afterwards the young Countess Helen to Count
such and such a one; then he died. It all
appeared so real to me, that a tear of self-com-
passion for an instant dimmed my eye. No doubt
the elders were much impressed by the feeling their
young Pastor had shown when they were telling
him about the lives of his predecessors. Such
instances of morbid sensibility were by no means
rare at that time. The Werther period had not
quite passed away, and I first entered on it after I
had come through the phase of storm and stress at
the University.

The ladies at length took leave of my mother,
and went to their carriage, bowing to me as they
did so. On entering the house, my mother greeted
me with a perfect torrent of words in praise of the
Countess and her daughter, and the dear old lady

grew a little cross with me for sitting there so silent, when she was talking of the satisfactoriness of everything connected with the living of Seeried. It was as though I did not care, she said, and such ingratitude was flying in the face of Providence.

As time went on I gradually learnt resignation from the beautiful bit of God's world in which my lines were cast, and also in trying to comfort others, comfort came to me, although a slight sadness remained hidden away in my heart. I never allowed myself to dwell on the subject, but when my thoughts involuntarily turned to it at sight of the low hedge in the orchard, I took myself severely to task for my weakness.

I often dined at the castle, and saw Countess Helen growing day by day in sweetness, grace, and beauty. The Count treated me with the greatest trust and kindness, the Countess with the gentle amiability and high-bred ease of a thorough aristocrat, and the little lady Helen with a mixture of shy confidence and respect for my calling. We talked a good deal of the literary movement in Germany, a subject in which the Countess was deeply interested, and to which she continually turned the conversation during our after-dinner strolls in the garden. On such occasions Helen would sometimes hazard an opinion, which delighted me with its freshness and justness of view.

She once surprised her mother and me by

saying, 'How I wish I were a clergyman's daughter!'

The Countess asked her in astonishment what could have put that into her head, and she replied :

'From all the descriptions I have read, life seems to be much simpler and more practical in a Parsonage than elsewhere.'

Her mother answered that poetry was to be found in every state of life, if people only knew how to look for it, and that it was a mistake to imagine it everywhere except at home.

But it was true for all that could be alleged against the narrowness of the assumption, that life in a country Parsonage was then thought the most idyllic that could be imagined. Although the ' Luise ' of Voss was as yet unknown, the literature of the day was more or less permeated by this sentiment, which perhaps had its birth in the *furore* caused by the publication of Goldsmith's ' Vicar of Wakefield,' and was kept alive by the fact that Hölty and Bürger, the most notable members of the Göttingen ' Hainbund,' were clergymen's sons, and that their poems contained many allusions to the homes of their childhood. Helen's wish was therefore a very comprehensible one. I heard it, however, with a silent transport of delight, as though her words meant more than she, in her innocence, understood.

The day before she said it, there had been many visitors at the Castle ; people of rank who lived in

the neighbourhood, and all of them, as old Peter
had taken care to inform me, had been much impressed by her beauty.   More especially had this
been the case with the heir of one of the largest
estates in the province.   It was in vain that I took
myself continually to task, and asked myself 'what
did it matter to me?'   I could not stifle the dull
pain at my heart.   This mood still prevailed when
I dined at the Castle on the following day, and
after dinner accompanied the ladies in their walk
in the park.   There it was that I was surprised by
Helen's remark, which brightened all the world to
me, like sunshine after rain.

I indulged in happy thoughts for some time after
this, and then became aware of my folly in thus
acting, and threw myself into the labour of my
calling more persistently than before, in order to
prevent myself thinking.   I had grown to love my
profession, especially since Helen had spoken in
praise of life at a Parsonage.   I was strong enough
to hide my feelings when in her presence; to appear
always calm and collected.   I saw a great deal of
her and her mother in those days, both at the
Castle and out of doors.   And sometimes in the
evening the Count would join us when we made
some longer expedition to the sea shore, or went
boating on the river.   Then again I would see the
Countess Helen helping her foster-sister, Christina,
to sprinkle the linen that was spread out to bleach
in the meadow near the sacristan's cottage, and

would sometimes speak to both the girls over the Parsonage hedge.

I never sought such opportunities ; but I often found it difficult to help availing myself of them when they came in my way.

I always met the Countess Helen with a distinct consciousness of the gulf that separated us. I should have despised myself had I forgotten it for a moment.

CHAPTER VIII.

' Und mich ergreift ein längst entwohntes Sehnen
Nach jenem ernsten, stillen Geisterreich.'

Faust.

' *Countess.*—The astrological tower ! How happens it
That that this same something, whose access
Is to all others so impracticable,
Opens before you even at your approach?
Thekla.—A dwarfish old man with a friendly face
And snow-white hairs, whose gracious services
Were mine at first sight, opened me the doors.'

The Piccolomini (Coleridge's Trans.).

ND so the summer passed away.
My mother would have been thoroughly
happy, if she had not felt that something was
amiss with me. I had won the goodwill of my
parishioners, and knew that I had warm friends
both in cottage and castle.

And yet I was not happy.

I was sitting in my study one day in the early
autumn. A sharp breeze was blowing up from
the Baltic, making the vane on the church tower
creak loudly. The storks had long ago forsaken
their nest on the roof of the Parsonage, and had
flown south to some milder climate. I was alone,

and a prey to despondency. I debated whether it would not be better for me to follow the example of the storks, and leave Seeried far behind me. Then, and then only, I thought, should I succeed in uprooting the love I felt for one who was so far removed from me by worldly fortune, and who yet grew dearer to me day by day.

As I sat there pondering over the sadness and hopelessness of my fate, I began unconsciously to turn the leaves of the Bible that lay on the table before me, and then to read the words on the open page mechanically. The writer described himself as a 'mortal man, like to all.' When he was born he had breathed the 'common air,' and the first word he had uttered was crying. He had been 'nursed in swaddling clothes, and that with cares'; but even kings had had no other beginning. He had prayed, however, and 'understanding' had been given him ; he had 'called upon God, and the spirit of wisdom' had come to him. And, he went on to say, 'I preferred her before sceptres and thrones, and esteemed riches nothing in comparison of her. .   . I loved her above health and beauty. . . . All good things came to me with her, . . . and I rejoiced in them all. . . . She is a treasure unto men that never faileth : which they that use become the friends of God, . . . because it is He that leadeth unto wisdom, and directeth the wise. . . . For He hath given me certain knowledge of the things that are,

namely, to know how the world was made, and the
operation of the elements. . . . For wisdom,
which is the worker of all things, taught me. . . .
She is the breath of the power of God, and a pure
influence glowing from the glory of the Almighty.
. . . She is the brightness of the everlasting
light, the unspotted mirror of the power of God,
and the image of His goodness. . . .'

And so it went on in the same strain. My
attention became gradually rivetted on what I was
reading, and it was not until I had finished the
chapter, that I looked to see which book of Holy
Scripture contained these remarkable words. It
was, as I had thought, the apocryphal ' Book of
Wisdom,' which is said to have been written by an
Alexandrian Jew in the time of the Maccabees,
and the word 'wisdom' as I had formerly heard,
and was now convinced, meant neither more nor
less than the occult teaching of the Jews—the
Kabbalah.

I was just in the humour to regard the accident
of my attention having been drawn to the subject
as an omen encouraging me to return to the study
in which I had formerly taken such intense delight,
and thus seek to allay the disquietude of my spirit.
When I read the next chapter, the eighth, it
seemed to be addressed to me individually, and it
was with inward emotion that I repeated the
words :

' Wisdom reacheth from one end to another

mightily : and sweetly doth she order all things. I loved her, and sought her out from my youth, I desired to make her my spouse, and I was a lover of her beauty.   .   .   .   She is privy to the mysteries of the knowledge of God.   .   .   .   If a man desire much experience, she knoweth things of old, and *conjectureth aright what is to come :* she knoweth the subtilties of speeches, and can expound dark sentences : she *foreseeth* signs and wonders, and the events of the seasons and times.   Therefore I purposed to take her to me, to live with me, knowing that she would be a counsellor of good things, and a comfort in cares and grief.'

These words came home to me with power.   As a youth I had longed for this wisdom too ardently to forget it now that I was a man.   I started to my feet, and paced the room.   A voice within me seemed to cry out : Yes, wisdom is the true love of my soul, and it were well to dedicate my life to her service.

Once more I approached the table, determined to try my fate after the fashion that has been handed down from generation to generation.   I opened the Bible, and my thumb pointed to these words of the Prophet Jeremiah :

'What wilt thou say when he shall punish thee . . .   shall not pangs seize thee, as a woman in travail ?'

Afraid ? I was not afraid.   Was I not as ready and willing to bear anything to attain my object now, as in the old days at home when Bachur Benasse had warned me against it?

It was with me as with so many other people under the same circumstances, I wished to force a favourable answer from my oracle. Again I tried my fortune, and opened the Bible at the 6th chapter of Ecclesiasticus, in which Jesus, the son of Sirach, says of this same wisdom :

'Come unto her as one that plougheth and soweth, and wait for her good fruits; for thou shalt not toil much in labouring about her, but thou shalt eat of her fruits right soon. She is very unpleasant to the unlearned : he that is without understanding will not remain with her. She will lie upon him as a mighty stone of trial ; and he will cast her from him ere it be long. . . Search and seek, and she shall be made known unto thee : and when thou hast got hold of her let her not go. For at the last thou shalt find her rest, and that shall be turned to thy joy. . . Stand in the multitude of the elders ; and cleave unto him that is wise.'

That was clear enough.

I could not bear to sit still any longer, and getting my hat, went out through the village and into the country beyond. I wanted to go down to the sea. The afternoon was cold and raw, and the sails of the windmill creaked dismally as they turned.

I met Count Arthur soon after passing the mill.

He was standing on one of the sandy dunes talking encouragingly to some of the cotters in their own Low German dialect, and telling them not to be weary of doing their best by the soil though it was poor, for careful cultivation did wonders. On seeing me, he came forward to meet me, and asked me to go back to the Castle with him. He looked rather grave and troubled, but seemed glad to see me.

He showed his trust in me that afternoon by speaking of his family affairs.

'We ought not to put the thought of death so far from us as we are in the habit of doing,' he began calmly. 'I feel that it is high time for me to set my house in order. My son Frank is in Paris just now, at least his last letter was dated from there; he is in good hands. But my daughter! You see, Herr Bergmann, my wife is a very good woman, and wise too in her way; but still she has her own notions, and her opinions on the subject of marriage are slightly romantic. She thinks that the heart goes for something in the matter. The heart! That is all very fine, you know, but it does not do for us. I cannot be called a prejudiced person, and am as liberal-minded as any one; but I maintain that if the peerage is to be kept up, we must look to securing brains and understanding in the marriages we make for our children. The Reichsgraf . . . (mentioning his name) has expressed a desire to enter into an alliance with my family, deeming that it would be advantageous for him. The boy would suit me well enough as a son-in-law. He comes of one of the oldest houses in the country, and so, although I have hitherto declined to listen to any of the applications I have received for my daughter's hand, I am now tempted to accept this offer.'

'And Countess Helen?' I forced myself to ask in as quiet a tone as though the subject were not of the utmost interest to me.

'There it is,' replied the Count. 'My daughter has the same romantic ideas as her mother. She calls one of her wooers unmannerly, another a sybarite, a third a fop, a fourth a boor, and so on, always ending by saying that she is far too young to marry. What do you think of it, Herr Pastor?'

'The Countess Helen *is* very young,' I answered.

'I believe that early marriages are much the happiest, Herr Bergmann,' he said quickly, almost vehemently.

'Well, my lord, why do you not use your authority, and bring about the wedding at once?' I answered rather impatiently.

The Count seemed a little astonished at the tone in which I had spoken, but not angered by it, and after walking silently beside me through the breezy wood for a short distance, he said gravely:

'Authority? I have not been fortunate when using authority to bring about a marriage that I considered thoroughly good in every respect. I deeply repent having done so then ; it cost me the trust and affection of a brother whom I loved as my own son, and who is now lost to me for ever. But enough of that—he deserved his fate.'

'If you are speaking of Count Hermann, my lord,' I answered boldly, 'I know that he was worthy of a better lot. I was slightly acquainted with him at the university, where he was loved for his bold, chivalrous disposition. It is true that he often used to take part in some wild piece of mischief that perhaps roused the anger of the authorities, but he never did anything that was either malicious or base.'

Count Arthur fixed his grey eyes upon me piercingly, as though he would read my very soul.

'You knew him then?' he said. 'Well, so did other people. As regards his conduct at Halle I have sufficient proof of its perversity. Say no more about him, Pastor, if you want us to remain friends. But if you really wish to be helpful to my family, you could not have a better opportunity than now. The ladies have a high opinion of you, Pastor Bergmann, and your advice on a certain subject would have a more beneficial effect than my authority, which, by the way, I should never have the heart to use with respect to my gentle little girl. I only want her to be happy, and even to ensure her being so, should not like to force her to take so grave a step against her will.'

The Count von Seeried-Strandow had won my

heart by these last words. I swore to myself that, so soon as I was convinced of the worthiness of the young Reichsgraf, I would do what little lay in my power to induce both mother and daughter to consider his pretentions favourably, for the sake of their husband and father. For, if he, a stern man, accustomed to rule himself and others, gave up from love to his child all attempt to enforce upon her the darling wish of his heart, surely I should be strong enough to sacrifice my own feelings, and plead his cause. Nevertheless, my thoughts at the moment were in such a tumult, that I was thankful to be obliged to turn my attention to the Count, who began to speak again, as seriously as before. And as we talked, we wandered deeper into the forest, through which the wind whispered and moaned, and made the branches of the trees sway hither and thither in every direction.

' If I trouble you with my private affairs,' said the Count, ' it is because you are, in right of your office, the spiritual director of everyone in this parish ; but I have yet another reason for doing so—you know how much I despise superstition of every sort—but still, I cannot deny that such prophecies come true now and then—by accident.'

' What prophecies ?' I asked.

' Well, those of the kind the Amsterdam Kabbalist made about me. The principal result of his computation was this, that I should not out-

live the twenty-fifth year of my marriage. And
this twenty-fifth year ends next winter.'

In saying this, he spoke with quiet gravity, un-
tinctured by the light mockery that usually
characterised him when talking of such things, and
yet with perfect indifference. I saw that he
believed in the possibility of his death taking
place as had been foretold ; perhaps even thought
that it would be so ; but that this foreboding
caused him no terror was equally evident.

So this was the secret at which old Peter had
hinted.

I was much startled at the correspondence
between what I had just heard, and one of the
verses I had read before coming out, in which it
was said of 'wisdom' that 'she knoweth things of
old, and conjectureth aright what is to come.'
But recovering myself as quickly as possible, I
could not help saying a few words to the Count
such as befitted my calling, and they came from
the bottom of my heart. I fared badly in so
doing. He turned upon me with all his old wit
and scepticism—then begged me earnestly to say
no more on that head, and ended by saying, he
could see that I did not altogether disbelieve in the
wonder-working powers of the Practical Kabbalah,
and would therefore take me where I might satisfy
any craving I entertained for the prosecution of
my studies on this subject. As my curiosity with
regard to the Red Tower, and the wizard's library

had been long awakened, I entreated him to do so
as soon as he could.   After a moment's hesitation,
he said that he would take me that very day.

So we went on together through the wood
towards the Castle.

He talked in his usual quiet clear-sighted way
about business matters.   And thus conversing, we
came to the edge of the wood near Castle Secried.
There we were startled by seeing some strange-
looking black carriages, draped with black, and
drawn by black horses coming down one of the
roads that led through the wood at a furious pace.
As they passed, we could see that the arms of the
Counts von Seeried-Strandow were painted on the
panels of the three carriages that formed the
procession.   One would have thought it was a
funeral, but for the pace at which they were driven.
And yet the only sound we could hear was the
rushing noise of the wind among the branches of
the trees, for the rolling of the carriage wheels was
inaudible.   We watched the mourning-coaches—
that was the only name for them—drive into the
Castle court, and draw up before the great entrance
door.

The Count frowned darkly as he stood looking
after them, and I felt as though I were turned into
stone.   Then he suddenly stamped his foot with
such vehemence into the soft soil of the woodland
path, that it was with some difficulty he freed

his spurred heel from the ground into which it had sunk.

'Back again,' he muttered wrathfully. Next moment he caught sight of my pale face, and asked: 'Why Pastor, what is the matter? You look as if you had seen a ghost!'

I stammered something about the mourning coaches, and their noiseless motion; upon which the whole expression of the Count's face changed, and he burst out laughing so heartily that he had to hold his sides :

' Ha, ha, ha! I must tell my brother Leo and my saintly step-mother that the enlightened Pastor of the parish of Seeried mistook their carriages for a ghostly funeral procession. You are a daring ghost-seer, reverend sir!—Oh what times we are living in, what times.'

I was so much ashamed of my mistake, that the Count was good-natured enough to pity me, and made excuses for the blunder I had made. He said that the softness of the ground, and the noise of the wind in the trees had prevented our hearing the sound of the wheels, and then went on to explain that Count Leo and the widowed Countess made it a part of their religion to avoid the use of all bright colours, while retaining the insignia of their rank. He quite admitted the ghostly look of the whole procession, and maintained that a natural cause might be found for every ghost that ever was seen. For ghosts, he said, had no existence outside

ourselves.   They were the creation of our own
brain and imagination, and he was certain that
when I had studied all the Kabbalistic books in his
ancestor's library I should come to the same conclusion as Ephraim Lebrecht, that *everything* was
an illusion.   I must look in the Red Tower, he
added, for the *Book of the Baal Teschuba* (*i.e.* of the
Penitent) by means of which his ancestor, Count
Ruttger, had tried to practice theurgy, and had died
in his madness.   That very book would perhaps
teach me better than aught else that there was
nothing behind the *hocus-pocus* of the adepts.

I was too much ashamed to say anything in my
own defence, and soon afterwards we reached the
Castle.   The Count took me through a side door
to the steward's room on the ground-floor, where
the keys were kept.   As chance would have it, we
met the sacristan coming out of the room as we
approached it, and the Count exclaimed :

'There you are, old Peter, you could not have
come at a better time, for in right of your name
you are well fitted to take charge of the keys.   Go
and get the keys of the Red Tower, and take
Pastor Bergmann to Count Ruttger's library.'

So saying, Count Arthur bade me farewell, and
went away to see his 'dear relations.'

Peter meanwhile stood before me, pale and silent.
I asked him to fetch the keys as he had been desired,
and he answered :

'Do you really care to see the library in the Red

Tower? Take an old man's advice, and do not go.'

'Why?'

'I have already told you why, sir. Going there will bring you no good. Be warned.'

A vivid recollection of the nervousness I had shown that afternoon came over me, and made me ashamed to yield to the old man's entreaty:

'Get the keys at once,' I said.

He obeyed in silence, and returned bearing two great keys of an ancient Franconian pattern that seemed more fitted to open dungeon doors than anything else. Without a word, and without even vouchsafing me a look, he led the way across the great hall; then up one flight of stairs and down another, and along a stone passage past cellars and vaults. Our footsteps sounded hollow in the empty corridors. At length the old man stopped before an arched doorway made of hewn stones of immense size, and standing in the middle of a rounded and projecting piece of masonry. Within this door-way was a heavy oak door clamped with iron. Before putting the key in the lock, the old man once more looked at me in silent entreaty, his silvery hair gleaming like a point of light in the surrounding gloom. I signed to him to proceed. The key grated loudly as it turned, and the door opened noisily. A damp mouldy air greeted us on our entrance.

Peter shut the door carefully behind us. Then

I followed him up a broad, winding stone stair-
case, lighted here and there by a window, and having a door leading from it on each storey.   When
we had climbed two storeys high, the old man
broke the silence to tell me, as he pointed to one
of these doors, that the family archives were kept
within the room beyond.

After that we continued to ascend the spiral
stairs for a long way, passing one narrow window
after another, until at last my guide stopped out of
breath and exhausted.

'If you are determined to go into the room,
reverend sir,' he said at length, 'take the key in
your own hand, and open the door for yourself.   *I*
will not.   The Count is always laughing at me
about my name, and saying that I ought to be a
worthy namesake of S. Peter and look well after
my keys; he shall not have to say that I have ever
opened the gates of Hell for any man.'

With that he gave me the key.   I took it, and
when I had put it in the lock, he whispered :

'If you should happen to find anything there
that alarms you, put your head out of the window
that overlooks the garden where you found the
young lady sitting the first time you came to the
Castle, and call me.'

He then went down stairs again.   I turned the
key in the lock, and the carved oak door opened as
easily as if it were often used.   I entered the room,
and found myself in a light, airy, and almost cheer-

ful-looking ante-chamber with a stone floor, vaulted roof, and curious, old-fashioned wainscotting on the walls.   It had probably been used as a servant's room in ancient times, while the chambers in the highest and lowest parts of the Tower may have served as cells or dungeons.   At the other end of the room was a door opening into a bedchamber, containing, amongst other things, a huge four-post bed, the wood work of which was ornamented with much delicate and intricate carving.   From thence I went into a lofty hall with a vaulted roof and tesselated pavement.

The first glance convinced me that I had come to the right place, for, hanging against the wall was the portrait of a pale, noble-looking man, attired in the costume of the early part of the Seventeenth Century ; he was dressed in a black velvet doublet —in a word, dear Reinhardt, it was the picture that you know as the 'Portrait of the Black Count.'   Another picture was hanging near it, a hunting scene.   The landscape depicted that part of Seeried park which is known and dreaded as the 'Slough of Blood.'   It is surrounded by great gnarled beeches, and there it was that Count Ruttger was once attacked by a furious stag, and was in imminent danger of losing his life.   This was the *motif* of the picture, and was marvellously delineated.

The hall had obviously been used as a laboratory in former times.   An ancient furnace that had fallen a great deal out of repair, some broken retorts, and other appliances of a like nature, were still to be seen in different parts of the room.

An enormous cabinet was standing in a sort of niche in the wall, and I at once perceived from the characters engraved above the lock that it must contain the documents of which I was in search. The key was difficult to turn, but when the cabinet opened I could not help starting on seeing the diagram of the ten Sephiroth, the Kabbalistic holy thing.

I stood before it, feeling like an acolyte about to be initiated into those sacred mysteries which have hitherto been kept from him. I need not further describe the cabinet and its contents, for you have often seen it in my study. I little thought that day, when I saw it for the first time, that it would ever come into my possession.

My heart beat quickly, but did not stifle the gnawing hunger I felt for the study of the Kabbalah. Come what might, I was determined to persevere. I drew back the curtain on which the Kabbalistic Tree was depicted.

Nothing alarming was to be seen. There were rows of beautifully bound books on alchemistic and Kabbalistic subjects, some of which I already knew. I took out several of the others, and at once perceived that they would not further the attainment of my object. They were either full of an unfruitful, metaphysical speculation, or merely led the enquirer up to the door of the mystery, and there left him abruptly, or else recommended him to seek further enlightenment from the personal instruction of an adept.

I knew as much as that long ago.

The evening was beginning to close in and I was about to give up my vain search for the day, when I chanced to lift a book under which another ragged little volume had been lying concealed. On opening it, I at once perceived from my knowledge of Oriental languages, that it was an introduction to the Practical Kabbalah written in Chaldæ. Now, at last, I had a book that would help me to understand the Kabbalah *Maschiith*. The desire of years was accomplished! Was this the book of mysteries of which Ephraim Lebrecht had told me? It must be so. I trembled and rejoiced at the same time, and then fell upon my prize with the appetite of a hungry wolf. There were a number of Kabbalistic forms of prayer, and there were also magical propositions to which no solutions were given. At last, at last, I thought that light was beginning to glimmer faintly through the gloom, that one of the mystical explanations was becoming clearer to me, and promised to reveal some portion of the secret.

I need not describe my sensations—I trembled. The long-wished for teaching had come, the secret was about to be disclosed. I read on eagerly— and lo, the book came to an end in the very

middle of a sentence. All that followed had been
torn out.

I could have wept with rage and disappointment.

I was so lost in my own thoughts that I did not
hear the door open, and some one come into the
room, until I was startled by a voice at my elbow,
saying :

'How now, Pastor, what is the matter with you ?
Why are you so excited ? '

Turning round, I found that Count Arthur had
followed me. I told him something of the contents of the book I had discovered, and he exclaimed :

'You have done very well, more than well, for
your first visit to this room. That is the Book of
the *Baal Teschuba*, that we thought was lost years
ago. Perhaps if you continue your search you
may find the missing pages, and then you will be
able to study the incantations, and other arts, the
secret of which my forefather is said to have
carried off with him when he was hurried out of
the world. You can come here whenever you like.'

He then advised me to give up all further
researches for that evening, so I took leave of him,
and set out on my homeward way in the growing
darkness.

I paid no attention to the questioning looks old
Peter cast upon me, and a few days later I returned
to Count Ruttger's room in the Red Tower.
When I took the Book of the *Baal Teschuba*

again in my hands, I found a folded paper within the cover, the first page of which was filled with writing, that I at once recognised as Count Arthur's. It contained an account of the circumstances connected with the death of his ancestor, close to whose body the Book of the *Baal Teschuba* had been found lying tattered and torn on the floor, and an old Jew had afterwards told the family 'that so many pages having been torn out proved what valuable secrets they had contained.' Count Arthur had written this short biographical notice in much more old-fashioned Franconian than he usually spoke.

I laid down the Sybilline book, and instituted a thorough examination of the cabinet, and all it contained. I was fortunate enough to discover a secret drawer, and, on opening it, perceived, to my intense delight, a manuscript written by Count Ruttger, the alchemist ; he who had died in that very room more than a hundred years before, the victim of some mysterious chemical experiment.

I was again disappointed.

The manuscript contained nothing but a slight biographical sketch of certain events in Count Ruttger's life. It told how he went to Brussels when quite a young man, devoted himself there to the study of the occult sciences, and fell in love with a clergyman's daughter, whom his father would not allow him to marry. How he went home to Castle Seeried. How he had lived apart from the proud woman, whom he had been obliged to make his wife, ever since the day, when, in a fit of jealous anger, she had burnt the portrait of the gentle Dutch girl he had loved so dearly.   After that time he had shut himself up in the Red Tower with his books and chemicals.   The narrative went on to state that the Book of the *Baal Teschuba* had been found in the possession of a dying Jewish penitent, and that, by means of its teaching, Count Ruttger had been enabled to call the spirit of his dead love to his presence, and, moreover, that he had persisted in doing so in spite of the warning that a speedy death would be the consequence of such conduct.   The story was told in the quaintly *naïf* style of the period at which it was written.   Much to my disappointment, it broke off at the most interesting point, when the spirit warned Count Ruttger to beware of holding personal communion with the dead, and he, persisting in his entreaties that she should continue to appear to him, was informed that after he had departed this life, his ghost would be condemned to wander, seeking rest and finding none for full two hundred years, when one of his race should at length set him free by . . .   Here the story ended abruptly.

I was interested in comparing this prophecy with the tradition old Peter had related to me a few days after my arrival at Seeried, when he told me how the dying priest had exclaimed, during the massacre at the Slough of Blood, that the guilt of that day's work should rest on the family of Seeried-Strandow until certain of their daughters became the wives of country clergymen, and a clergyman's daughter, lady of the Castle.

I was well aware that there was hardly a noble family in Germany that did not possess some curious legendary prophecy peculiar to itself. And yet, I could not help being impressed by the way in which the two predictions fitted into each other. On showing Count Ruttger's manuscript to my patron, he read it eagerly, and seemed to be rather startled by its contents.

'Strange, strange! he ejaculated, as he read. 'Helen Vanburgh was the name of the Dutch girl whom Count Ruttger loved when he was young, and my wife was a Baroness Vanburgh. Why did she insist on our daughter being christened Helen? I must ask her whether she had any reason for it, or if it was only that she had a fancy for the name.'

Then turning to me with a smile, he continued: 'Why, Herr Bergmann, perhaps I have in all ignorance set the ghost of my ancestor free from the doom that was laid upon him. But, *morbleu*, the two hundred years prophesied have not yet passed away. Perhaps though, that may not matter. The Dutch parson's daughter may have made a slight error in her calculations!'

He thus endeavoured to throw off the uncomfortable feeling that the perusal of the manuscript had undoubtedly occasioned, but did not entirely succeed.

He now begged me to have Count Ruttger's papers and the Book of the *Baal Teschuba* bound up together, after which he wished them to be put back in the secret drawer of the cabinet.

Whether the Count ever asked his wife the question he had intended, I do not know ; but I found out long afterwards that he had guessed aright.

Count Arthur's humour was very changeable in those days. Sometimes he seemed to be brooding over matters of deep and serious import, while at others, he laughed and jested as though he had not a care in the world.

CHAPTER IX.

'Whence is that knocking?'
                                        Macbeth.

'He was a man, take him for all in all.'
                                        Hamlet.

MY former passion for the Kabbalah had re-vived in all its intensity, and my regular work fell into a secondary position during these autumn months, for my whole interest was centred in the search I was making through Count Ruttger's books and papers, in which I hoped to find some-thing that would more than reward me for my trouble.

I encouraged my thoughts to dwell on the sub-ject hoping thereby to kill the love I felt for the young Countess.

In order, if possible, to effect a radical cure, I had seized the earliest opportunity that presented itself of carrying out her father's behest, and telling her what he wished her to do. At the same time I reminded her of her duty, representing that the path of obedience was the only path it would be right for her to tread. I had sworn to myself that

I would not betray my feelings, and I kept my word.

Helen became very pale, and listened to me in grave silence. Then she turned to her mother with a look of reproach, and the latter gave me gently, but decidedly, to understand that this was a matter that must be left entirely to her daughter's decision.

Ought I to have regretted my failure? I do not know. But if I was not distressed by it, neither did it make me happy. And it was in order to stifle the dull pain at my heart, that I threw myself so vehemently into my Kabbalistic studies that they soon absorbed all my attention. I continued to fulfil the duties of my profession; but it was only mechanically that I did so.

My low spirits were the more increased by the miserable weather that prevailed. But in spite of rain and storm I made my way, day after day, to Count Ruttger's Tower, and sat there for hours together endeavouring to discover the secret that was not to be made known to me until afterwards, and by another agency. My cheeks grew hollow, and my face so pale that the Countess often advised me not to study so hard. Even Helen once asked me compassionately if I were ill. My mother looked at me sadly, and old Peter shook his head in silent disapprobation. At last I saw the vanity of my efforts, and ceased to visit the Red Tower.

I tried to gain comfort from a more unwearied exercise of my pastoral duties, and was, to a certain

extent, successful in the attempt. But when I was
once more alone the old pain overmastered me,
and the whispers of the Tempter sounded again in
my ears.

Autumn was drawing rapidly to an end. The
family were still at the Castle, and the villagers
wondered why they remained there so long, for
they generally went to Strandow in September,
and from thence to Berlin. The heavy rains of
October had given place to frost, and slight snow
showers.

It was on the 25th of November that my mother
came to tell me Count Arthur had ridden up to
our gate followed by a groom. I changed my
coat as quickly as possible, and hastened out to see
why I was wanted. The air was heavy and grey
as though presaging a storm, and a few snowflakes
were falling at intervals. Count Arthur received
me with a peculiar smile.

'I have come to see what you are about,' he
cried, holding in his horse with difficulty. 'You
have quite deserted the Red Tower. Did you see
a ghost the last time you were there? and did it
frighten you away? Or is it as I imagine—have
you found out that the whole thing is a delusion,
a figment of the brain. It always comes to that in
the end!'

The Count was in curiously high spirits. He
could not refrain from jests at what he called the
clerical weakness of wishing to appear to know

more on certain subjects than the rest of the
world, and so imposing on the ignorance of the
multitude.   I could not understand him.   He
seemed to be what the Scottish Highlanders call
'fey.'   He continued to talk in the same strain,
saying that it had always been so from the beginning of time, for the priests knew that thus, and
thus only, could they retain the power they had
won over their fellows.

'It is the old story over again,' he said ; 'the
great secret of Sais, which was hidden behind a
veil.   Now, my dear ghostseer, what do you think
was concealed behind that veil ?   Can you not
guess ?   Well, come and dine with me to-morrow,
and I will tell you.   We go to town in a day or
two, and I want to see you.'

He was about to set spurs to his horse and ride
away, but turned to me again, and said :

'I will put you out of pain at once, for fear the
puzzle should keep you awake to-night.   The veil
hid—*nothing !*'

Then he rode away laughing loudly, and I lost
sight of him in the grey mists of the gathering
snowstorm.

When he had left me, I stood for a moment unable to move.   After that I turned and went up
the path leading to the church.   A faint rosy light
was indistinctly visible in the south-west, marking
the hour of sunset.

Nothing !   The word rang in my ears, and made

me shiver. Nothing? nothing? I asked myself, as I fixed my eyes on the setting sun, the only bright spot in the general greyness of the landscape.

I sought, I struggled for light, and the light of day was sinking.

Nothing! The word had struck me to the heart, and filled me with woe unspeakable.

I sought the light, that primæval light of which the Kabbalah teaches. Was it the sun? I knew that there are many suns throughout immeasurable space, each with its earth, like that on which we dwell. Are these suns ruled by a central sun, the primæval light, or by—nothing? That is the question.

My brain seemed on fire, and I turned and went back to my study.

To change the current of my thoughts I determined to get the church Registers of the parish of Seeried, and make a copy of all the marriages, baptisms, and deaths of the family at the Castle that I could find in the church books. While so employed, I came upon the notice of the marriage of Count Arthur von Seeried-Strandow to Baroness Cornelia Vanburgh. The wedding took place on the 26th of November, 1756—this very day, therefore, completed the year, the twenty-fifth of his marriage, which, according to the Rabbi's prophecy, was to be fatal to Count Arthur.

I thought that I now held the clue to his extra-ordinary behaviour that afternoon.

My mother called me to supper. When we had finished, I returned to my study ; but feeling dis-inclined to go on with my work of copying the parish Register, I went to the window and gazed out into the night. The ground was covered with snow ; but the heavy clouds had cleared away, and the moon and stars were shining overhead. Long I stood there seeking enlightenment ; but the light that I desired was not to be found in moon or stars.

My eyes fell on a book which was lying on the window-sill. It was a volume of Klopstock's poems. I opened it at the ' Psalm,' and read :

> ' Um Erden wandeln Monde, Erden um Sonnen,
> Aller Sonnen Heere wandeln
> Um eine grosse Sonne :
> Vater unser,
> Der Du bist in Himmel !' *

These words were in accordance with the Kab-balistic idea of the Central Sun, which it calls ' primæval light.' Was this light God ? And who could prove its existence to me ? How was I to obtain certainty that ' all the hosts of suns ' did not circle round *nothing ?*

---

* Moons circle round the earths, earths round suns, and all the hosts of suns do circle round a greater sun : our Father, which art in Heaven.

I turned to the Bible, which speaks of the beginning and the end. My cheeks were pale, and my hands were cold and trembling. I opened the book, and it was but a dark oracle I received. I could make nothing of it.

The old curse had come upon me.

The terrible word 'nothing'—of which the Kabbalah speaks mysteriously, and which Philosophy has reintroduced to the world hidden under a thin veil of subtle phraseology—threw me back into the questioning and despair of my student days. But in one respect I was changed since that old time. I could no longer arm myself with the *insouscience* that had then dulled my sense of misery. The pain was almost more than I could bear, and I could neither laugh nor sneer it away. I groaned when I thought of my holy office, and of how human ignorance was obliged to content itself with the knowledge conveyed in a few dark sayings of Holy Scripture—with the limits of Revelation, was it wonderful that recollections of the Kabbalah should now have returned to me, although it had so often stolen away my peace of mind in the days that were gone.

The question of questions to my mind now was whether the teaching which represented that it was able to unfold all mysteries, to foresee what should come to pass, and to lead its disciples nearer to God than aught else—whether this sacred wisdom

was indeed 'nothing,' a mere figment of the imagination, a delusion of the brain !

I threw myself upon my bed without undressing.
Racked by doubt, I found it impossible to lie still,
and springing to my feet went to the cupboard
where Pastor Engelreich had seen the ghost. Had
it appeared to me, I should not have been afraid,
for I longed to force an answer from the unseen.
The church clock struck eight, slowly and hoarsely,
the sounds dying away gradually in the frosty air.
Nothing else was to be heard or seen ; the ghost
declined to appear.

I complained that Scripture had taught me to
hope when all hope was vain.

I went to the window. A thin covering of
freshly fallen snow was lying on the village street·
Lights were still burning in a few of the neigh-
bouring houses ; and generally speaking most of
the villagers had already retired to rest. None of
them guessed through what deep waters their
Pastor was wading. They trusted him, and were
at peace. I felt the difficulties of my position
bitterly, and thought my fate exceptionally hard.

The greater question had never presented itself
to me in this guise before.

As I stood there a prey to the most dreadful
uncertainty, the most despairing doubt, I felt a
deep compassion for my parishioners.

'How can I, who am blind,' I asked, 'lead these
poor blind folk out of darkness into the light ?   If

one of my people who has died were to come to
life again, I could not look him in the face after
having prepared him to meet another life *which
does not really exist.'*

Again I threw myself upon my couch, and
buried my feverish head in the pillows. Outside
the house all was still. So quiet was it that I
could distinctly hear the chirping of the cricket in
the adjoining room where my mother was seated
with her spinning-wheel.

.   .   .   .   .   .

There was a knock at the front door.

Quite a common every-day knock, such as I had
often heard before, when some messenger had
come to summon me to visit a sick or dying
person. And yet when the stillness was broken
by this most commonplace sound, my heart beat
quickly. I felt as though my fate were at the door
demanding admittance.

I was on my feet in a moment ; but had hardly
left my room when the knocking was renewed with
greater violence than at first. My mother was
already at the door, and was demanding to know
who was there.

'Open the door. Where is his reverence?
Where is Pastor Bergmann?' answered the visitor.

I opened the door while my mother stood beside
me with the lamp in her hand. It had begun to
snow again, and the draught was so great that the

light was nearly extinguished. Two men were standing outside, wrapped in large cloaks, and their hats were drawn low down over their faces. The first to enter was as pale as death. He shook the snow from his hat and cloak. Close at his heels followed the other—old Peter, who looked as though overwhelmed by some misfortune. No sooner had they come in than, the first—a servant of Count Arthur's—said :

'For God's sake, come quickly, reverend sir.'

'Where,' I asked.

'To the Castle,' was the answer, 'and take everything you will need to comfort a dying man.'

My heart stood still, and I gasped for breath :

'Who is dying?' I enquired in an awed whisper.

'Count Arthur is dying. Make haste, reverend sir.'

I stood as though turned to stone. Old Peter collected all that was wanted with my mother's help, and then I followed him and his companion to the carriage that was waiting for us, hardly knowing what I did. The sacristan got into the carriage beside me, and we were soon driving rapidly through the village, and the wood to the Castle.

While I sat thus silent and motionless, old Peter whispered :

'The Amsterdam Rabbi was right, and so was I, sir.'

We had reached the middle of the wood before

I could rouse myself sufficiently to ask what had happened. I was then informed that the Count had taken a longer ride that afternoon than usual. He had been mounted on a fiery chestnut that he had lately bought from his brother Leo, and had been accompanied by a former groom of his brother's, whom he had engaged when he purchased the horse. For the last three weeks the groom had exercised the chestnut regularly in the woodland roads, and to-day Count Arthur had tried it for the first time. It was growing dusk when the Count and his servant had entered the wood on their way home. The ground was slightly frozen, and a thin carpet of snow covered the road. When they came to the Slough of Blood, the Count, who was a thoroughly good horseman, had wished to ride over the frozen marsh, but the chestnut, either startled by the weird shadows cast by the great beeches over the morass and pool, or from some other cause, had suddenly shied, and thrown his rider with such force against the stem and gnarled roots of one of the beech trees, that the blood had streamed from his mouth and nose, and he had fainted. He had been carried home, and when he had come to himself again, the family doctor had declared himself powerless to help him.

I was much moved by what I heard, and gazed sadly out of the carriage window at the familiar scene. The park was bathed in the pale moonlight, which made every well-known object take weird and unaccustomed shape, and then the Castle rose before us, and the Red Tower in the background added a mysterious gloom to the picture. I shivered as I thought of the thick darkness that surrounded our fate, and of the sudden blow that had fallen on Castle Seeried, turning it into a house of mourning. A few hours before Count Arthur had ridden up to the Parsonage, and there in all the pride of health and strength had given utterance to those evil words that had haunted me ever since. Now he was dying, and I had been sent for to give him the last consolations of religion. And that mysterious power, that wisdom that 'knoweth things of old and conjectureth aright what is to come,' was justified in my eyes after a most remarkable fashion.

I ascended the steps leading to the front door sadly, and old Peter followed close behind. A servant received us at the door.

'Thank God you have come, sir,' he said, with tears in his eyes. 'You are much wanted.'

He preceded us, walking softly. We passed a good many of the servants, all of whom seemed overwhelmed by the sudden calamity that had befallen the Seerieds. Some of the old people were collected in an ante-room. They all looked distressed, and one or two were weeping. Our guide asked one of the men, who had just come from the inner room, how Count Arthur was.

'It will soon be over,' was the answer, and the

sobbing of the old people grew louder. 'Come, Herr Pastor,' he continued, 'come in.'

I went into the room, which was faintly lighted. Heavy green silk curtains covered the windows. The bed was draped with hangings of the same material, which were partially drawn aside. The Countess was bending over her husband, while Helen knelt at her side, her hands clasped in bitter sorrow. Two gentlemen were standing somewhat apart, and the Count's faithful *valet* came and went with all that might be required.

When I saw the Countess and her daughter in their grief, my heart grew heavier than before, and my lips trembled.

The *valet* informed his mistress that I had come. She turned to me. She was not weeping, but— never before or since did I see a face on which was the stamp of such immeasureable woe. She took my hand, but said nothing. Helen was crying softly.

The Countess led me towards her husband's death-bed. There he lay quiet and motionless.

I wondered whether he might not dislike to have a priest brought to him at that last hour, and hesitated to advance; but the Countess whispered so low that I could scarcely hear :

'You are his friend—he wanted to see you.'

As I came up to the bed to offer the dying man the consolations of religion, his consciousness once more returned. He recognised me, and a look of pleasure came into his face. Then he tried to speak.

'So—the—Rabbi was right—after all,' he whispered. 'Do what—your office demands of you—pray with my dear ones. Come, Cornelia, Helen—Pastor Bergmann—will comfort you.'

My voice trembled as I read the prayers for the dying. The Countess and Helen knelt with clasped hands.

One of the gentlemen, who was standing in the background, came forward, bowed his head, and seemed to join in our prayers. When I paused, he began, much to my astonishment, to repeat one of those almost hysterical prayers, which the Pietists of that day were in the habit of using at the death-bed of their friends. I looked keenly at the stranger. He appeared to be about my own age; was tall and thin; had a pointed nose over which his eye-brows met, and a gloomy, disagreeable, expression, and was, moreover, dressed in dark, quaker-like garments. I thought I had seen him before, though I could not remember where. He was standing close to the bed while he prayed, and I noticed that the dying man grew restless and uneasy as he listened, and that he looked at me entreatingly. I bent over him, and he said faintly:

'I hear—a false—voice. Silence! silence!'

Count Arthur uttered the last two words in loud and angry tones, so that the stranger could not help hearing. He ceased therefore to pray aloud, but remained with his eyes fixed on the ceiling, and looked as though he were finishing his devotions in silence. Then Count Arthur raised his eyes to mine and said, or rather gasped :

' Be a faithful friend—to my wife—and daughter. O, my son !—O, my brother—— '

The stranger came a little closer to the bed, saying :

' Here I am, Arthur—beside you in life and death.'

' In life and death,' he repeated after a pause.

The dying man fixed his eyes on him, and distrust and indignation were plainly to be read in his face. At length he stammered, making a great effort to speak distinctly :

' You ? ' and there was a world of horror in his tone and expression. ' Go away—go away ! Evil counsellor that you have ever been, what brings you here ? Away with you, and send me back him whom you drove from my side !'

But Count Leo took no notice of his brother's words, or of the Countess's gesture of entreaty. He continued to stand by the bed with the same look of unctuous solemnity as at first, while the doctor, with whom he had been talking when I entered the room, still remained in the background. I went to the latter, and begged him to induce Count Leo to retire, as his presence was obviously hurtful to the sick man ; but he shrugged his shoulders despairingly as a sign that he could do nothing.

'I, therefore, determined to make an appeal to the young man's good feeling, and entreat him not to embitter the last hours of his dying brother, by forcing himself upon him against his will. No sooner had I spoken than Count Leo laid his hand on my arm, and glared at me. There was a cruel look on his face. His forehead was contracted with a heavy frown, and his lips curled sardonically.

'Herr Pastor,' he whispered, 'you forget that as my brother is dying, and his son is absent, it is *I* who have to give orders here. You need not remain any longer, my brother does not want you.'

With that he turned away, and went back to the bedside. Count Arthur hung for a few minutes longer between life and death. Almost his last words were :

'My son! My brother Hermann! O Cornelia, Helen, my dear ones! Herr Pastor, be a friend— to my dear ones !'

The Countess hid her face beside her husband's. Helen wept, and held her father's hand, while old Peter sobbed like a child. My heart felt very heavy as I stood beside them.

Count Leo held his clasped hands over the dying man, who looked at him once more, and moved his lips as though he were trying to speak. He therefore bent over his brother, but immediately afterwards started back as if he had been stung.

Count Arthur had uttered the one word 'traitor' so distinctly that it could not be mistaken. It was his last effort. He then looked at his wife and daughter lovingly—and so passed away.

I prayed inwardly, and then I prayed aloud, unheeding the order Count Leo had given me. The Countess and her daughter were kneeling by the bed. I longed to give them comfort in their grief.

Count Leo raised his arms, and cried :

' Lord, judge him mercifully, and reckon not up his blasphemies against Thee.'

At these words old Peter started out of his sorrowful reverie, and going up to Count Leo, said in a voice that trembled with excitement :

' My lord, your brother was perhaps over-bold of speech ; but his heart was gentle—and he was true and just in all his dealings.'

And I added :

' God does not judge us according to our words ; but according to our deeds and thoughts.'

Count Leo glanced at me with contempt and dislike, and then left the room accompanied by the doctor.

Old Peter closed his master's eyes, and helped the *valet* to arrange the room, while I endeavoured to comfort the widow and daughter of the dead man.

On going through the ante-room, I found the servants collected there weeping. Count Arthur had been a strict master ; but just and generous at

the same time.   The servants knew what they had
lost in him.

The Castle bell began to toll as I came out into
the corridor, and at the same moment I heard a
horse galloping down the avenue.   I was so much
astonished that I asked who was leaving Castle
Seeried at that late hour, and was informed that it
was a groom Count Leo was sending away with
dispatches, probably to the young Count to tell
him of his father's death, and summon him home.

I remained talking with the house-steward for a
short time, for I saw how much it comforted him
to speak of his master.   While I was still sitting
with him, old Peter came in search of me with a
message from the Countess.   She hoped that I
would help her in her great affliction, for no one
was more in need of a true friend than she, her
children, and dependants.

The steward wanted to order a carriage to take
me home ; but I declined, as I felt that the walk
would calm me, and do me good.

The moon was shining dimly.   The clouds
driving up from the Baltic scudded in heavy
masses across the sky, and the wind swept the
rain and snow in gusts against the battlements of
the Red Tower.   It was a wild night.   The
steward lent us cloaks to shield us from the storm,
and sent a servant with a lantern to guide us
through the wood.   And so we set out on our
walk, leaving behind us, what, in the morning, had

been the abode of joy, and was now turned into
a house of mourning and death.

A cold rain was falling mingled with numerous
large flakes of snow, and as we crossed the open
space in front of the Castle I glanced up at the
dimly lighted windows, and thought sadly of the
widowed mother, and her fatherless daughter. I
swore to myself that I would be their faithful
friend through life, and, seeking no advantage for
myself, would live, and if need be, die in their
service.

Meanwhile old Peter and the servants walked on
before me through the wet snow. At first they
were silent ; but after a little they began to speak
of their dead master who had been so strict and
yet so kind. He never would suffer any injustice
to be done, they said, was wise and active in the
administration of his estate, and there was none
like him in the whole land. I listened sorrowfully.
Seeried would never again have such a master,
they went on, indeed bad times were coming, if it
were really true that the young heir was leading
a wild life abroad under the tutelage of Ephraim
Lebrecht. The two faithful old servants went on
talking after this fashion until we approached the
Slough of Blood, and then they began to speak of
the accident, and of how it had happened. The
light of the lantern fell tremulously on the stems
of the great beeches that surrounded the fatal spot.

'Ah, I knew what would happen,' sighed the

sacristan. 'I have felt all this year that I should help to bury Count Arthur before the twelve months were out, and now it has come to pass, though he never would believe it.'

'They say,' answered the servant, 'that the accident was as much the fault of the groom as of the restive horse. They both came from Count Leo's stables, and had our poor master not mounted that vicious brute, and ridden out with that groom ——'

'Stuff and nonsense!' interrupted old Peter. 'The people at Strandow have many a sin on their conscience—that cannot be denied—but what took place to-day was predestined to happen; Count Arthur could not escape his fate.'

These words recalled to my mind all that the Count had told me respecting the prophecy; and as we walked on through the sleet and snow, and heard the wind moaning in the dry branches of the trees, I began to reflect on the prognostication of the Amsterdam Rabbi, and on the strange story of Count Ruttger. I remembered how he was said to have called up the spirit of his dead love by means of a spell he had learnt in the Book of the *Baal Teschuba*, and pondered what connection there was between this and the older tradition, and how far either or both were in agreement with my own experiences during the past year. Was there, then, really an art such as those verses of the Apocryphal Book of Wisdom seemed to teach, by

means of which one might foresee the future?
Was what I had witnessed that very day an extraordinary proof of the correctness of the Kabbalistic
method of reckoning, or was the Count's death a
mere accident, that cast no doubt on the truth of
the assumption made by him that very day, when
he had called on me at the Parsonage.

My thoughts were gloomy as the circumstances
that had called me out that night ; gloomy and
dismal as the storm that was howling through the
wood.   I was once more standing face to face with
the dark problem of human existence, and asking
questions of Fate, to which no answer was vouch-
safed me.   I therefore felt all the more keenly
what I afterwards read in Shakespeare, who makes
Hamlet say to the friend with whom he is walking
on the terrace of Kronburg Castle, at Elsinore :

> ' There are more things in heaven and earth, Horatio,
>   Than are dreamt of in our * philosophy.'

The death of the man, whose body was lying in
state at Castle Seeried, bore witness to the truth
of this.

On coming out of the wood, the village lay
straight before us.   Heavy clouds were driving
over the sky from the Baltic, so that the moon
shone fitfully with a spectral light, like a dim lamp

---

* 'our,' White, Dyce, Knight.

in the death chamber of the world. We went
through the village, Peter and the servant still in
front, and I following a few steps behind them.
The cottagers were all asleep ; not a light was to
be seen in any of their windows. The only sound
to be heard was when some watchful Pommeranian
or Spitz barked at us as we passed. The inhabitants of these small houses knew nothing of the
sorrow and anxiety that prevailed at the castle,
they slept in peace.

We had at length nearly reached our destination.
The church and parsonage lay before us. The
road was in a dreadful state of mud and slush, so
old Peter proposed that we should take the path
leading through the churchyard and past the
sacristan's cottage. The church clock was striking ten as we entered the burial-ground, and all
around was so dark that we could hardly discern
the grave-mounds, and sometimes nearly tripped
over them as we felt our way, for the light of
the lantern was thrown too far in advance to let
us see the ground at our feet.

We made our way round one side of the church,
and as we did so, we could hear the wind howling
and groaning through the building as though the
spectral pastor were holding his ghostly service
within. The moonlight fell here and there for a
few moments in patches on the ground. Then we
came to the new mausoleum with the great coat-

of-arms hewn in stone : the resting-place Count
Arthur had built for himself.

I was startled out of my brooding by the action
of the two men who accompanied me. They had
been walking a little in advance, but now came to
a sudden halt, and began to retrace their steps
with every sign of fear. Old Peter was the nearest
to me, so I asked him what was the matter.

' Herr Pastor, reverend sir, do you hear nothing?'
he said, while the servant with the lantern quietly
slipped behind me.

' Yes, I hear the wind in the church porch,' I
answered. ' Come, let us make haste and get
home.'

The sacristan seized my arm, and clung to it in
terror.

' The noise does not come from the church,' he
stammered. ' It comes from over there in front of
us.'

I listened attentively, but could hear nothing
except the wind.

And yet—what was that ! A wild cry came
out of the darkness, followed by moans.

Then all was silent, but for the voices of the
storm.

CHAPTER X.

' A sound—a voice—a shriek—a fearful call !
A long loud shriek—and silence.'
                                        —*Lara.*

' Die Geisterwelt is nicht verschlossen,
Dein Sinn ist zu, dein Herz ist tot ! '
                                        —*Faust.*

IT was a terrible, heart-piercing cry, and the
silence that succeeded it was not less startling.
We stood as though rooted to the spot. Old
Peter was still clinging to my arm, and I felt that
he was trembling in every limb. Even I could
not help shuddering as I stood there listening
intently, in the gloom of that dark November
night. I could not determine from which direction
the cry had come, although it still seemed to be
sounding in my ears.

' It came from the graves over there,' said Peter
at last, in a quavering voice.

I now desired the servant to precede us with the
lantern, as I wished to see what was the matter.
But the man was far too frightened to obey ; he
slipped behind me, and stood there shaking from
head to foot.

A low plaintive moaning now became audible in the darkness. It seemed to proceed from the graves, and could not by any means have been made by the flagstaff on the church tower, as I was at first inclined to believe.

'Is God calling the dead to arise?' I asked myself. The moon was hidden behind a cloud so that nothing could be seen distinctly.

'Go on with the light,' I repeated. 'I must find out what this means.'

Upon this, the terrified servant dropped the lantern amongst the graves, and ran to take refuge against the church wall. As Peter made no movement to pick up the lantern, I did so myself, and advanced determinedly in the direction of the moans, looking heedfully to my steps the while. The snow on the grave-mounds was half melted, and, clinging to the blades of the coarse church-yard grass, hung thousands of rain drops, that shone for a moment in the rays of the lantern, and then fell back into the darkness.

I made my way as far as the hedge that bordered the burial-ground without seeing anything unusual, and it was not until the moon came out from behind the clouds, that I thought I could perceive a human form stretched between two newly made graves.

The figure was lying on its back. On coming up to it, I caught sight of a countenance so grey and cadaverous that it might readily have been supposed to have but just arisen from the dead. I should pretend to be braver than I was, if I do not confess that an irrepressible terror seized me at the sight of that ghastly object.

I stood for a moment holding the lantern so as to see better, and could dimly discern the outlines of a bald head, and a long grey beard that lay on the breast of the dead, or dying man. His head was leaning against one of the grave-mounds. I shivered as I caught sight of his drawn and wasted features, and the cold, hard expression that seemed as though frozen into his eyes.

I then approached the figure more nearly, shivering as I did so, and it appeared to me as if a slight twitch agitated the limbs of the seeming corpse.

My courage grew. Quickly placing the lantern on one of the graves, I bent over the figure, and found that life was not yet extinct. I raised the grey head ; but it sank back stiffly on the cold, damp ground. Vainly I tried to lift the body, it was too heavy to manage alone.

So I called old Peter and the servant to come to my assistance. They did so ; but started back in amazement when they saw the strange bearded figure, clothed in a long caftan, that rested motionless in my arms. At length, seeing that there was no question of having to do with a ghost, Peter obeyed my reiterated order, and came to my help, and the other man followed his example after a moment's hesitation. Together, we carried the stranger to the Parsonage.

My mother was sitting up waiting for me, and praying for Count Arthur, so that she was ready to open the door when we knocked. She was much startled when she saw us, and the burden we were carrying into the house ; but she wasted no time in asking questions, and at once led the way to a bedroom.

We laid the old man on a couch. It was terrible to look at him. His wide and staring eyes, his haggard face, blue, foam-flecked lips, and stiffened jaw alarmed us. His body and limbs were motionless as those of a corpse ; but we could hear a faint gurgle in his throat, which convinced us that he was yet alive.

My mother was the first to recover herself sufficiently to act. She looked at the old man's hand, the fingers of which were closed over the thumb.

' He is an epileptic,' she said tremblingly, ' and the fit is on him now. We must wait till the worst of it is over ; meanwhile, loose his neck-cloth and belt—I will go and prepare some camomile tea.'

As soon as old Peter was convinced that the stranger's peculiar appearance was due to natural causes, his benevolence was at once awakened, and he proceeded to obey my mother's directions.

When he had done all that he could for the sick
man, he turned to me, and whispered :

'He is a Jew.   Look, here are his phylacteries
and the ten commandments.'

'Never mind them, Peter,' I said, 'but do what
you can for the poor man.'

The servant now wished to return to the Castle,
and took leave, saying that he intended to avoid
the wood, and go by the windmill-hill.

The stranger seemed to be getting better of his
own accord, and when my mother had forced some
of the hot tea between his clenched teeth, his face
lost its blue look, and became more natural in its
colouring.   At length he fell into a deep sleep,
accompanied by heavy stertorous breathing.

My mother and the sacristan begged me to go
and lie down, assuring me that they could not
sleep, and would therefore remain with their
patient till morning.   At last they persuaded me
to go away, and after lying awake for a long time
thinking over the strange events of the day, I fell
asleep.

When I awoke, it seemed as though all that had
happened were a bad dream ; but I was soon
brought back to a sense of the reality of things by
the tolling of the church-bell that published abroad
the news of Count Arthur's death.   I then got up,
and no sooner was I dressed than my mother came
in, and told me that Rabbi Meier wanted to see
and thank me.

'Rabbi Meier!' I cried. 'Thank me for what?'

'For having saved his life,' answered my mother. 'He is the old Jew you found in a fit in the churchyard last night. He would have died to a certainty had he remained out in such weather.'

I went to the old man's room, and knocked at the door. A voice called me to come in, and on entering, I perceived a venerable figure clothed in a long caftan, over which descended a white pointed beard, while long grey locks fell over his shoulders.

The old man rose to meet me with a friendly : '*Sholem Alechem*' (Peace be unto you).

When I had enquired after his health, he asked whether I was the clergyman of the parish, and, on receiving an answer in the affirmative, he overwhelmed me with expressions of gratitude for what I had done for him. I had difficulty in preventing him kissing my hands.

'God of my fathers, O Lord of Sabaoth!' he cried. 'I pray Thee, reward this, my benefactor, unto the third and fourth generation. May this petition of Thy servant find grace in Thy sight. O Lord God, give him joy and gladness, a noble mind, wisdom and grace, and may his children and his children's children be held in honour, and be rich in all good things of heaven and earth. Thou alone canst give, and take away ; blessed be Thy holy name for ever and ever. Amen.'

Having thus spoken, he sank back exhausted in his chair, and gazed before him thoughtfully. One

N

could see how weak he was.   His face even was
worn and sunken.

'Sir,' he said, addressing me after a few minutes'
silence, 'I can never repay you for your kindness
to me otherwise than with my prayers.   Now, give
me your good wishes for the long journey that lies
before me—I shall have need of them,—and give
me also a staff to support my aged limbs, and help
me to reach the goal of my wanderings.'

'You cannot go, old man,' I said gently.   'Why
should you attempt a long journey?   You are not
fit for it.'

'The weaker I am, the sooner I shall reach my
destination,' he answered.   'I shall die in misery,
and shall be buried in a strange place.   Let me go,
reverend sir.   The burden I brought to your house
is heavy enough as it is.'

He rose from his chair; but I made him sit
down again, and said :

'You must not leave me until you are strong
enough to pursue your journey.   Do not distress
yourself, old man ; let this house be your shelter—
call it your inn, if you refuse to be a guest under
the roof of a Christian priest, or to receive, from the
hand of one of another faith, what is offered in
brotherly kindness.'

He fixed his dark, deep-set eyes upon me, and
gazed at me for some time in silence.   Then he
said :

'Nay, not so.   I bless you for your kindness.

But tell me, I pray you, where I am, and what is the name of this village to which the Providence of God has led me?'

'It is the village of Seeried, and lies in the property of the Count von Seeried-Strandow,' I replied.

'Count von Seeried-Strandow,' he repeated thoughtfully. 'Is there not a Count Arthur von Seeried-Strandow?'

'Yes, until last night,' I said.

'Until last night?' enquired the old man. 'What do you mean by that? Speak, man of God, and tell me what you mean.'

'Count Arthur died last night, and his mortal remains will be laid in the vault in a few days' time,' I answered.

Rabbi Meier was silent for a few minutes. He remained sunk in deep thought. Then he strove to rise from his chair, took my hand in his, and said:

'Let it be as you wish. It is God's will that I should remain here—but not for long. May the reward of Abraham and David be with your house, I will pray for that, I can do no more.'

I tried to comfort the old man, assuring him that my house was his home until he had regained his strength. And so it was settled. He quite distressed my mother with the little trouble he gave, for he would have nothing more than a jug of milk in the morning, and an egg at night.

I have little to tell regarding my own doings during the next few days. Every morning I went to the Castle. Count Arthur's body was lying there in state on a bier hung with black, and placed in a large room. Around it candles were kept constantly burning. Everyone who liked was allowed to go there and pray, and I often saw the Countess and her daughter kneeling by the bier.

The Countess often sent for me when she heard I was at the Castle, and asked me to read prayers. She bore her sorrow with dignity, and Helen's was a gentle, silent grief. Letters had been sent to the young Count, who was still in Paris, to announce his father's death, and entreat him to come home as quickly as possible, and take possession of his heritage, for there were many things that wanted seeing to. Meanwhile Count Leo drove like an uneasy spirit between Seeried and Strandow. He offered to help the Countess in all her arrangements, and she could not well refuse his assistance as he was the only male representative of the family in the neighbourhood, with the exception of Baron Karl, the youngest son of old Count Frederick by his third marriage, and he was not yet of age.

The days before the funeral passed sadly for me, as for everyone at Seeried. My mother told me that Rabbi Meier spent most of his time in prayer. When in my study I occupied myself with the work I had undertaken on the day of Count Arthur's death, *viz.*, with making a copy of all the notices of the Seeried family contained in the church books. The baptismal registers of the young Count, and of his sister Helen were each written on a separate page of the great book, while those of Count Frederick's twin sons by the second marriage were placed side by side on the same page, and I saw that Count Hermann's birth was registered as having taken place six hours before that of his brother Leo. I should not have paid any particular attention to this circumstance, had it not been that a loose sheet of paper fell out of the book at that moment, containing a duplicate of the notice in Pastor Schimmelmann's writing ; but with two important differences. The ink in which it was written was not yellow and faded like that used by Pastor Schimmelmann in the church-book, but much bluer, and, as it appeared to me, more lately written. It was the same kind of ink as that in which Pastor Lebrecht had made his entries in the book. And besides that, this other document made Leo, and not Hermann, the elder of the twin brothers. Such an essential difference as this could hardly have been made by accident.

Strange and inexplicable as the circumstance appeared, I laid but little weight upon it, for the duplicate was valueless, and the true date of birth was safely entered in the church register. But all the same I made a note of it, as you will see on looking at my diary for that year. I determined to speak to old Peter about it on the first opportunity, but all my thoughts were soon occupied by other matters. I made a discovery on that very day, which not only helped to soothe my grief for the death of the Count, but also enabled me to put my unavowed attachment more into the background of my thoughts. It was therefore not wonderful that I forgot the forged certificate. A few minutes after restoring it to its place, I heard someone tap three times at my door.

On calling out, 'Come in,' the reverend figure of Rabbi Meier appeared in the doorway, leaning on his stick. He excused himself for disturbing me ; but I thanked him for coming to see me in my solitude, for little as I knew of him, he had yet awakened my sympathy if not my trust. I drew an easy chair forward, and begged him to sit down. He told me that he had come to bring back a book which he had borrowed, and again begged me to excuse him for having disturbed me. So there was nothing for it, but to tell him what my very unimportant labours had been. I further informed him of the duplicate certificate, and even gave him the paper to look at. He examined it silently, and without showing any apparent interest. He then asked a few questions about the Seeried family, and as it did me good to speak, I have no doubt that I told him a great deal more than he cared to hear. My sympathies for the

Countess and her daughter could not be altogether repressed. In the course of my story I mentioned the prophecy that the Amsterdam Rabbi had made concerning Count Arthur. Then I went on to talk of Count Ruttger, of the Red Tower, and of the Kabbalistic books in the library there, and this in due course led me to speak of the Kabbalah itself, and to confess what a tempting study I had found it.

Rabbi Meier listened to me calmly, almost indifferently. From the few remarks he made from time to time, I gathered that he did not belong to the orthodox Talmudist party, who reject the Kabbalah *in toto*. Little as he said, and reserved as he was, he yet gave me the impression of being deeply versed in the ancient lore of which I was speaking. His sayings were unconsciously oracular, and the more laconic he endeavoured to make them, the more sibyline they appeared. When he saw that I really knew something of the Kabbalah, he asked me point-blank what I thought of it, what conclusions I had come to regarding it.

I found the question rather difficult to answer at first ; but as I had really gained a good deal of information on the subject since ny undergraduate days, I collected my thoughts, and began to explain the light in which I held it.

I now looked upon the Kabbalah as the religious philosophy of the Hebrews, which had been propagated as a secret science ever since the time of the Babylonish Captivity ; as a system which had assimilated the ideas of all the ancient races with respect to the Divinity, after having worked them out after the manner of the Talmudists. I could not deny that the Emanation theory of the Kabbalah, that the idea of spirits and worlds proceeding out of Space, as well as the doctrines of the Trinity, of the incarnation of the Deity, of the immortality of the soul, and its return to God after its probation on earth, one and all formed the basis of the ancient religion of India. Elements of Egyptian Theosophy, such as the idea of the veiled divinity of Elemental Light, might also be discovered in the Kabbalah. Zoroaster's Parsi-ism, or, in other words, the reformation he introduced into the religion of the Chaldæan Magi, was the connecting link between it and Hindu Theosophy. During the time of the Babylonish Captivity, or even later on, these doctrines were further worked out by Jewish sages, who incorporated with them the Indian decimal system. This teaching was brought into Europe by the Moors in the 11th century. From the same source, I continued, comes the Pythagorean Philosophy ; for Pythagoras, and those disciples whom he collected around him that they might worship God together, already felt a foreboding of the great secret hidden in numbers. They recognised, and explained the existence and essence of all things which revolve round the One, the central fire, by the relation and

connection of figures. That their ten Spheres
resemble the Sephiroth cannot be denied. Again,
what Plato dreamt of as an Ideal, is also to be
seen in the teaching of the Kabbalah, and the
influence of the same ideas is to be found amongst
the gnostic sects of early Christianity.

The old man listened to me calmly. Now and
then a smile hovered about his lips. When I had
ceased, he said:

'Nothing can come out of nothing, so the Kabbalah must have had a beginning like everything
else. If you will not believe the ancient tradition
that God's angels taught Adam and his descen-
dants these holy lessons, in order that fallen man
might sooner learn the way of blessedness, or that
to Abraham we owe the Book Jetzira; you might
—seeing you do not doubt that the teaching is
ancient—go so far as to hold that the Patriarch
brought it from his home in the far East. He left
Ur of the Chaldees with his father Terah, and
went into the land of Canaan, where he built altars
to the God of his fathers. But that is not what I
want to speak to you about. I wish to know this.
Do you not consider that the Kabbalah, is, as it
were, a ray of divine wisdom and knowledge?'

I was silent for a few moments thinking what
was the right answer to make, and then said without further hesitation:

'I used to look upon it as a science revealed by
God, by means of which we might learn what has

been hidden from the multitude. But, as I said before, I now regard it as one of those systems by means of which man seeks to gain light in the darkness that encompasses him, and endeavours to sound the depths of the gulf that divides him from the unknown. The only difference between the Kabbalah and other systems, is that it is yet darker and more mysterious than all the rest.

Rabbi Meier looked at me enquiringly as I spoke, and when I had ceased, he murmured so low that I could scarcely hear him :

'Light is as darkness to him whose eyes have not been opened by God—the pure light of wisdom blinds those whose eyes are unaccustomed to look upon it.'

Then turning to me, he continued aloud : ' You have never realized the marvellous power of this divine Wisdom ? '

'I believed in it, until I found that it was the self-deception of a heated imagination, which made me see wonders where none existed.'

'The spirit of Count Arthur rests upon you,' answered the Rabbi ; 'and yet,' he added quietly, ' the prophecy of the Amsterdam Kabbalist ought to have taught you something.'

I was taken aback, but only for a moment.

' Accident almost always counts for a good deal in such cases,' I replied.

' " *Almost always*," ' repeated Rabbi Meier, shaking his head sadly and thoughtfully. ' But you told me about the Red Tower, in which a Count Ruttger von Seeried-Strandow kept his Kabbalistic books and papers, and where he called up the spirit of his lost love by the aid of the Book of the *Baal Teschuba.*'

'Yes, Count Ruttger, the alchemist, as he is called in the family chronicles. He wrote down his experiences,' I answered.

'And you will not accept his testimony?'

'I have lately proved in my own person how great is the power of imagination.' I returned, remembering with shame how I had thought I had seen a funeral procession passing through the woodland drive, and also how a belief in ghosts had affected my two companions in the churchyard, while I myself had not been untouched by tremours on the same occasion, owing to having nursed a feeling of awe at the sudden death of the Count happening at the time prophesied. Still, boldly as I spoke, I knew that I did so in consequence of a secret shame, and a desire to make myself appear stronger than I really felt.

After a short silence, the old man asked me if I would take him to Count Ruttger's Tower.

I gazed at him in doubt.

'I know,' he said, 'that it is a great deal to ask, more perhaps than I ought. But it is not curiosity that induces me to make the request—I am too old for that, and my experience has been too varied. My days are numbered, and I would not spend the short time that remains to me in vain. To speak frankly, reverend sir ; will you do this for me, or do you think that evil would come of it, as when Abimelech, son of Gideon, went to the Tower of Shechem ?'

'I do not know any reason against granting your request,' I answered at length. 'It can do neither the family nor me any harm to take you there.'

'Then let us go at once, the Lord gives me but a short time more to live,' he replied, taking up his stick and going towards the door.

It was a few days before the funeral of Count Arthur that this conversation took place.

Rabbi Meier and I set out on our way to the Castle without further delay.

A thick fog had come up from the Baltic, and covered the dunes and the forest of Seeried. It was so dense that we could not see three feet before us. We walked down the village street almost unnoticed, and when we reached the end of it, I turned into the road that ran across the windmill hill, thinking it the safer of the two. No sooner had we reached the top of the sandy, heath-covered knoll than the curtain of mist parted, and floated away leaving no trace behind. We walked on without meeting any one. Whenever I glanced at the figure of the old man beside me, my thoughts turned involuntarily to Old Testament times, and I called to mind pictures of the prophets of old.

The story of how Elisha had accompanied his master, Elijah, across the heath from Beth-el to the other side of Jordan became, as it were, alive to me, so vividly did I realize it. I did not then know what was hidden in the heart of my companion, and yet I felt as though I could say to him what Elisha had said to Elijah : ' I pray thee let a double portion of thy spirit be upon me.'

But we soon left the hill behind us, and when we reached the pathway through the wood, I went on in front. The strength of my impression faded as we made our way through the damp leafless woodland. It was very cold and dreary, and we were glad when we saw the Castle through the mist that was once more rising in the low ground, and seeming to gather force, and spread over the landscape.

A servant, whose curiosity did not appear to be in the least aroused by my companion, admitted us by a side door. I was so well known to every one, and was trusted so implicitly that I might have taken any one I liked there without causing the least uneasiness or astonishment. The old servant evidently thought that we desired to visit the great hall in which the bier was placed, for he took us into the corridor that led to it. When I told the Jewish Rabbi where we were being taken, he begged to be allowed to go in, if I did not fear that an old man's prayer would hurt the dead. I bowed my acquiescence, and we went in together.

The room seemed to be deserted. In the midst of it stood the bier on which the body of Count Arthur was laid, covered with a black and white pall. The light of the tapers that were burning around it fell upon the face of the dead man, and served to accentuate the marked features which had always distinguished him. The portraits of his ancestors hung round the walls of the room, and seemed to gaze down at him as he lay there. Right in front was the picture of his father, Count Frederick, and a little further off was that of Count Ruttger, the alchemist, a copy of the original portrait in the Red Tower. The wife of the latter, a fair-haired, handsome woman, with strongly marked, energetic features, hung close beside it. From her picture alone, it was easy to believe the truth of the story that she had burnt the portrait of the Dutch girl, her rival. These, and all the other family pictures, hung round the room in which the dead man lay. Together they formed a quiet, ghost-like company.

It was not until the old man and I had approached quite close to the bier, that I perceived two female forms kneeling behind it. The Rabbi saw them also, and stood still, bending his head, and murmuring so low that I could not hear what he said. When the Countess and her daughter rose to go away, he bowed in silent reverence for their grief.

As soon as we were alone with the dead, I closed

my eyes and prayed, so that I did not see what my companion was doing. I was at length aroused by hearing a strange murmur, and when I looked up, I saw the Rabbi bending over the corpse, his lips close to Count Arthur's ear. I shivered, and stood irresolute for a moment, not knowing what to do. Then the old man raised his head, and coming towards me with a far-away look in his face, said, as though to himself:

'He is satisfied that all is well, and will not make accusation against me. If Samael* was not accursed to all eternity, why should I be?'

Horror seized me as I listened. I touched his arm, saying:

'Rabbi, we must go away from here.'

'Then let us go,' he answered quietly. 'Our time is short.'

We went out into the corridor again, and found it but faintly lighted by the windows, so dark was the grey, misty atmosphere without. Our steps made no sound on the thick carpet. I could not

---

* 'The demons are the grossest and most deficient of all forms. Their ten degrees answer to the decade of the Sephiroth, but in inverse ratio, as darkness and impurity increase with the descent of each degree. Their prince is *Samael*, SMAL, the angel of poison and death. Samael is considered to be identical with Satan.'— M'Gregor Mather's *Kabbalah Unveiled*.

Samael was regarded by Kabbalists as the old Serpent of the O. T., and was therefore the tempter of Eve.—See Emanuel Deutsch's *Literary Remains*.

M. W. M.

help feeling in awe of my companion, and yet I walked on boldly as if nothing were the matter. I led the way downstairs to the steward's room, in which the keys were kept, and there learnt that Count Leo was in the Red Tower examining the family archives in the muniment room below the library. The door into the Tower would therefore probably be open. This news struck me disagreeably.

We descended the stone passage, which I knew so well, to Count Ruttger's Tower, and our footsteps sounded hollow in the silence. The scene in the picture gallery still lay heavy on my heart, and, in order to change the current of my anxious thoughts, I stopped and asked Rabbi Meier if it was a Jewish custom to whisper in the ears of the dead—a useless ceremony it seemed to me.

'Our law,' he answered gravely, 'does not command it, and yet the words I uttered were not in vain. Nothing is lost in this world, not even the breath of our mouth—God makes use of every thing that is. Nothing is without effect of some kind, not even the words and voice of man, as the aged stranger said to the disciples of the great Simon ben Jochai, from whose teaching the book Sohar was written down. So why should my words be of none avail, and vanish as though they had had no being? If you knew the effect of a word, you would not question me about what concerns you not.'

We had reached the end of the great hall outside the Tower. The door was locked. I was raising my hand to knock when a grating sound was heard, and the door opened slowly.

CHAPTER XI.

'Anbetung dir, der die grosse Sonne
    Mit Sonnen und Erden und Monden umgab.'
                                —KLOPSTOCK.

    'O Ewigkeit, O Ewigkeit !
      Wie lang bist du, O Ewigkeit !'—*Old Song.*

'He questioned me on many points ; for instance,
  When I was born, what month, and on what day,
  Whether by day or in the night.'
          The Piccolomini. (Coleridge's Trans.).

A MAN came out of the doorway, and stopped
in amazement when he saw us. It was
Count Leo. It was easy to understand his astonishment at unexpectedly meeting two men, one of
whom was such a remarkable looking figure as
Rabbi Meier, standing there in the half darkness.
Although I knew that Count Leo was by no means
well disposed towards me, there was nothing else
for me to do, but to approach him, and ask whether
I might go to the Tower as usual, for I wanted to
show the Rabbi Count Ruttger's library.

After a moment's hesitation, Count Leo answered:
'Most certainly, Herr Pastor. You may visit
Count Ruttger's library as freely as if my brother
were still alive. Here is the key. Show your

friend the room, as a place which the Evil One has
marked for his own. I intend to come and see you
one of these days at the Parsonage, and have a
little talk with you. A heavy responsibility rests
on me at present as the eldest of the family, and I
must try to gain the assistance of all the friends of
our house.'

'You may count upon me, my lord,' I replied,
'in every matter that relates to the well-being of
the family.'

'I am sure of that,' said Count Leo, 'and the
Lord,' casting up his eyes, 'will help us.'

We then left him and went on our way up the
turret stair, which the old man found steep and
difficult.

When I described Count Ruttger's apartments
before, I forgot to mention that the view over the
lake was splendid from his windows, which were so
high that we were able to see over the low-lying
mist, and far out to sea. As the library had in a
great measure lost its charm for me, I contented
myself with pointing out and explaining whatever
seemed most interesting, although from the Rabbi's
manner it seemed hardly necessary. He appeared
to understand all about the curious cabinet, and
busied himself in searching through its contents,
whilst I amused myself with watching him, and
gazing out at the window.

Once when I looked round I saw Rabbi Meier
standing on a chair feeling all round the frame of

Count Ruttger's picture, but so little did his actions interest me that I soon turned to the window again. When I next looked round, he was examining the books in the cabinet.

I told the Rabbi about the secret drawer, not noticing that he had already discovered it, and was busy turning over the books and papers it contained. At last he put them all back in their places, and, drawing the curtain on which the ten Sephiroth, or Kabbalistic Tree, was depicted, joined me at the window, and said :

'That cabinet contains great treasures for him who knows how to use them.'

'Indeed,' I asked somewhat incredulously. 'If Count Leo had known that, he would hardly have been so willing to let us enter this room.'

'We read in the Book of Wisdom,' answered the old man solemnly, '" if riches be a possession to be desired in this life, what is richer than wisdom, that worketh all things." And again, "I preferred her before sceptres and thrones, and esteemed riches nothing in comparison of her. Neither compared I unto her any precious stone, because all gold in respect of her is as a little sand." Yea, verily, he who knows how to use the power of wisdom, without abusing it, is the happiest of men ; and as for him who misuses it—he is accursed, accursed, accursed ! '

The old man's voice had risen almost to a shriek. I gazed at him with startled wonder. His last words seemed to echo through the room, making my blood run cold. Flinging his thin hands over his face, he stood as though possessed by some evil spirit, like one of the demoniacs of old, his knees trembling, and his teeth chattering. Suddenly I remembered the illness from which he suffered, and sprang to his side, that I might catch him should he fall. But scarcely did he feel my arms around him, than he let his hands sink from his face, looked round him wildly, and asked :

' Where am I ? Where have you taken me, my benefactor ? '

' I brought you here, to the Red Tower at Castle Seeried, at your own urgent entreaty.'

He passed his hand across his brow, and once more became calm and quiet. Then turning to me, he said soothingly :

' Do not be alarmed, Herr Pastor, the evil spirit has no power over me here. Had I longer to live, I should beg you to let me come back to this room alone, and prepare for death, doing expiation for my sins. But my time is short. Let us go now. May I lean on you ? '

Without another word, I led him downstairs, through the stone passage, and out into the open air. We walked on in silence. The fog had grown more dense, and the evening was drawing on apace, so that we could see very little of our surroundings. But every now and then the mist parted for a few seconds, giving us a momentary glimpse of the sky.

It was very cold. The old man walked as quickly as he could. We had not exchanged a single word since we left the library, and I did not like to be the first to break the silence. But all at once Rabbi Meier turned to me, and said :

'So you never understood what treasure was hidden in that old Tower ?'

'To speak frankly,' I answered, ' I did not think much of it ; because I conceived that its value had been much over-rated.'

'Have you ever tried to learn its real worth?' he enquired.

' In the first place,' I said, ' let me ask you what it is you think so highly of, if it is not the Book of the *Baal Teschuba* ?'

'Of that, there is only one thing to be said, its tattered condition is an undoubted proof of its great value.'

'Your words surely have a double meaning,' I exclaimed. 'According to what you say, the strongest proof of its value would have been that nothing should have been left of it but its binding.'

'Yes,' answered the Rabbi with a sigh, 'for those who know not how to stop at the limits that have been set for their good.'

My attention was aroused by this. The old man evidently saw much more in the book than I had been able to discover. But he now went on to speak as though he wished to avoid the subject.

'He who knows how to devote himself humbly to the study of wisdom, will find much profit in perusing the books in Count Ruttger's library.'

'Do you really think so?' I cried. 'I have examined them closely, and have found but little profit in so doing.'

'It may be that you were like the goats that spring from rock to rock without seeing the meadows that lie in the valleys below,' said my companion, 'or perhaps the fault lay in the object of your search. What did you wish to find?'

'Light, light!' I exclaimed passionately.

Question and answer awakened all the old pain in my heart, and I went on in great excitement.

'I desired to find light in the darkness that surrounds us, that weighs upon our souls, and destroys all pleasures in life.

'And you did not find it?' enquired the Jew.

'No, neither there nor elsewhere. Whenever I thought I had discovered the way to it, I found only the appearance of light, not the reality. Nowhere could I gain any knowledge of the essence of Things or of God. Nowhere could I find the means by which to comprehend God and His dealings with the Universe.'

'And did you think you could have borne the weight of such knowledge?' asked Rabbi Meier. And then with a deep groan, he went on in a voice

that trembled with emotion, 'Your demand is bold
—and yet it is not more sinful than that of many
another.   O, that everyone were humble!   God
may be approached in His revelation of Himself;
but the veil beyond that revelation is not for you
to raise.   For His nature and attributes cannot be
apprehended by you, so long as you are conditioned
by this earthly existence.'

We had meanwhile left the wood, and had
reached the open country near the windmill hill.
The fog had lifted for the moment, and we could
see the sky sparkling with innumerable stars.   The
Rabbi stood still, raised his hand to the heavens,
and said :

'These are His work.   Can you comprehend
them?   Have you any wand by which you can
measure the visible revelation of God?   Look at
those stars through a telescope, and you will see
that their numbers form a total which your mind is
powerless to grasp.   The Kabbalah offers you the
means that you need—though the first is inade-
quate, and the second is hard to understand.'

'And these are?'

'Imagination and figures,' replied the old man.
'By the aid of these the Kabbalah endeavours to
render the works of God and His infinity comprehensible to our limited faculties ; and how far the
effort has been successful may be seen, not only in
the progress that has already been made in science,
but in that which may be confidently looked for in

the future. The Pythagoreans were not ignorant
of the deep mystery of figures and geometrical
signs, for their Master had learnt so much from the
Eastern Magi—men who were deeply versed in
knowledge of the stars. Figures can go beyond
the point where imagination folds her wings unable
to proceed any further. Can you form a clear idea
in your own mind of a billion?'

I looked at him in silence.

We walked on and had passed the windmill
before he spoke again. Then he said :

'If the first man had lived till now, the seconds
composing his life would number something like
the sixth-part of a billion seconds. The sun,
which forms the centre of a system of planets,
like our earth with our moon, and of comets still
more numerous, is so far removed from us, that a
cannon-ball would take twenty years to reach it
going at the rate of two miles a minute ; and yet,
it is only the fifty-thousandth part of a billion miles
distant from us. What we call fixed stars are suns
like ours, and each of them has its planets, moons
and comets. The nearest of these stars is four
billion and a half miles distant from our earth, so
that their light needs hundreds and thousands of
years to reach us, although light travels at the rate
of forty-two thousand miles a second. You look
at me in surprise ; but ask your astronomers if this
is not the case. Millions of solar systems like ours
exist in space, their suns perhaps form another

Milky-way like that which we see, and the eighteen million suns or stars are at a distance of some nine thousand billions of miles from the earth. Innumerable such Milky-ways are existent in immeasurable space. Astronomers have seen some of them faintly as ethereal forms in the distance, and reckon that they are about five hundred thousand billion miles away from us. Think of that! Think whence they get their light!'

The words of the old man made all the more impression upon me that they were spoken in that solitary place, and under the light of the stars. Moreover, they were in perfect harmony with the astronomy of the day—Herschel had already made his great discoveries. I remained silent, intent on what should follow ; and he went on, even more solemnly than before.

'Thus figures bring us to a point we should never have reached through thought alone. And yet, even by their means we can measure but a small part of what exists. The suns in immeasurable space are more numerous than the drops of water in the ocean. And then, each of these suns has its centre round which it revolves. Ours makes its revolution in a length of time to which our year is as a moment, and the centuries that have elapsed since the days of Adam are as a week. And yet, one year of the sun, which as you see embraces millions of our years, is not a second of Eternity.

Consider again this central sun, with others re-
sembling it, all of which revolve round a central
point of worlds, and so on step by step until you
come to the inconceivable—to the Primæval Light.
The Kabbalah contains this truth, and teaches it.
There we read of the 'point,' the point of Primæval
Light, from which the 'white light' streams, that
enlightens the worlds, lending them its radiance
without losing aught of its own glory. It is the
highest manifestation of that which is hidden, the
first revelation of the Eternal—the Crown of the
Sephiroth in the Kabbalistic Tree. The Idra
Suta of the Sohar teaches us that the essence of
that light is inconceivable even to the wisest. Who
can comprehend its glory, greatness, power and
action? And you, you think that *you* can do this!
A mere mortal! Dust upon a speck of dust!'

'And this primæval light, as you call it,' I
answered shyly, 'this primæval light is—?'

'The throne of the Most High God,' said the old
man solemnly. 'Have you not read in the Sohar
of where the Inconceivable, the Eternal and Everlasting, He who is without beginning and without
end, is enthroned! His dwelling-place is in the
white light, and by that light, whereby He also enlightens us, is He to be recognised. The worlds
proceed from him, and are, as it were, sparks in
His garment of light. He alone is the Eternal.
One of the sages of the olden times has said—and
he was of your religion—'A thousand years are

but as a day in the sight of the Lord.' A thousand years! Reckon up time by millions of years, and even then you will have no idea of a second of His life. And as for the greatness of His person? When Rabbi Akiba tried to make his disciples in some measure apprehend the greatness of the appearance of God, he wrote : ' The greatness of the Eternal may be compared to a thousand milliards of miles ; each of these miles contains a million ells ; each of these ells consists of four spans and a handsbreadth, and each span reaches from one end of the universe to the other.'

Long before this, my brain had grown dizzy with trying to follow what Rabbi Meier said. The sight of the starry heavens no longer raised my thoughts to ecstacy ; but rather depressed me unutterably. I was not able to follow the drift of his last sentence.

' What then,' I asked bitterly, ' is the value of this life of which man makes so much ado, of those actions he calls great, when our earth itself is but as a speck of dust in the Universe ? What is the use of all our striving and labour in a world that is as a grain of sand, uncounted, and unseen amongst myriads of others ? '

' But not in the eyes of the Eternal,' answered Rabbi Meier. ' Nothing is small, nor is anything great in His sight. He has counted the lives of the millions of living creatures that sport in every drop of water. And to men He has given souls, which had their origin in Him and in His light, and which still retain a dim consciousness of their spiritual birth. He has given us the means whereby we may approach Him, and has left us faint memories of the way that leads to His throne, the way by which we shall go back to him when our mortal bodies return to the dust from which they sprung.'

'And you regard the Kabbalah as one of the means by which we may approach God?'

'Certainly—as the chief means.'

'The old story! I have wasted only too much time and thought on this so-called occult science, and it has had exactly the opposite effect upon me.'

We had now come in sight of the village.

I did not notice that the old man's eyes were fixed upon me, until I turned to him enquiringly, and continued:

'Why did God plant the desire of knowledge in our hearts if He did not intend to satisfy it? What will prove to me that those are not right, who maintain that our striving, knowledge and faith are of no avail, that there is *nothing* beyond the laws of nature?'

'And what proof should you regard as sufficient to content you—to satisfy your reason?' asked the Rabbi gravely.

'The magic properties of the Kabbalah are often asserted,' I said. 'Now, I should like to have a visible, credible proof of the truth of this assertion, otherwise, I cannot help looking upon the whole thing as self-deception and vain imagining.'

'That is not the way to speak of the holy teaching,' said the old man sternly. 'You want to have a mere sign, saying that will content you, and yet, you will not accept the mighty wonders that God has done in this universe of His.'

As he spoke he raised his hand to heaven.

We walked down the village street towards the Parsonage in silence. At length, as we reached the garden gate, he said more gently :

'If you do not believe in the wondrous works of the Almighty, would the small marvels a human being is able to accomplish by the aid of the ray of divine light contained in the Kabbalah, really convince you?'

'Yes, if I could comprehend the process by which they were brought about?' I replied, as I opened the hall door, and followed my guest into the house.

'What of Count Arthur's story?' enquired the old man, laying his withered hand upon my arm.

'His death may have been nothing more than an accident, and therefore only an apparent fulfilment of the prophecy,' was my answer.

Rabbi Meier had slipped his right hand beneath the folds of his caftan. He now extended it, and I saw that he had taken a thin book from his pocket.

'May I come to your room this evening?' he said. 'If you allow me, I shall go to you about an hour after supper, and then we can have a little further conversation on this subject.'

I willingly consented, upon which he gave me the book, saying:

'Read that, perhaps it will convince you.'

He then went to his own room to eat his egg, while I supped with my mother, and afterwards went to my bedroom that I might examine the book the old Jew had given me. I did not expect to gain much assistance from it, and was therefore not disappointed when I found that it contained a carefully written copy of the psalms which Luzzato had composed in the Hebrew language to the praise and glory of wisdom, and which gave undoubted proof of a rich and glowing imagination. Besides these, there were also extracts from the second Sohar, written by the same author, and purporting to be conversations between the Prophet Elijah and the Patriarch Abraham. Then there were sundry signs and figures that I did not understand, and lastly, quotations from the *En Rogel*, the Book of the prophecies of Rabbi Löw, with an incomprehensible commentary. I knew the sort of thing—a book that sets forth mysteries, but does not explain them.

I turned to the window and looked out into the night. Involuntarily I began to repeat the following lines of Klopstock in a low whisper:

* ' Wie schön und wie hehr war diese Sternennacht,
  Eh' ich des grossen Gedankens Flug,
  Eh' ich es wagte, mich gu fragen :
  Welche Thaten thäte dort oben der Herrliche ?

† Mich, den Thoren, den Staub !
  Ich fürchtet', als ich zu fragen begann,
  Dass Kommen würde was gekommen ist.
  Ich unterliege dem grossen Gedanken ! '

And then I remembered that part in which he says :

'Here stand I, O Earth! What is my body in comparison with these heavenly bodies that are too numerous for even the angels to count.'

One passage of Klopstock's Odes after another flashed into my mind as I stood there gazing up at the starry sky, and thinking of the 'great white throne' of God, which Rabbi Meier called ' Primæval Light,' and in which he maintained that all the heavenly bodies had originated. His ideas regarding it much resembled those of the author of the 'Messiah,' as shown in certain of his poems, such as those entitled, 'Spring,' 'The Psalm,' and

---

* How glorious and how fair was that starlit night, until I allowed my thoughts too bold a flight, until I dared to reason concerning the actions of the Most High, desiring to know what might not be known.

† Fool, that I was and dust of the ground ! I feared, when I began to question, that that would happen which indeed has come to pass. The burthen of such thought is far too heavy for me ; it crushes me !

the 'Ode to the Eternal,' in which the suns are described as rushing out like streams of fire. In the 'Hallelujah' again, the same spirit is manifest:

> ' A flame from the altar near the Throne
> Has flashed into our souls.'

What flame? I asked myself. Is it the flickering weakly flame that burns in the lamp of life, or is it that faint spark of light called human understanding, human wisdom?—a mere glow-worm radiance at best! Can it be true that a brighter ray than these exists between us; a light, to which, in our ignorance, we are blind? And if this be the case, can we learn to recognise it, and fan it into a flame? Yes, if the teaching of the Kabbalah is true—if it is not a delusion, or a phantasy like a poet's dream.

Who can prove to me that it is no delusion? Who can disprove the mocking words uttered by Count Arthur on the afternoon of his death?

I returned to the document in my hand, and read some more of the wild, incomprehensible things it contained. Tired of the useless effort to discover the meaning of what I read, I was on the point of throwing it down impatiently, when I heard Rabbi Meier's voice behind me, saying:

'Did you understand what you were reading just now?'

I answered in the words of the chamberlain of Candace, Queen of Ethiopia, whom S. Philip met on the road from Jerusalem to Gaza, and whom he questioned as to his understanding of the Book of the Prophet Isaiah, which he was reading as he drove homewards: 'How can I, except some one shall guide me?'

With that I turned from the window and faced the old man. He was looking dreadfully worn and ill, as though he had newly recovered from one of his epileptic attacks, and seemed too weak to stand. I, therefore, hastened to draw an easy chair close to him, and made him sit down. A silence of several minutes' duration ensued. At length he said in a tone of heart-felt sorrow:

'What if I were to open the seals you cannot break? What if I were to unfold more than you yet comprehend of the divine mysteries of the works of God, and thus show you that the wonders of the Kabbalah *Maschiith* are poor and worthless compared with the spiritual insight which may be gained by studying the divine wisdom and order as they are revealed to us in the Kabbalah?'

I was silent for a moment, and then said:

'Do not let us discuss the matter any more tonight, Rabbi. You are not well, and ought to go to bed. Besides that, I must tell you plainly that I am weary of the transcendental speculations contained in the theoretical Kabbalah; they no longer interest me.'

'What is it then that you want to know?'

'I will tell you,' was my reply. 'I will tell you, if you have forgotten what I said before. You cannot inspire me with faith in the power of that occult teaching, to the study of which I vainly sacrificed my youth, by any mere phrases. No vague assertions, dark sayings, or metaphysical philosophisings will suffice to convince me of the truth of its doctrines. I need an *actual, undoubted* proof of the powers ascribed to the *Practical* Kabbalah before I can believe.'

'Look at me, then ; look at me,' said the old man in a hollow voice, 'I, Rabbi Meier, your guest, am a living proof of it.'

I gazed at him in speechless amazement. His words sounded as though he might be speaking in a parable. What did he really mean. I shivered in the silence that seemed almost palpable, and which was only broken by the striking of the clock on the church tower.

My mother had gone to bed, and we two were quite alone. I was so nervous and excited that no sudden metamorphosis in the old Jew, no magical portent would have surprised me.

But Rabbi Meier sat motionless as a dead man.

At last he opened his lips, and said with slow emphasis and hollow voice : 'Or would you rather give heed to the words of the Amsterdam Rabbi, than to those of your guest ?'

I was too sad at heart to be able to answer at once. A pause ensued, and then I said :

'After all that has happened lately, I could not help believing him if——'

Here the old man interrupted me by raising his withered hand. He looked at me with a fixed and sorrowful gaze, and then went on slowly, stammeringly, and in a hoarse voice that scarcely rose above a whisper :

'He who made the Kabbalistic computation long years ago at Amsterdam, by means of which Count Arthur's fate was revealed—sits before you.'

There was a long silence.

The death-watch ticked in the wainscot. I could hear the beating of my own heart, and shivered as at the presence of something unearthly.

We continued to sit thus for many minutes.

At length a new feeling awoke in my breast, and I struggled for mastery over the sensation of horror that had at first overwhelmed me.

'You,' I muttered.

'I,' he answered in the same strained tone of voice. 'But this confession of mine proves nothing to you—why should it? You want deeds, not words. Well then, my kind host, I feel that my hours are numbered. Ere many days have elapsed, the Angel of Death will stand by my couch with a flaming sword in his hand, and summon me before the judgment-seat, where the archangel Rasiel, who is guardian of the mysteries of the Kabbalah, awaits me, and where my body will be crushed into dust. I cannot repay you for all the kindness you

have shown the poor, sick, homeless and helpless
man, whom you mercifully took into your own
house although he was a stranger, and a heavy
burden on your hospitality. In spite of your unbelief, your soul belongs to a higher world than
this. I would fain leave you something that would
be of value in your life.'

He ceased speaking.

I said all sorts of things in my endeavours to
calm him, assuring him that I had simply done my
duty, and had behaved as one human being was
bound to do to another. I needed, and expected
no reward. But he was not to be soothed into
quietness. He began to speak again, and I listened
with a beating heart and deep amazement.

'My end approaches—I shall expiate my sins.
But as for you, sir, I pray that all happiness may
attend you. I am a poor old man, and have
nothing that I may call my own, but misery. And
yet there is *one* thing I possess. The curse of my
life may now be turned into a blessing; the source
of my woes may bring joy and contentment to you,
for its origin is good and beneficent. And I
already know that the consequences of what I am
going to tell you will be good. Have you no
question to ask me?'

I started to my feet, but no words would come
to my lips until I had sat down again. Then I
said·brokenly:

'What do you mean?'

'Well, as regards the future.'

'Can you forsee what will come to pass? Do you really know that secret?' I cried, scarcely venturing to credit what I heard.

All the longings of my youth, all the wild excitement I had felt in the old times at Halle, had been aroused by the desire to look into the future, for the power of so doing had, strangely enough, always seemed to me the acme of magical wisdom. And now, at last, I was sitting face to face with a man who acknowledged that he possessed the powers of prognostication, a man who could teach me the secret I had so long sought in vain, and in the reality of which I had afterwards doubted.

Rabbi Meier answered sadly, 'try!'

'Must I ask a particular question, or will a general one suffice?'

'The latter will do quite well,' was his reply, as he rose and began to push his chair nearer the table.

I came to his assistance, and when he was seated, he asked me to give him a sheet of paper and a pencil.

He then took the book he had lent me, opened it, and placed it beside him on the table. If I had expected him to want any magical apparatus I was mistaken. Nothing could have been simpler than the preparations he made, and his questions were put with a total absence of necromantic fuss.

'You must answer me truly and exactly, otherwise I can tell you nothing,' he said, and then proceeded to question me concerning my age, the hour
of my birth, when I had arrived at Seeried—in
short made a number of the sort of enquiries that
are usual under such circumstances. He wrote
down all my answers on the sheet of paper before
him, and then said :

'That will do.'

I shall tell you very little about his manipula-
tion ; indeed, my excitement was so great that I
was able to take in few of its details. I only
saw that he bent so low over the book that his
white beard flowed down upon it. The page he
had opened contained magic quadrates, and Kabbalistic devices and figures on a very small scale·
He translated the words into figures and the figures
into words ; wrote, reckoned, and completely
buried himself in his work. He would have made
a splendid model for a painter, as he sat there with
the lamp light falling on his bowed head.

But at that moment, I felt nothing of the artistic
beauty of the picture. I watched the old man's
every movement with an anxious intensity of gaze,
desiring that nothing he did should escape my
vigilance. His eyes were fixed on the figures and
letters on the paper before him, and it almost
seemed to me as though something prevented the
lamp light resting as warmly upon them as elsewhere,

But—what if he were a charlatan, and were only to pretend to read my future from the hieroglyphs he was making!

No sooner had the thought flashed through my brain, than I started from my seat, and walked across the room. The noise I made did not disturb the Rabbi in the least. He did not seem to have heard me. I seated myself again, and looked at him attentively. His face was of a ghastly pallor like that of a dead man.

All at once, he flushed up in a moment. He raised his head, heaved a deep sigh as though of relief, laid down his pencil, and exclaimed, rather than said :

'Blessed be He who bringeth peace! Praised be Thy holy name, Lord of Sabaoth! I have good tidings for you, my kind friend, for although a great danger will soon threaten you, your life will yet be a happy one. You will live through that time of need, and your days will afterwards be more full of pleasantness than falls to the lot of the generality of men. The desire of your heart will also be granted you.'

'This is a most oracular saying,' I thought within myself, somewhat disappointed by the vagueness of what I had heard, and then added aloud : 'What kind of danger is it that threatens me? And how will my desire be fulfilled?'

'No outward danger will come upon you ; but a storm within your own breast ; a wild, destructive tempest, which nevertheless will pass away, leaving a beneficial influence on your character,' answered the Kabbalist. 'And,' he continued, 'must I tell you of the secret feelings that you hide away at the bottom of your heart?'

I was much startled by the unexpectedness of these words, and turned crimson. The old man went on unnoticing:

'She whom you love returns your affection, and will joyfully descend from . . .'

'Hush, hush!' I cried; 'no more of that! Does your art tell you nothing of the present, by which I may judge your prognostications of the future?'

'Yes, there are several things to which I paid no attention at first,' was his reply. And then, after consulting his figures once more, he proceeded to relate sundry incidents that were only known to myself, and which it is unnecessary to repeat here.

I was convinced at last. My heart seemed to stand still, and I remained motionless for a full minute. Then the fever of excitement came upon me once more.

I looked at Rabbi Meier, who was leaning back in his chair supporting his head on his hand. He was exhausted by all that he had gone through. I gazed at him, and still struggled against my burning curiosity, still hesitated.

'At last I went up to him, and laying my hand on his shoulder:

'Rabbi,' I said, scarcely above a whisper, 'you must teach me your secret.'

'On hearing this, his head sank back upon the cushion behind him, and his arms fell limply on his knee.   He looked at me fixedly with open mouth and eyes, a very picture of terror.

'You must teach me your secret,' I repeated in louder tones than before.   'I cannot let this opportunity escape me of freeing my spirit from the bonds that confine it.   Teach me your wisdom ; give me your power of foretelling events.'

Upon this, he sank from his chair upon the ground where he lay prone at my feet in anguish of heart.

But this availed him nothing.

CHAPTER XII.

' Kein Sterblicher, sagt sie,
  Rückt diesen Schleier, bis ich selbst ihn hebe.
  Und wer mit ungeweihter schuldger Hand
  Den heiligen, verbotnen früher hebt,
  Der, spricht die Gottheit '—Nun ?—'der sieht die Wahrheit.'
SCHILLER.

' Ich bin ein Baal Teschuba, bin ein Sünder,
  Der wallend durch das Elend Busse thut,
  Und jetzt der eignen Missethat Verkünder.'
A. VON CHAMISSO.

GERMANY, in those days, was full of charlatans. Belief in magicians and magic had reached its height. Every one spoke with bated breath of the mysteries and occult teaching of the Rosicrucians, and other secret societies. Men, who had spent their whole lives in confuting mysticism, suddenly announced themselves fully convinced of the reality of the wonders done by Illuminati, or betrayed a leaning towards the secret sciences. The whole educated world took an enthusiastic interest in such subjects, without troubling themselves to study the Kabbalah deeply, or perhaps without having the opportunity of doing so. Conjuring ghosts, magic experiments, theosophic philosophy, and alchemy, were the order of the day, and, moreover, it was just at this time that magnetism, and the spiritistic mysticism of Lavater and Jung Stilling were first published. What wonder then that my honoured old teacher and friend, Professor Semler, was also carried away by the general delusion. It was about this time that he was employing all his energy on experiments with ' aerial salt,' as it was called, which was regarded by him and many others as a remedy for all diseases. A short time afterwards he wrote three pamphlets on the subject. Later again, he thought he had discovered the secret of the hermetic tincture, and proceeded to try to make gold, loudly proclaiming his good fortune. But the gold proved to be nothing but gilt foil, which had been secretly put in his retort by the soldier's family whom he had taken into his house from charity. The poor people acted from ignorance, thinking they were doing their benefactor a kindness and nobody any harm. Bnt the old man never recovered from the shock of the deception, and soon afterwards died of a broken heart. I have mentioned these circumstances here although they did not take place till several years later.

But at the time when Rabbi Meier was staying with me at Seeried parsonage, magic was, as I said before, firmly believed in. Schröpfer indeed was dead, having shot himself at Rosenthal near Leipzig ; but there were many other teachers of occult mysteries going about the country.

Amongst others I may mention Samuel Rosa, whom I had seen at Halle ; Baron von Prinzen, the ' moon-doctor ;' the enthusiastic Gugomos, and the exorcist Gassner ; besides these there were Count St. Germain, who was supposed to be a thousand years old, and last not least, Cagliostro, the most impudent and the most ignorant of all these adventurers. When the Kabbalistic movement in Judaism died out in 175- with Rabbi Eibenschützer, it only continued to affect the minds of a few students, utterly unknown to fame, in the east of Europe, and especially in Poland, so that the mysteries practised by the adventurers of twenty or thirty years later had very little to do with it except in externals. Just as the hollowness of the pretentions made by these charlatans became manifest through their own unexampled impudence, the Patriarch Frank made his appearance in the early days of the French Revolution. He excited very little attention, and did not wish to arouse it. Times were changed. The world was tired of occultism, and wanted something new ; the Revolutionary tempest had cleared the air, and brought plenty of excitement of a different kind.

In 178-, when Rabbi Meier was my guest, I had seen so much of what was going on in the world, that had he attempted any sort of hocus-pocus, I should at once have suspected him of trickery. The very simplicity of his proceedings impressed

me favourably, and his every word bore the stamp
of inward conviction and truthfulness.

I had watched him with bated breath, and careful intentness.   No sooner, then, did I know the
result of his computation than my resolution was
fixed.   Nothing could change it.   I *must* know
the secret for which I had so long sought.   The
cruel hunger of a wild beast filled my breast,
shutting out all feeling of compassion for the
miserable old man on the floor at my feet.

'You must teach me your secret, Rabbi,' I once
more repeated.   'Do not be afraid—I will go
through any preparation that may be deemed
necessary.'

'O God!' cried the old man.   'What have I
done!   I have shown the poisonous apple to a
child, and now he wants to taste it.   But no, no,
no—you shall not have it.   I will not poison your
life.   Have mercy upon yourself and me!'

'Get up, Rabbi,' I said sternly ; 'Get up.   You
can say nothing to change my determination.   I
intend to learn your method of computation.'

He rose, clasped my hand in both of his, and
looked at me imploringly.

'Give it up, man, give it up!' he said.   'Expel
the poison from your heart, the vehement longing
for this knowledge from your mind.   It destroys
the house that contains it.   The power of looking
into the future brings no joy with it—only pain
unspeakable.   It is better to float into the un-

known on the stream of faith, than to play with this fire, and then fly through the air—only to fall at last with your wings scorched.'

My face did not change, so he went on :

' I could leave you no heritage that would be more dangerous than this. It were better for you to drink hemlock-juice than that I should accede to your demand. O have mercy on yourself ! The burden you would take upon you is too heavy for you to bear.'

' Am I weaker than you ? ' said the wild beast within me.

The old man let me go, and stood for a moment as though thunder-struck. Then he moaned :

' O righteous and jealous God, the curse doth indeed rest upon me to the bitter end ! Sir, do you know that it is this very knowledge of mine, that you covet, which has driven me forth as a fugitive and a vagabond throughout the earth, and that wherever I rest, it is as though I were lying upon red-hot coals ? I was once young, bold and audacious like you, and like you, I sought for knowledge. The wisdom which God had revealed to us, which He had given us in order that we might learn moderation, and the just proportion of things, was not sufficient for me. I wanted to raise the veil that hid the future from my eyes. I listened to the whispers of the Serpent, who showed me the forbidden fruit. I left the other fruits of Paradise untouched, and tasted that after

which my soul hungered, and so my eyes were
opened that I could see. The Serpent had told
me that this would be the consequence of my eating of it. My eyes indeed were opened, and I
could see—but at the same time I saw that I was
turned out of Paradise. Yes, there I was outside
the gates, a miserable man—cast out, banished,
condemned, cursed. With that demon in my heart
I could not choose but listen to his whispers. He
tore me away from all that I loved—consumed me
—tortured me Many and many a time, he rent
my body as he had already done my soul, holding
it firmly in his clutches. The Angel who brings
us our blessings from on high came near me no
more. I saw wife, children, friends die long years
before they really passed away. At length I was
alone in the world, a homeless wanderer. My
name was posted as that of a heretic in every
synagogue of my people—and now, old and dying,
I am tottering to my grave. O let me entreat you
to preserve your faith, and not to take upon your
shoulders a burden they are not strong enough to
bear. Tear your eyes out of their sockets rather
than let them gaze into futurity. Did not your
Lord and Master say : " Be ye innocent as doves."
Banish then, let me implore you, this evil desire
from your heart.'

Much as these words of the old man might have
moved me at another time, they had no influence
upon me that night. I was as implacable as a

thunder-bolt, as immovable as a rock. I walked up and down the room several times, and then said, vainly striving to make my meaning clear without harshness :

'Old man, grant my request. Do not give me your advice ; but the information that I want. How I bear the burden of such knowledge is *my* affair. I have no fear of the pain you tell me about. You must remember that we are also told to be 'wise as serpents.' The yoke of faith will crush me, if I am not enlightened with a ray of divine wisdom. I will pluck this fruit of the tree of knowledge, even if by doing so I lose all earthly joy.'

Rabbi Meier looked at me for some moments in silence. Then he said :

'Sir, you know not what you ask. He who is once initiated in this art can never give it up. An unquenchable thirst for more and more knowledge is the punishment laid upon those who have given way to the temptation of learning what was meant to be hidden from them. The Kabbalah itself warns us against such abuse of its teaching.'

'If it possesses this wondrous power, and if it was revealed to man, why should we be forbidden to make use of it ?'

'O it can work marvels,' cried the old man ; 'but that is quite different from being made the tool of idle or impious curiosity. Listen. Rasiel, the Archangel of the mysteries, of the seals of

Kabbalistic wisdom, watches jealously over the actions of those mortals to whom he has entrusted any knowledge of the secrets under his charge. And the Angel of the Face of God,* Metatron, the Chief of the High Council of Heaven, tries our souls to see how they have behaved during their probation here on earth ; he looks into the use we have made of the talent that was given us, and judges us accordingly. The Angel Jophiel, administrator of the Kabbalah, tries the soul, on its return to the place from whence it came, with great severity. And all the great masters, even Rabbi Luria, tell us that madness and death may come upon those who insist on going on in their own way unheeding the warnings given them. Hence the fear in which the secret teaching was held in the old time. Did not the Angel Jophiel say to Rabbi Ishmael ben Elishah, who was called the High Priest : ' What is this thou darest to do, O child of man, mere worm that thou art ? ' And Rabbi Ishmael was in the end flayed alive by the Romans,—yet his mind was much stronger than either yours or mine. And what does the Talmud say ? Four men went to the Garden of Delight, that is to say, were deeply versed in the secret science ; Benasa looked in and died, Bensoma looked around him and went mad, Acher tore the

---

* Metatron was the Angel who led the children of Israel through the wilderness.—M. W. M.

plants up by the roots, that is to say, he became a heretic. Rabbi ben Akiba alone, who lived to a very old age, went in and out in peace. Later on, he was slain by the Romans. Yes, Acher tore out the plants, and became an heretical backslider, for he could not understand how *Metatron, the Angel of the Face, sat beside the Almighty, who ruled the visible world through him. So Acher became a Manichean, and accepted the theory of the dual governance of the universe.'

I let the old man go on thus for some time, but at length I interrupted him by saying :

'That is all very good. I know the sagas and allegories of the Talmud, and the language of mysticism. But they are beside the question. Let us leave such Phantasmagorias alone for the present, and attend to the purely mathematical problem before us. I am determined to learn your method of computation.'

The Rabbi shook his head sadly, and sat down.

'Very well,' he said, 'I will tell you my own story, Herr Pastor, perhaps it will serve as a warning. I shall not keep you long; sit down. Did you ever hear of Rabbi Löw, who travelled through Germany some fifty years ago, and therefore pre-

---

* What with Plato were the Ideas, with Philo the Logos, with the Kabbalists the ' World of Aziluth,' what the Gnostics called more emphatically the wisdom (σοφία) or powers (δύναμις), and Plotinus the νοῦς, that the Talmudical authors call Metatron.' ' Literary Remains of Emanuel Deutsch," p. 5.

ceded Rabbi Eibenschutzer and Luzzato. I heard
of him when I was a young Bachur, and started
off to see and learn of him, but found on my
arrival that he was already dead.   After that I
entered the service of an old man, who had
retired from the Jewish ministry, and lived a very
quiet life withdrawn from all society. My reason
for doing so was that I needed money to support
my wife and child. My master gradually became
attached to me, and interested himself in me. As
I was with him a great deal I soon noticed that he,
like many others in his position at that time, was
learned in the secret arts and sciences. Before he
died he sent for me into his sick-room, and said :
' My son, I intend to reward you for all your faithful service. That desk over there contains my
legacy, and the key will be found under my pillow.
In the top of the desk are two drawers, one of
which is painted black, while the other is gilded.
In the black drawer I have placed certain papers
showing the amount of my money and jewels, and
where they are hidden ; the gilded drawer, on the
other hand, contains a dangerous heritage, which I
trust will fall into the hands of that avaricious
wretch, who already regards my wealth as his own.'
By this he meant his nephew, and heir. He little
knew that I coveted his secret knowledge as
passionately as the other did his gold, and I
guessed that the desire of my heart was hidden
away in the gilded drawer. The dying man con-

tinued : ' According to my will he is to have his choice of the two drawers, the other falls to you. I am sure he will choose the gilded one, and so you will inherit all my money.' The old man had always been eccentric, and showed himself so to the end. After he had spoken he fell into a deep sleep. I made use of the opportunity this gave me, and led away by my covetousness, carefully abstracted the key from under his pillow, opened the desk, and examined the contents of the gilded drawer which consisted of this little book, and a sheet of paper covered with pencil marks explaining its use. The solution of all the mysteries I had desired to know ever since I could think at all lay before me. I did not hesitate for a moment ; what were my master's earthly treasures to me ? When one of my people sets his affections on the treasures of abstract thought, he does it with passion, and has no room for that love of Mammon that fills the hearts of so many of my brethren. So I took the inventory out of the black drawer, and laid it in the other, putting my find in its place. After which, I locked the desk, and replaced the key under my master's pillow. Everything happened as I had hoped when the old man died. The heir chose the gilded drawer, and rejoiced in his good fortune, laughing heartily over my legacy, which he did not grudge me at all, for he was a child of Mammon. I was now able to keep my family

comfortably, for my secret had taught me wisdom.
I saw what was hidden from others ; but I could
not learn moderation.   My fame spread abroad.
Many persons of distinction came to consult me,
Count Arthur von Seeried-Strandow, who was then
staying in Amsterdam, amongst the number.   But
alas, the worm of sorrow was already growing at
the root of all my happiness.   I knew when my
wife, my children, and my gentlest friends were to
die, and mourned their loss while they were yet
alive.   I was miserable.   My passion grew with
what it fed upon, and became a consuming fire,
which yet did not burn me up.   I suffered un-
speakably, until at length I stood alone in the
world.   And yet I could not give up the art which
was the source of all my grief.   Despair seized
upon me, and my weakened frame became the
prey of epilepsy.   The Amsterdam Rabbis heard
of me and my doings.   I was thrust out of the
great Synagogue, the curse of God was called
down upon me, and I was excommunicated.   I
fled before their wrath.   But wherever I went their
interdict followed me.   I was accursed before the
Lord, and wandered miserably throughout Europe,
until at last I came to Poland, where I found a refuge amongst the Chasidim.   There I remained a
long time in retirement, became more deeply
versed in the secret arts, and spent my hours of
solitude in conversing with the dead.   But the
longing to visit the graves of my family became

too strong for me, and drove me back on my long
and weary journey to Holland where I hoped that
no one would remember me, I had changed so
much. I saw the graves of my dear ones in the
Beth Chajjim—and wept, wishing with all my
heart that I were lying beside them. Soon afterwards, I was recognised and excommunicated
again. I fled to Hamburg in a vessel whose cap-
tain had taken pity on me ; but even there, I was
not safe, for the curse of the Rabbis pursued me
wherever I went. The mark of Cain seemed to be
stamped on my forehead, for every Jew fled from
me. And yet I only wished to find the place
where I might die in peace. I dragged my weary
way across the country, and at last one day sank
down exhausted in the midst of a heavy shower of
rain. A lady dressed in mourning was driving
past with her little child, and saw me fall. She took
compassion upon me, and, poor old vagabond as
I was, made me get into her pony carriage, and go
home with her. When she heard that I came from
Holland, she sighed, and pressed her child to her
heart. From what you have told me since I came
here, I know now that she was the widow of that
Count Hermann who was disowned by his family. It
was from her I learnt where Seeried was to be found,
unwilling as she was to speak of it. The time I
spent with her and her child is one of the pleasantest
memories of my life, and it was in her house that
the art to which I had devoted myself first brought

me comfort, for it showed me that her little boy would one day be the father of a rich and powerful Count. When I told the mother, she shook her head and—wept. My art does not deceive,—but it consumes. O Adonai,* I have done penance, and shall soon be completely consumed by the restless fire in my soul. The lady would have had me stop a little longer and rest ; I could not ; so she gave me some money and let me go. At last I came here, as you know, in the midst of the snow-storm, and had an attack of epilepsy when trying to find my way through the church-yard. You discovered me lying there, and brought to your house, and now, here I am waiting for death—still burdened with the curse.'

I had listened to the old man's story inattentively and with conflicting feelings ; but it must be confessed with an ever growing impatience. So entirely was I under the influence of the burning desire for knowledge of the Kabbalistic secret, which I had indulged until it had overpowered every other sentiment, that even had I paid greater heed to what Rabbi Meir was saying, his story would have failed in having the desired effect. Once more, I rose, and began to walk up and down the room, while my companion remained sitting by

---

* IIIVII (Jehovah), the Tetragrameton, is so holy a name that He is generally called ADNI (Adonai), Lord. He is the King of the Kabbalistic Sephiroth, the Christ of the Christian Trinity.— *M. W. M.*

the table, his grey head sunk on his breast. At
length I turned to him, and, in my blind delusion,
was not ashamed to say :

'Rabbi, your history is a sad one, there is no
doubt of that ; but it does not prevent me persisting in my wish to learn the Kabbalistic method of
reckoning. Let me entreat you to teach me, and
may the consequences be on my own head. If
you really wish to repay me for the hospitality I
have shown you, you will teach me.'

The old man was conquered. He said in a tone
of sorrowful resignation :

'Then it cannot be helped. I can say nothing
more after that. May God take the worst sting
out of the legacy. I will pray for you, for myself I
will implore the kiss * of the Righteous One. Let
it be as you will. This sin will not be counted
against me. But you must promise three things
before I begin.'

'And these are ?'

'First, that you will not try to practise the art
until I am dead.'

After a few minutes thought, I answered :

'Very well, I promise.'

'Secondly, that you will bury me exactly where
you found me.'

I bowed gravely in acquiescence, and the
Kabbalist went on :

* Death.—M. W. M.

'And that you will faithfully discharge a com-
mission that I shall leave in your hands. It is a
further part of my legacy—it's heir is as yet unborn.
But you will take it to the place to which it
belongs, and where your house will be blessed in
years to come. Do you promise this?'

'Yes.'

'And now one thing more,' pursued the old
man.

'What is it, Rabbi Meier?'

'Promise me by the Holy Scriptures that you
will never ask how long any one will live who is
near and dear to you.'

I did not fail to perceive the good intention of
this requirement, and therefore took the oath that
was demanded of me. After which I said :

'But, Rabbi, what question remains for me to
ask of fate?'

'Be humble and moderate in all things,' he
answered. 'You will always learn more than you
will be well able to bear. From the calculation I
made respecting your destiny, it was clear that
your life will not be unhappy, nor will you die in
despair. God grant that it may be so. Now sit
down and attend to me.'

I did as he desired.

It had grown very late. The lamp was burning
low. The clock outside struck twelve as I drew
my chair to the table.

Rabbi Meier laid his hand on the Kabbalistic

book, and began in a low solemn voice to speak of
God as without beginning and without end ;
eternal, everlasting. Again the Logos, or creative
Word, was from the beginning. After that he
went on to speak of the power of the Word in the
Prophets belonging both to the old and the new
covenant. Of how it was able to perform miracles
to the glory of God and the Prophets. He told of
the operation of the Word in the mouths of the
saints, of the leaders in the time of the captivity,
of the Rabbis at the head of the great schools of
Babylon and Alexandria, and of those at home in
Jerusalem. Then he spoke of the mystery of
figures, of the sacred numbers that spell the name
of God. He told why the simple figures one, three,
four, seven, and ten, are specially holy, and how as
soon as their real meaning is known, the Christian
book of mysteries, the Apocalypse with its seven
seals, becomes perfectly clear and comprehensible.
Besides that, he explained to a certain extent the
signification of the strange Easter hymn, which is
used by the Jews after the fourth cup on the Eve
of the Feast of the Passover. It was nearly to
this effect, (of course I only give a very slight and
superficial sketch of what he told me): *One* is
God, one the origin of all numbers : *three* signifies
beginning, duration, end,—past, present, and
future,—threefold is the Being of God, three are the
Patriarchs : four, the elements and climates, four
letters are needed to spell the name of God in

most languages : seven are the days of the week,
and the same number stands for the omnipotence
of God : ten are the commandments, and ten pre-
figures eternity.　　He then proceeded to explain
the essence of the Hebrew letters, which are also
numbers, and, at the same time, pictures and
names of things.　In their figures great mysteries
are hidden.　He interpreted the symbolic Kabbalah in a few words, defined the uses to which the
geometrical figures and signs were put, and showed
me how words and signs must be translated into
numbers, which is done by the permutation of
words and letters as they become known through
the Notarikon and Themurah.　Last of all, he told
me of the results to be attained by the pronuncia-
tion of certain words and verses.　It is unnecessary
to add that he taught me the use of the magic
quadrates and Kabbalistic equations, and their
relation to the mysterious name of God.　The key
which he gave me soon smoothed away all the
difficulties in my path ; but for reasons that you
will easily understand I do not intend to tell you
or anyone else what it was.　Suffice it to say that
it is hidden in the sublime word Jehovah.

　　After he had shown me how to write the cyphers
properly, he gave me some examples.　My zeal
helped me over all difficulties.　The sight of the
figures caused me none of that mental trouble the
old man had described.　I rather felt as though a
rich and wonderful feast were spread out before

me, an intellectual treat which stimulated every faculty. A new world had opened out before me. At length I had conquered all hindrances, and was able to calculate any of the problems given me by my master with ease and quickness. The night vanished like a dream.

It was not until we heard the first cock crowing and the lamp had grown dim for want of oil, that the Rabbi rose from his chair, and said :

' It is done. We have little more to say to each other. I shall pass away in three days time, let me die quietly in your house. Do as you have promised after my death, and leave me alone with God during the short remainder of my life. I have much to say to Him, many things to pray for—for you as well as for myself.'

My head was burning and my hands were cold as ice. I caught his right hand, and would have spoken ; but he stopped me, saying :

' Do not thank me, sir. It would cut me to the heart if you did. Purify your heart that you may be worthy of her who is destined for you by Almighty God.'

I blushed deeply at these words, for I knew the Kabbalistic idea that true marriage consists in the reuniting of two souls, which, before they descended from heaven to this earthly sphere, were united in one being.

' Do not be ashamed of what is the will of God,' continued Rabbi Meier. ' I will ask to be enlightened as to what must be done to change past, present, and future wrong into right. The family and Castle of Seeried are burdened with endless wrong. But those sins will one day be expiated— how I know not yet. Leave me alone—we shall meet no more in this world. For seven days after my death keep a basin of water and a towel laid out ready in my room—as the Kabbalah ordains. And now farewell; do not curse me in the evil hour that is sure to come.'

With that he left me, and went to his own room, closing the door behind him.

A curious feeling of sympathy for him came over me. But my selfishness was still greater than my pity, stronger than my sympathy.

The dying light of the lamp fell upon the papers scattered on the table. There was something in me, it is true, that softened, that even tried to stifle the pæan of joy in my heart at having at last attained the object I had for so many years regarded as the chiefest good. But still triumph predominated as I looked at the calculations scribbled on the sheets of paper. These figures! Who had discovered them? Who had first written down these magic characters, behind whose mysterious forms a spiritual world was hidden? How strange they looked! How they trembled and danced in the faint glimmer of the dying lamp.

But something was wanting! It was only now that I perceived that the old man had taken his

Kabbalistic book away with him. The lamp flickered up once more, and then went out altogether, and all was dark.

But turning my eyes to the window, I could see the stars shining in their immeasurable distance.

CHAPTER XIII.

'Drum hab' ich mich der Magie ergeben,
  Ob mir durch Geisteskraft u. Mund
  Nieht manch Geheimnis würde kund.'

   .   .   .   .   .   .

'War es ein Gott, der diese Zeichen schrieb,
  Die mir das innere Toben stillen?'
                                    —*Faust.*

IT was late when I awoke. At first I could not remember at all clearly what had happened the night before, and when all the circumstances at last returned to my recollection, it almost seemed as though they belonged to a wild, improbable dream.

But there were the papers still lying on the table where I had left them, and there was the pencil with which Rabbi Meier and I had worked out our Kabbalistic problems. I jumped out of bed, dressed as quickly as I could, and then seating myself at the table, went over all the calculations again. No, it was not a dream, but sober reality, though it was difficult to believe it in the clear light of day. I had forgotten nothing of what I had learnt the night before—I held the key to all the Kabbalistic mysteries in my own hand.

Very often in the morning, we cannot understand the fear, excitement, delight or horror awakened by the events that have taken place during the night, and look back to such feelings with astonishment. So it was with me on this occasion. When I remembered all that had happened, I felt thoroughly ashamed of my conduct. Of what passionate folly and selfishness had I not been guilty, and all for the sake of an illusion. Even granting that the calculations were correct— what proof had I that they could be used for the purpose I desired.

Doubt after doubt flashed through my mind. Was Rabbi Meier one of the numerous impostors, pretending to a cognizance of occult secrets, who were then going about Germany. Well, I thought to myself, if his death really takes place in three days time, I shall regard it as a proof of his knowledge of the black art. But should he live beyond the date he specified, I shall consider the Kabbalah as a mere phantastic philosophy, and the practical side of it as a delusion, and never again shall I be induced to believe in such necromantic folly.

My mother summoned me to breakfast. While I was eating it, Count Leo came in wrapped in a large cloak. He shook hands with me condescendingly. I was very much surprised to see him, as I knew that he disliked me. He was most patronising, and said it was high time that we should begin to be on the friendly footing that

R

beseemed good neighbours, for, as the eldest of the family, he was the natural adviser of young Count Frank, and would therefore be a great deal more at the Castle than of old. He then asked me in a tone of easy benevolence, if the Parsonage was quite comfortable, or if I wanted anything done to the house. After a little conversation of this kind, he enquired whether he might see the church books, for he wished to look for something in the Baptismal Register. He had been puzzled by an entry he had found in the family archives, the explanation of which he was sure he would find in the register.

I took him to my study. He asked me for a pen and ink, and was soon deeply engaged in making notes of what he found in the baptismal records. Meanwhile my thoughts returned to the prognostications Rabbi Meier had made respecting my future, a subject that interested me so much that I quite lost sight of my surroundings, and was scarcely conscious of Count Leo taking leave of me.

In the afternoon I was called away to the other side of the parish on professional business, and during the two next days my time was very much occupied in one way or another. I was a good deal at the Castle, as there were many arrangements to make about Count Arthur's funeral. The widow of Helen's grandfather and young Baron Karl had arrived, that they might be with the rest of the family at this sad time. But busy as I was,

I must confess that my thoughts often turned
involuntarily to the Kabbalistic reckonings I had
made, and which I repeated every evening, only
wishing that my promise did not bind me to
attempt no new ones.

Rabbi Meier kept his word. He saw me no
more. And when my mother went into his room
to look to his comforts, she always found him
sitting in his arm chair buried in silent meditation
or prayer, for his lips moved, though they uttered
no sound.

The day of Count Arthur's funeral arrived.

Everything was done with the usual pomp and
circumstance, and kept me employed all day. The
new mausoleum had first to be consecrated, then
the funeral took place, after which I held a service
for the servants and tenants on the Seeried estate,
and then went up to the Castle to read and pray
with the family. When I returned home in the
evening, my mother met me at the door, with tearful eyes and a somewhat nervous manner. She told
me that when she had gone into Rabbi Meier's
room a few minutes before, she had found him in
bed, and that as she approached him, he had
suddenly raised his clasped hands, had called upon
the God of Abraham, of Isaac, and of Jacob, and
immediately afterwards had fallen back on his
pillows. She had spoken to him several times,
calling his attention to the egg she had brought
him, but had received no answer.

I hastened to the old man's room. He was lying stretched out in bed, his long white beard flowing over his breast, and his face absolutely unchanged. But his hand was cold, his pulse had ceased to beat.

Rabbi Meier was dead.

I stood by the bedside in emotion. Many and various were the thoughts that crowded into my mind.

The old man's weary pilgrimage was over. He had died in a foreign land, in the house of a stranger, and alone. Had the curse been taken from him at the last? My hands joined in prayer for him as for one of my own people.

When I looked round the room, I saw a small parcel lying on the little table beside the bed. It was very neatly done up, and was fastened with a Kabbalistic seal. Besides this, strange and incomprehensible characters were drawn on the edge of the address. I was astonished to see that the packet was directed to that Bachur Benasse who lived in the country town in Thuringia, where I was born. It was that part of the Rabbi's legacy which was not intended for me. A few days later, I despatched it to the nearest Post-office, from whence, as I afterwards learnt, it reached its destination in safety. But the Kabbalistic manuscript which Rabbi Meier had lent me on the memorable evening when he taught me his secret was gone. I could find no trace of it.

I buried the old man after the Christian manner
close to the hedge that bordered the churchyard,
and in the very same spot as I had found him on
the night of Count Arthur's death. According to
his desire, I laid a basin of water and a towel in
the room where he had died, and kept them there
for seven days; for Kabbalists hold that the soul
of the departed returns every night for a week to
the place where it was set free from its earthly
tabernacle, in order to perform certain Parsi-like
ablutions. I put a headstone on the grave to mark
the spot, and had Rabbi Meier's name and the date
of his death carved upon it in Hebrew characters·
An elder-bush blossoms every spring close to the
grey and moss-grown memorial-stone, and when
the sun is setting in the south-west horizon, and
its golden beams are falling on the roof and tower
of Seeried Church, its light resting softly the while
on the churchyard graves, then it is that the shadow
of Count Arthur's tomb is thrown upon the humble
mound that covers the mortal remains of Rabbi
Meier.

.   .   .   .

Every day the weather became more severe.
One snow-storm succeeded another, and covered
the country with a thick white shroud.

The storms that come up from the Baltic in
winter are terrible to witness, especially those
towards the end of Advent and at Christmas time

—that Yule-tide when the old heathens used to think that the gods were journeying through the land. The nights are longest then anyhow ; but often and often the clouds are so thick and heavy at that season, that the inhabitants of these Baltic Provinces are tempted to think that daylight will never come. The people are obliged to sit at home quietly, for it is impossible to work at sea or on land. Then it is that, as they sit round the fire, busied with some handiwork, old stories are told and old songs sung—all telling of the past, and keeping the spirit of poetry alive in the hearts of the people to an extent that is scarcely understood in many a more favoured clime. Ancient customs are also kept up amongst them, customs that date from the time of the heathen observance of Yule-tide.

I was much alone during these dark tempestuous days, and had ample time for thought.

Count Leo spent more of his time at Castle Sceried now ; he was looking after his nephew's interests, he said. For the young Count had never come home. The letters summoning him could not have reached him, as he had written to his mother—sadly enough ; but making no allusion to his father's death. He and his tutor had left Paris, so his mother wrote to the new address, begging him to return at once.

Meanwhile the Countess and her daughter lived in the strictest retirement, their only hopes fixed on the coming of the son and brother, who was now the head of the house.

My feelings would have been even more gloomy than the weather was sufficient to account for, had it not been for the studies to which I devoted all my leisure time. I mean the Kabbalistical algebriac speculation, the magical reckoning, which I had learnt from Rabbi Meier, and by which I desired to prove the infallibility of his knowledge of the black art. First of all, I tried its effect on questions regarding my past life. Then I enquired respecting certain events in the parish—and the calculation always came out right. After that I turned to historical subjects, and the answers were as correct as before. Once or twice, however, the result of my calculation was not what it ought to have been, and I felt a painful uneasiness lest my supposed knowledge should melt away as the morning mists before the sun ; but on every such occasion I found that I had made some mistake in the position or reckoning up of my figures. I sometimes sat up a whole night hunting after the error in my calculation, fearing that I should not find it, and should thus prove that the so-called science was a delusion. I had often read in Rabbi Vital's 'Ez Chajjim' of his Master, Luria, who had continually spoken of the danger of this art, because a single mistake might bring confusion into the spiritual regions, and bring about the madness or death of the foolhardy person who tried to solve such problems. The same warning might be read in any of the Kabbalistic documents in Count Ruttger's library. My feeling of triumph was therefore all the greater, whenever, after long and unwearied search, I succeeded in discovering the error of my labours, and in making the calculation perfect in every point.

My whole heart was set upon the study of this mysterious art—everything else had become subordinate to it. I employed whatever time I had at my disposal in practising it, especially 'deep night, dark night,' which, as Shakespeare holds, is the most proper time for such experiments.

So I went on my way, making my mind familiar with the great secret I had been taught. By dint of patience and perseverance, and also by the help of the books in the Red Tower, which, thanks to the Countess' permission, I visited more frequently than before, I succeeded in perfecting myself in the Kabbalistic method of calculation.

I always avoided making any enquiry into my neighbours' affairs. An indescribable feeling restrained me from doing so. It was to matters of public interest that I confined my questioning. I used to consult the Hamburg paper which Count Arthur had taken in, and which still continued to come to the Castle, and by this means found out that my prognostications always came true. I looked upon my art as one that through its divine power raised me far above my fellows. I had indeed tasted of the fruit of the Tree of Knowledge.

And so I thought that I had drawn nearer to the 'throne of flaming light' of which the Kabbalah teaches, nearer to Him from whom all the worlds proceed, and in whose laws they abide for ever. It was with a feeling of estatic delight that I now repeated the words of the poet :

> ' A flame from the altar near the Throne
> Has flashed into our souls.'

Nothing seemed beyond my reach, and I smiled superior to the old Rabbi, who had warned me that he regarded his secret as the curse of his life.

Although I had at first felt no inclination to take anyone into my confidence, after a while I was very much tempted to share the results of my researches with others. My mother and old Peter were the most natural people for me to speak to on the subject. The latter especially, for he used to look at me enquiringly, and shake his head in disapproval of my frequent visits to the Red Tower. He had, moreover, noticed the custom that had grown upon me of sitting up late at night. His garrulousness or curiosity enticed me to tell him how this or that affair would turn out, and no sooner had the newspaper confirmed my prognostication than I would triumphantly read the paragraph aloud to the old man, although in very truth it needed little magic to foresee how the affairs in question were tending. On such occasions he

would stand open-mouthed before me with astonishment, a sight that caused me much inward joy.

'But, Herr Pastor,' he would say, recovering
himself, and shaking his head thoughtfully, 'how
did you find that out?'

I would then smile, or look mysterious, or else
answer:

'That is my secret, Master Peter.'

'Your secret,' he would repeat. 'Can it be a
good secret? Why do I see your lamp burning in
the study at midnight? Why do you spend so
much time in the Red Tower? Herr Pastor, Herr
Pastor, I am an old man, who has grown grey in
the service of lords of Seeried and the clergy of
the parish, and, as I have told you before, no good
will come of your visits to Count Ruttger's library;
indeed——.'

'Never fear, Master Peter, it is all right,' I would
interrupt him by saying abruptly, and turning
away at the same time to break off the conversation.

But one day the sacristan asked me, quite
innocently, how I thought some matter in which
he was much interested would turn out. I could
not resist the temptation to put one or two apparently indifferent questions to him, and taking a pencil
and piece of paper—the example was one of the
simplest order—told him the answer. He stared
at me in blank amazement for a few moments.
At last he said:

'Is that your art, sir ; your whole secret ?'

'You see that there is no danger in it, Master Peter. It is a very simple affair.'

'So it seems, sir. I will wait and see whether your fortune-telling comes true. It looks very simple, Herr Pastor, but—forgive me, I am an old man and wish you well—I can't help thinking there is something more in it than meets the eye, and should very much like to know who it was that taught you.'

Indignant as I felt at his continued mistrust, I answered :

'I can easily tell you that, Peter. It was that same Rabbi Meier, whom we buried near the hedge in the churchyard, that was my teacher.'

'Then I wish the old Jew had been dead when we found him that night. Sir, you are a clergyman, and know the Scriptures. Is it not written : " Thou shalt not seek for that which is hid from thee." Are we not told that knowledge of the future "belongeth to God alone," and that the wizard should be "put out of the land ?"'

I was now really angry with the boldness of the old man.

'Be silent !' I said sternly, and then added in a somewhat milder tone : 'You do not understand what you are talking about. Did not God send forth the Prophets of old ? Were they not His servants ? And as for the present day. Do you not use the Almanack, which foretells eclipses, occultations and other celestial phenomena? Do you think that it is more difficult, and less useful, less allowable, to calculate what is going to happen in the small events of human life? Do you think that the heavenly bodies alone are governed by law, and that our lives are quite apart from it? Why should no researches be made into the law of life?'

Master Peter was silenced. He could not controvert what I had just said, so he scratched his head, and held his peace. At last, after a long pause, he answered:

'I believe that you are right, sir. You are a clever man, and I am not. I never thought of the Almanack, and it is quite true that what we read about the stars there has been reckoned up by learned people before it happened. Well, well, if you are right about my little affair, I'll say your art is a very useful one.'

I was right, and old Peter became a convert to my opinions. He went about everywhere praising my wisdom, and the villagers all came to consult me in any of their difficulties, more especially after I had foretold that the fishermen would have a great haul if they broke holes in the thick ice of the Baltic. Some of them drove out in sleighs, broke holes in the ice, and caught a number of herring. As soon as it was known what good fortune they had had, the whole fishing population in the parish went out and followed their example.

I was told that the herrings were so numerous they might have been ladled out in buckets! Henceforward I was regarded as an infallible oracle, although it had needed little art to make such a prophecy, as I had read of the same thing having been done elsewhere.

The people held me in great honour, and treated me like a saint. I became puffed up, and haughty, and wise in my own conceit.

The following incident gained me as much renown in the country-side as I already enjoyed in my own parish.

One evening in the ghostly time, between Christmas Day and Twelfth Night, or during the winter solstice, old Peter came to me with a very long face, and said that the villagers would not leave him in peace; but insisted on his going to tell the Herr Pastor that the devil was abroad. He was even going on worse than usual at such times, they said. Some people who had passed the church in the dark that evening had heard the ghostly preacher's voice distinctly, and even Peter himself, when ringing the six o'clock bell, had trembled to see the black-gowned figure in the pulpit thumping the book-board and drumming on the Bible.

Now, as it happened, I had forgotten all about the story the sacristan had told me on the day of my arrival at Seeried, and so:

'Who do you think it was, Peter?' I asked.

'Well, sir, it is Pastor Lebrecht, who is ranting in the church after his old fashion.'

' Is it ?' I answered boldly, 'then we will go and tell him that he has no business to take possession of our pulpit.'

With that I stepped out into the church-yard, followed by the sacristan. I found a good many people collected in the road in front of the church, listening with bated breath to the howls that obviously came from that building.

It was a clear moonlight night, and only a few small grey clouds were being driven across the sky by the wind which was rising to a gale. As I came nearer to the church, I could distinctly hear a hollow, gruff murmuring within. I asked Peter for the keys, and told him that he might wait at the door if he liked until I had exorcised the ghost.

Entering and glancing at the pulpit, I saw a sight that was calculated to make the boldest pause. By the faint light from the window I perceived a dark figure waving its arms vehemently. For one moment I stood stock-still, after which I moved determinedly up the aisle towards the pulpit, where I was accustomed to preach every Sunday. The figure grew more indistinct, the more nearly I approached it ; but the arms continued to move as wildly as before.

A few minutes later, I went out to the villagers, and invited them to come into the church with me. They did so ; but cast many frightened glances at the pulpit. I advanced, and before their very eyes, ascended the steps, and walked, as it were, right into the middle of the ghost. After which I explained to them that the appearance was caused by the moonlight falling in a certain position on the tree outside the church window, while its trunk and branches were waving in the wind. The shadow cast by the tree exactly resembled a human figure waving its arms. This accounted for the fact that the ghost was only seen when the moon was at the full in windy weather ; and the noise caused by the draught from an ill-fitting casement, humming and roaring through the empty building, and sometimes even banging a loose shutter, was quite sufficient to give rise to the superstitious belief that the church was haunted. This explanation convinced the villagers, and covered Master Peter with shame. 'Ah, yes,' they said, 'our Pastor is a clever fellow.'

I do not mention this insignificant fact from any wish to praise myself—although, to tell the truth, I had by no means too low an opinion of my own merits in those days—but in order to show you that I was not wanting in courage or boldness, in case you may afterwards deem that I was too easily alarmed by supernatural things. If you bear this in mind, you will be able to give more un-prejudiced attention to what I have yet to relate, for I am now approaching the fateful moment which formed the turning point of my life, and the memory of which still fills me with affright.

But I will go on with my story.

Whenever I thought of the admonitions of Rabbi Meier, and the warnings and reprobation of Bachur Benasse, I smiled involuntarily at the fears of these foolish Jews. I felt proud and happy in the possession of the secret, to the knowledge of which I had so long desired to attain ; far from regarding it as a 'curse,' as the 'mark of Cain' on my brow, I looked upon it as a thing to treasure, a source of satisfaction, and a well of comfort, whenever I began to despair of my love for the Countess Helen coming to a good end.

But I was soon to regard my art with other eyes.

CHAPTER XIV.

'Was er allda gesehen und erfahren,
Hat seine Zunge nie bekannt.'

'Weh' dem, der zu der Wahrheit geht durch Schuld;
Sie wird ihm nimmermehr erfreulieh sein.'
—SCHILLER (*Das vershleierte Bild zu Sais*).

THE young Count von Seeried-Strandow did
not come home. I saw his mother sometimes. She was anxiously awaiting his arrival.
Helen, I had scarcely seen. The worst part of the
winter was over, and a few premonitory signs of
spring might be noticed; but the weather was still
very wild, and the road leading to the Castle as
slushy and disagreeable as it could well be. Had
wintry weather followed the thaw? But it mattered
little to me. I visited the Red Tower very often,
unheeding whether I waded through the mud or
slipped upon the ice. Count Ruttger's library had
become a sacred place to me—a spot where I liked
to be alone.

One day when I went to the steward's room as
usual to get the keys, I was told that the Countess
wanted to see me. I went upstairs at once, but
felt strangely uneasy as I approached the suite of

S

rooms to which the two ladies had removed. I tried to calm myself by the thought that my disquiet was perfectly natural, seeing that I loved the Lady Helen, in spite of her being so far above me in station, and that, by the aid of the Kabbalah —the holy art—it had been foretold that she was intended for me from the beginning.

But however I might reason with myself, I knew that it was not only the shyness of untold love, but also a foreboding of evil that oppressed me.

The servant who conducted me said that Count Leo was with the ladies, and would I be so good as to wait for a few minutes in the ante-room. The tone in which he pronounced the Count's name showed that he, like all the other servants, had a hearty detestation of that gentleman. While waiting in the ante-room, I became, much against my will, an auditor of the following conversation. Count Leo was talking louder than usual, but still in his ordinary unctuous tones, while the Countess spoke with the gentle dignity for which she was always remarkable.

'You are somewhat in error,' I heard her say, 'in assuming that my son is under your guardianship. Frank is of age, and so, according to the laws of the country, he is entitled to enter at once into full possession of his inheritance, and must therefore be regarded as head of the family. Should he need advice at any time, his mother is the natural person for him to consult. He alone has a right to express an opinion about my daughter's decision in this matter, and he will certainly put as little pressure upon his sister in respect of an affair in which the heart alone can decide—such as marriage —as his father did, or his mother would permit him to do. Helen is *my* child, and Frank is her brother.'

'And, as head of the family, has a right to dispose of his sister's hand, my dear Madam,' said Count Leo. 'That this alliance was desired by his father, will be a sufficient reason to determine my nephew to carry out a policy that would be so advantageous for his family, as the projected marriage of his sister to the noble Reichsgraf . . . .'

Helen must have entered the room as he spoke, for I now heard her sweet voice in reply.

' Uncle,' she said, ' do not put yourself in opposition to my mother, or you will force me to resist your assumed authority. You know that in such matters as these I can be guided only by my own heart, and my mother's will.'

There was so much gentle determination in her voice that my heart leapt for joy, and such was the confusion in my thoughts for a while that I did not distinguish what followed, until I heard the Countess say :

' Besides that, I had no idea, that my husband Count Arthur, had confided his last wishes on this subject to his brother Leo, and to him alone.'

I then heard the Count pronounce my name, upon which a silence ensued. It was at length broken by his going on to say:

'Let us suppose that it pleased the Lord—which may His mercy forfend—that my dear nephew Frank should be taken away.'

He was here interrupted by a deep groan from the mother. But after a moment's pause, he resumed:

'I only mean that God, in His inscrutable purposes, may have decreed that Frank should pass away from amongst us without leaving a son to inherit his estates. In which case, I, as rightful head of the family, and with a view to compassing the spiritual welfare of my father's house—a matter that, alas, has been only too long neglected—should ——'

'*You*, Leo! What do you mean?' cried the Countess in a tone of the greatest amazement. 'Why do you pass over your brother Hermann?'

'Why do you remind me of my poor brother, dear Cornelia,' said the hypocrite with a sigh. 'Oh that he were yet alive!'

'I hope to God he is,' answered the Countess; 'but at any rate, his child is still alive.'

'*That* child,' said Count Leo with curious emphasis. Then changing his tone, he went on: 'You are in a strange humour to-day, my dear sister-in-law. Suppose my brother had made over all his rights to me before he disappeared, or else

that I really am, what some people maintain, the
first-born of the twins ——'

'Does any one say that?' interrupted the
Countess.

These were the last words that I heard, for at
the same moment the servant returned, and excused
himself for having kept me waiting so long, alleging
that he had thought Count Leo would have gone
away before. He then proposed to announce my
arrival, and did so without loss of time.

Count Leo came to me at once, and holding out
his hand graciously, said in a whisper:

'The death of my brother Arthur has had a very
sad effect upon his widow; her nerves are in a
terrible state, poor woman—we must have patience
with her, Herr Pastor.'

I made him no answer, and, as soon as he left
me, hastened to join the ladies in the next room.

I found them seated in a simply furnished apartment, the walls of which were covered with a dark
flock-paper, while the heavy damask window-
curtains were made of some colour suitable for
mourning.

The Countess' face still showed traces of the
suppressed excitement awakened by the conversation my coming had interrupted. She and her
daughter were dressed in deep mourning. I
thought that Helen's pale face flushed for a
moment when I greeted her; but if it were so, it
immediately regained its former palor. After I

had seated myself, there was a short silence, which
did not surprise me, knowing, as I did, what had
just taken place.

At length the Countess, who had vainly struggled
to hide all signs of her inward disquiet, thus
addressed me :

'Herr Pastor,' she said, 'my husband looked
upon you as a friend, and we lonely women do so
too.   Tell me frankly, here in the presence of my
child, did my husband ever tell you that he was
determined to insist on his daughter's marriage to
the Reichsgraf . . .?'

I thought I could almost hear the hearts of those
two high-minded women beat as they awaited my
answer.

'Madam,' I said, 'I cannot deny that Count
Arthur once confided to me his heartfelt desire for
this marriage ; but I am also bound to inform you'
—and it seemed to me as though Helen drew a
long breath—'that your noble husband told me
decidedly that he would never use his authority to
bring it about, for all he wanted was his child's
happiness, and he would not force her to take such
a step against her will, even to ensure it.'

The Countess pressed her handkerchief to her
eyes, and said :

'Ah, how like my Arthur!   Noble and generous
under a harsh exterior!   Thank you, Herr Pastor,
you have freed me from a great dread.'

Helen also was much moved; she looked up-wards, and murmured with tearful eyes:

'Dear, kind father, why cannot I fulfil your wish!'

The ice was broken. A gentle cheerfulness that did not at all interfere with their sorrow might be read on the countenances of both women. They spoke to me more cordially than they had ever done before. The Countess enquired for my mother, and surprised me by saying that her hus-band, shortly before his death, had expressed his intention of giving me Count Ruttger's books, as they interested me so much, and were not entailed. 'No one cares about them but Pastor Bergmann,' he had said, 'and they may be useful to him.'

The Countess then questioned me about the contents of the library, and I explained its character to her as well as might be. After that she made some enquiries regarding the document containing Count Ruttger's story, which I had discovered in the secret drawer of the cabinet. Her husband had told her about it, she said, and she remembered that there was a family tradition belonging to her father's house in Holland which agreed in every respect with the contents of the manuscript in the Red Tower. The forefather of her branch of the family was said to have been the son of a German Count. After the death of his poor mother he had been adopted by a rich rela-tion, and, entering the navy later on, had fought

288 of the Devil

under Tromp and De Ruiter with such gallantry, that the States-General (during the time of their alliance with the Emperor against Louis XIV.) had made him a Baron in reward for the services he had rendered his country.

The Countess seemed much struck with the strange turn of events which had brought her, the descendant of the Dutch clergyman's daughter, as mistress to the Castle from whence the cause of all the misery of her ancestress had come. Part of the prophecy was thus fulfilled, she said, and the rest, according to the legend, which was no doubt founded on Count Ruttger's account of what the ghost had said to him, was to come to pass in a later generation. She then asked me whether I considered that the touching story of the broken-hearted man conjuring up the spirit of his dead love was a real event in Count Ruttger's life.

'At any rate,' I answered, 'the Count himself had no doubt upon the subject.'

'Do *you* believe that it is possible, by means of the Kabbalah, to bring about results similar to those Count Ruttger describes in his autobiography?' enquired the Countess, looking at me piercingly.

'I cannot deny the possibility,' I answered, and then added : 'Although, as a general rule, apparitions should not be too closely examined.'

There was a pause.

The Countess looked down thoughtfully, and I

was almost afraid to ask myself what the object of her questioning might be. For even amongst women of the Countess von Secried-Strandow's strong common-sense, good judgment, and cultivated mind, one was not astonished in those days to find a vehement desire to conjure up the dead. She loved her husband, and mourned his loss deeply. His death had been so sudden that there were probably many things she would have liked to have consulted him about, and so what wonder if she desired to call back his spirit, as Count Ruttger had done that of the Dutch girl?

'My husband,' she said at length, 'did not believe that such things were possible, as you know, Herr Pastor. Nothing would have delighted him more than the way in which you got rid of the supposed ghost of Pastor Lebrecht. The villagers are full of it.'

I breathed more freely, and the Countess went on:

' I am quite sure that the strange things we hear of as going on in Germany just now are in some cases due to the over-heated imagination of superstitious people, and in others, to the trickery of imposters. My husband was right in that. But, Herr Pastor,'—here the Countess lowered her voice to a whisper—'My Arthur's deadly injury must have taught him, even before he passed away, that there are things beyond our comprehension. I mean the Kabbalistic prophecy made

by the Amsterdam Jew, who, I am told, died in
your house on the day of my husband's funeral.'

I was confounded at this turn of the conversation.

The Countess gazed at me searchingly, and then,
finding that I made no reply, asked in the same
low tone as before :

' Do you believe that it is possible to foretell the
future by the Kabbalistic process of reckoning?'

' I have no reason to doubt the possibility of it,'
I answered quietly, and the Countess continued :

' The world gives you credit, Herr Pastor, for
knowing something of this art ; indeed, for being a
master in it, since you had Rabbi Meier for a
teacher.'

I was again silent. I could not deny that I
possessed the knowledge, and I was unwilling to
confess it in so many words. She seemed to
understand the meaning of my silence. Her face
was very grave, almost solemn, as, drawing her
chair nearer to mine, she said :

' Pastor Bergmann, you are our friend, and I can
trust you. Since my husband's death, my children
are all that remain to me, and I am very anxious
about my son, whose return we may expect any
day. Although his travelling companion enjoyed
my husband's confidence, I never liked him. My
anxiety has been ten-fold increased by a remark I
heard lately, upon which I am perhaps laying too
much weight. What widowed mother does not
hope to see her son happily settled in his heritage,

does not wish—but enough of that. I want you to do something for me, Herr Pastor. Will you answer a few questions on this subject by means of your art? Speak frankly.'

'First of all,' I answered hesitatingly, 'I must know what your questions are. I will do what I can to comfort you, Madam, and dispel your fears.'

'Not so,' she said. 'I wish to have simple, categorical answers to my questions, the bare results of your reckoning, or whatever you call it. This curiosity of mine, which comes from maternal love and anxiety, *cannot* be sinful. Will you be perfectly frank with me, my friend?'

There was a moment's pause. I could not speak at first ; but seeing her eyes fixed on me entreatingly, I replied :

'Yes, Madam, I promise ; but on one condition.'

'And what is that?'

'That your questions are not of the kind forbidden by the oath exacted by Rabbi Meier before teaching me his secret. Tell me what you desire to know.'

'These are my questions then,' said the Countess taking a long breath. 'I want to know who will be my son's bride, and whether he will have children—an heir.'

The Countess spoke these words with difficulty, and as though she had made a great effort. I was so rejoiced that she had uttered nothing as to the duration of her son's life, that it seemed as though

a great weight had been lifted from my heart. I
told her that I thought I could easily answer her
questions, if she gave me a little necessary information, which she did most willingly.

I could not have reckoned up the problem in
Helen's presence—solitude was requisite for that,
so I took leave of the ladies, saying that I would
go to the Red Tower and make the needful calculations.

A February storm was howling round the Tower,
making the flagstaff at the top groan and moan
like a living thing in agony. The wind blew great
flakes of snow through the iron stanchcons against
the window-panes, making a sort of twilight in the
library. Count Ruttger seemed to be gazing at me
with gloomy eyes from his picture. The copy in
the gallery of the Castle had not half the effect of
the old brown portrait in the Tower.

I now began my preparations. I read several
pages of a Kabbalistic work in order to bring
myself into the proper tone of mind, and to gain
strength enough to insure that I should make no
mistake. I believed that I could almost force a
favourable answer.

After that I began the operation, set down my
figures, signs, and letters, and made my calculation
without a mistake. I overlooked none of the
proper manipulations.

And yet, before I had finished, or had begun to
translate the figures into letters, I tried my calcula-

tion over again by another method, and found it correct. My heart beat as I prepared to write down the result.

I formed the letters one by one, and turned deadly pale when I saw them. 'Oh, God!' I cried inwardly, 'what is this?'

In answer to the first question came :

'*His bride, the grave.*'

And to the second :

'*Dust and ashes, his children.*'

A cry of terror escaped my lips.

I sat there as though turned to stone, staring at the horrible result of my reckoning.

Again and again I read the words which I was to repeat to the anxious mother :

'The grave his bride. Dust and ashes his children.'

This was what I was to tell the poor woman, who was watching and praying for the arrival of her only son—this was the comforting assurance with which I was to soothe her fears.

There I sat, cast down and utterly miserable. It was of no use that I repeated the whole operation from the beginning. The pale face of the Amsterdam Jew seemed to be grinning at me from every cypher, and asking me why I had not listened to the words of warning that might have saved me from my present despair.

A consciousness of the curse I had brought upon

myself flashed upon me, and hiding my face in my hands, I groaned:

'Oh, fool and blind! I know now what the old Rabbi suffered; what the fiery rods were like that gave him no rest. And I, I have undertaken to tell Helen's mother, that her son, his father's heir, will sink into an early and childless grave.'

I sat thus for a long time in despair, and then began to pace the room feverishly.

It was growing late, and I could stay no longer. So I seized the written papers with loathing, tore them in pieces, and flung them out of the window into the storm, and the wind carried them away, whirling them amongst the snow-flakes.

And now, the sooner I was gone the better.

My knees trembled as I left the room, and softly made my way down the winding-stair to the entrance door, which I locked noiselessly. I then glided along the stone passage with a beating heart. 'Oh, God, if the Countess were to meet me by any chance,' I thought. Fortunately, I passed no one on the way, and the steward's room being empty, I returned the keys unnoticed, after which I slipped out by the side door—like a thief.

How thankful I was that it was already dusk.

I nearly ran across the lawn, and into the wood. The wind was blowing gustily, catching my mantle and whistling in my ears, but I did not notice it. Nor did I remark that I was wading through deep half-melted snow, and that heavy flakes were being continually driven in my face.

Where could I hide from the Countess? How could I ever again enter her presence?

I wandered in the woods for hours, a prey to distracting thoughts, and unheeding the inclemency of the weather. When I, at last, got home, my mother was much alarmed at my appearance. I threw myself exhausted upon my bed; but was afraid to go to sleep because then the morning would seem to come more quickly. And yet I longed for sleep, to still the pain at my heart, if only for a time, but it refused to come. I tried to pray, but my prayers brought me no comfort. I tossed about in bed, vainly striving to find a cool place on which to lay my beating temples. At length I took something to make me sleep, but whenever I closed my eyes I fancied that I saw the Countess approach my bed to question me about the bride, and the children of her son. And I started up again, unable to lie still.

To-morrow, to-morrow! What was I to do? How could I always manage to keep out of the Countess' sight?

What a change had come over me! My foolhardy pride of knowledge was broken. Were not the indignant expostulations of Bachur Benasse, and the warning entreaties of Rabbi Meier well justified? Ah me, I now felt the weight of the

burden I had so recklessly taken upon my
shoulders, and experienced the horror of the curse
that falls upon all the disciples of the black art.

CHAPTER XV.

'By the eternal God, whose name and power
Thou tremblest at, answer that I shall ask ;
For, till thou speak, thou shalt not pass from hence.'
—*King Henry VI.*

'Du hast mich mächtig angezogen,
An meiner Sphäre lang' gesogen,
Und nun   .   .   .
Da bin ieh !'
—*Faust.*

IT was only momentary exhaustion that at length enabled me to close my eyes, and I started up with a cry when my mother came into the room. She questioned me anxiously as to what was the matter.

'Nothing, nothing,' was my answer. 'I only want rest.'

It was quite true. I wanted nothing but rest, and that was exactly what I could not have.

I remembered the result of my Kabbalistic reckoning with terror. If anyone passed along the road, I imagined that it was a messenger from the Countess, who came to summon me to the Castle that I might give his mistress an account of how I had sped. If there was a knock at the door, my

T

heart stopped beating, and I listened in breathless suspense. It is wonderful how inventive real terror is, and on this occasion I suffered martyrdom.

I could not sit still, so, getting my hat, I went out, and wandered aimlessly into the wood. Like a criminal, the impulse seized me to haunt the scene of my crime.

The sole object of my existence in those days of anguish was to avoid both sight and speech of the Countess. I mounted the steps of the pulpit on the following Sunday as though in a dream, and I am sure that Pastor Lebrecht's ghost could not have preached more drearily on stormy nights, than I did that day. I had once exorcised his shade from the church ; but now his restless spirit seemed to have taken possession of my body in revenge, and to drive me forth into solitary places.

If I endeavoured to draw comfort from the Bible, the book always opened at some ill-omened place, and I shuddered as I recollected the verse of Jeremiah which I had once turned up when looking for guidance :

'What wilt thou say when he shall punish thee . . . shall not pangs seize thee as a woman in travail ?'

How true it was !

Little did I know how terribly the warning was yet to be fulfilled.

I could not bear to think of my Kabbalistic studies. They filled me with horror. Wrapped in my cloak, I wandered about the wood, or across the snow-covered fields unable to still the unrest of my soul. The villagers did not know what to make of their Pastor in those days, for, when they came to consult me about anything, I either looked at them vaguely, or turning away abruptly, begged them to leave me alone.

And old Peter would shake his head sadly and mysteriously, as he muttered :

' So I was right after all ! '

A hard frost set in. One day when I was walking over the dunes, and watching the waves dashing against the shore, peace returned in some measure to my soul. I know not how. But the sound of the sea soothed and calmed me.

I turned back and went inland again. The roads and the snow were hard frozen, and a fresh breeze was blowing over the heath. I then went through the wood, where the trees were glittering and beautiful with snow and hoar frost. Tiny little snow-flakes, or rather frozen particles, were dancing in thousands in the keen air, and then falling to the ground, as it seemed, when tired of their play.

I felt more cheerful, and looked at everything from a brighter point of view. What, I told myself, what if my supposed art were only an illusion after all, and the other answers had come out right by a mere chance !

When our reason needs comfort, it is very clever

in coining it for itself. So I arranged the matter greatly to my own satisfaction, and took heart again. A revolution had taken place in my senti-ments. I now pleased myself by imagining that the secret I had so long desired to possess was of no value; that its working could not be relied upon.

Immersed in these thoughts I turned into the broad road leading through the wood without noting where I was going. A two-horse sleigh came rapidly towards me. As the Countess could not be in it, I pursued my way quietly. The sleigh came on more slowly as it approached me, and I saw that a countryman was driving. A young man wrapped in furs was seated in it, but so bent and broken did he look, that anyone not seeing his face would have taken him for an invalid of sixty. I felt a lively compassion for the stranger, for, I thought, his unhappiness must be even greater than mine.

I remained standing in the road, looking after him, and wondering where he was going. Sudden-ly the horses were pulled up; the hollow-eyed, sickly-looking stranger turned his head and looked back at me, signing with his hand that I should approach.

'Are you not Pastor Bergmann of Secried?' he enquired in a weak, husky voice.

'At your service,' I replied.

'Will you get into the sleigh and drive up to

the Castle with me?' he asked, coughing as he spoke.

I naturally declined, excusing myself on the score of having no time to go.

'Ah well,' he said, 'I suppose you are thinking out your sermon. I will not press you to come with me, Herr Pastor. I see that you do not remember me.'

I looked at him more attentively. He had pushed the furs, in which he was wrapped, a little further back, so that his clothing was visible : a blue coat with brass buttons, an embroidered yellow waistcoat, white duck trousers, and top boots—in short, the 'Werther' costume, which was then in fashion. He shivered, and drew his mantle tightly round him, but I could still distinguish his features, which did not seem altogether unknown to me, although I asked myself in vain where I could have seen him before.

'And yet,' he continued, 'we often saw each other a few years ago ; but many things have changed since then. Do you not remember me at Halle in the days when you were a wild young undergraduate there ? '

I racked my brains to think who he could possibly be, and was at last obliged to tell him that I was sorry I could not recollect his name. He smiled sadly.

'Yes,' he said, 'I am a good deal changed since the days when I was renowned as one of the best

fencers at the University.   And when you were
called away from Halle by your father's illness, I
little thought that I should meet you again as the
Pastor of Seeried, respected, and, as I hear on
competent authority, justly respected, by the whole
parish.   And besides that, I understand that, since
the death of my father, you have shown yourself a
true friend to my dear mother and sister.'

I took off my hat.   Deadly pale, my pulses flying and my heart beating almost to suffocation, I
stood before the young lord of the place, Count
Frank von Seeried Strandow, whom I had last seen
in the bloom of his youth at the University of
Halle.   He had gone out to see the world, young
and inexperienced, his father's pride, and with his
mother's blessing, and now he had come home sick
alike in body and soul.

He saw the shock his appearance had given me,
and smiled faintly.

'I am a little changed,' he said.   'Ah well, what
can you expect, Herr Pastor ; I led a wild life of
the 'storm and stress' order in Germany ; then I
went to Paris, and associated with French women
of the Philosophical School, ending up with a duel,
in which I was wounded in the right lung.   Much
as I long to embrace my mother, and see Helen—
who has grown very pretty, I hear—I am yet
afraid of terrifying the dear women with my pale
face, should they see me unprepared.'

I was so deeply moved, so saddened by what I

heard and saw that I could not answer him at first.
But feeling the necessity of putting an end to the
painful silence that ensued, I began to speak, giving utterance to the first words that occurred to
me.

' And had you no friend, no adviser at your side,
my lord Count ? ' I asked.

He tried to laugh ; but the laughter ended with
a severe fit of coughing. When it was over, he
said in a weaker voice than before :

' Oh, Ephraim Lebrecht was a capital adviser ! '

There was unmistakeable irony in his tone. He
began to cough again, and signed to me to put on
my hat.

Then shaking hands with me, he whispered : ' *à
revoir!*' and desired the coachman to drive on.

It would be impossible to describe the feelings
with which I looked after the sleigh, which was
bearing the young Count—a dying man—back to
the home of his ancestors.

The possessor of one of the finest estates, and
most enviable positions in the country was coming
back to his fair domain a hopeless invalid ! What
would be the feelings of his mother and sister when
they saw their natural protector in so sad a case ?
I could not bear to think of their sorrow, and
rushed away into the wood, and there wandered
restlessly for hours.

The Black Art was then no illusion, no phan-

tastic hallucination of the brain or senses. I
would have given worlds that it had been.

I cannot describe my agony of mind. That and
the next few days were the most wretched of my
whole life. The curse that had lain on Rabbi
Meier now rested upon me. And often, and often,
I felt inclined to hold the art I had been taught by
the old Jew responsible for the Count's misfortunes.

'Why,' I cried in my misery, 'did God ever allow
men to become acquainted with the Practical Kabbalah? Did this art, which works as a devastating
fire, really come from Him, the Source of Light?
And if not, who was its author?'

These were the questions that now tormented me.

Manifold are the opinions of even the initiated
respecting the origin of this dread art and its
earliest discoverer. I had never heard or read any
satisfactory solution of these enigmas, and was
determined to find out whether the art was of God
or of Lucifer; whether the angels had taught it to
men, or some wizard of the olden time had forced
the secret from the spirit-world.

I had made up my mind irrevocably, and having
done so, set about my preparations for carrying out
the resolution I had formed. Some Kabbalistic
works belonging to Count Ruttger's library being
necessary for the purpose, I set out one stormy,
spring-like evening by the well-known woodland
path to the Red Tower, in order to fetch them.
It was beginning to grow dusk, and I knew there

was little fear of meeting the Countess at that hour.

The old steward received me sadly, and asked whether I had seen the young Count. I nodded. He then went on to say that nothing more melancholy could well be imagined than the quiet sorrow which filled the heart of everyone at the Castle. The Countess smiled whenever she saw her son, and told nobody anything about her feelings ; but the mournful expression of her lips betrayed her secret thoughts. It was the same with the young lady, he said, and added that everyone in the household was sad at heart, for they felt that the old rule was passing away, and Count Leo would soon come to Seeried as master. Indeed, he was already taking a good deal upon him as though he were quite sure of coming into his inheritance very shortly. Nobody knew what had become of the tutor ; but they were one and all certain that he would come back soon—before he was wanted, most probably.

The old man's voice sounded to me like that of the screech-owl announcing death and disaster, and rung in my ears even when I had left him, and was walking down the stone passage leading to the Red Tower. I opened the door, and hastened up the winding stairs to Count Ruttger's library, took the books I wanted out of the cabinet, and then made the best of my way from the Castle as quietly as I had come. When I looked back at it, and saw its faint outline in the gathering darkness, I little thought it was the last time I should behold it, that I should never again visit the Red Tower.

Turning my back upon it at last, I went home with the bundle of books under my arm, and a heavy weight of anxiety upon my soul.

.   .   .   .   .   .

The night was pitch-dark. Great drops of rain beat against the window-panes, and the wind blustered and howled round the gables of the house. I was alone in my study, and secure from all interruption, for my mother had gone to bed.

I seated myself at the table, desperate in my resolution to raise the veil, to force the knowledge I desired from the spirit-world.

I seized a pen, and drew a sheet of paper close to me, exerting all my strength of will to subdue the nervous horror that threatened to master me completely.

My Kabbalistic studies had shown me only too clearly that my enterprise could not fail to cause the greatest disturbance in the spirit-world. I knew that madness or death might be my portion. ' Benasa died ; Bensoma went mad ; Acher tore the plants up by the roots, he became a heretic.' The aged Rabbi ben Akiba alone succeeded. But what of that ! One man had done it, and why should I not be as successful as he ?

The wind was blowing harder than ever. It

came in fitful gusts, making the house shake to its foundation. A more suitable night for carrying out my project could not have been found.

Oh that my calculation might once more have a prosperous issue—only this once more.

'Dark mysterious art, from whence thou comest I know not ; but be true to me to-night. There is only one question I should ask of thee, O Kabbalah ; one single thing I would know.'

Such were my thoughts, and perhaps I may have uttered them aloud :

'Wast thou taught to man by an angel or a demon ?—that is what I desire to know.'

Again I laid the books and papers in readiness beside me. My hands were quite steady now, they had ceased to tremble even before I picked up the pencil. Daniel was not bolder in giving the explanation of the words *Mene, Mene, Tekel, Upharsin,* which had been traced by a spirit hand on the plaster of the wall of the banquetting room in King Belshazzar's palace at Babylon, than I was that night—but after a different fashion !

'If no one has ever dared to ask this question, I will dare it, and thy answer, Kabbalah, shall show me whether thou art truth or delusion—should I receive no answer, I shall know that thou art the latter.'

I may not have spoken aloud ; but these were the thoughts that filled my heart ; the words that rushed to my lips.

As soon as everything was prepared, and I was in the proper frame of mind, I wrote down the question :

' *Who taught man this mysterious art ?* '

I reckoned long and anxiously. I forgot no cypher, no letter, no sign—there was not an error or oversight to be seen. I conquered all difficulties, followed all the turnings and windings of the process, pursued the figures upon which the calculation hinged as a harrier pursues the hare, and at length approached the result. The storm all at once ceased, and the stillness was so intense that I could hear the beating of my own heart. The calculation was finished, and had only to be translated into letters. This was quickly done, and I read :

' *Rash fool, beware of that thou dost !* '

Weary, worn, and pale, I sank back in my chair exhausted—but not discouraged. This was no answer to my question, but only a piece of advice I could quite well have given myself, had I chosen. It was not necessary to go through the labour I had done that evening in order to attain so poor a result. If the Kabbalah *maschiith* could tell me no more than that, I should curse the memory of him who had taught me its secret.

I flung the paper on which the warning was written contemptuously on the floor.

Well would it have been for me had I remembered the verse of the Prophecies of Jeremiah

which I had turned up for luck just before leaving
my old home in Thuringia :

'The heart is deceitful above all things, and desperately wicked : who can know it ?'

But alas, even such words as these would, I fear,
have had little effect upon me at that moment, for
my fixed determination was rooted in despair, and
despair is hard to move.

All was still quiet outside. I heard the church
clock strike eleven. The first answer I had received to my question did not content me, nor yet
did it terrify me. I brought the occult power of
word and number taught me by the Practical
Kabbalah to bear on the matter. So deeply engrossed was I, that I paid no attention to the
rising fury of the storm, which now began to rage
more wildly than before. The noises made by it
were so weird and strange, that one could easily
have imagined a tumult had arisen in the spirit-
world, that the devils were unbound. But I cared
nothing for what went on around me so long as I
was left in peace, and so there I sat writing busily
in the midst of the wild hurly-burly of the tempest.
I exerted all my strength of will, and felt sure that
I should succeed this time. My mind was clearer
than it had ever been before ; the darkest and
most mysterious rules of Kabbalistic arithmetic
became easy as child's play.

Time passed on, and I had reached a point
beyond any that I had formerly desired to attain.

And now my labours were almost at an end, and I sat there with my back to the window, bending over the paper on which I had been writing, as unmoved as though I had not penetrated the deepest mysteries that numbers could open to me.

Calmly and quietly I set to work to complete the calculation. As the fisherman draws his fish out of the net, so I drew my figures from the arithmetical network before me. The storm had again subsided ; not a sound was to be heard without. The answer to my question was found ; but was as yet hidden by seven seals.

For one moment I hesitated—but not from fear. I did not want to be in too great a hurry.

At length I broke seal after seal—and—there it was.

I saw the words distinctly. Why did I not read them aloud ? Why did I sit there so pale, and silent, and motionless ? Why did my hair stand on end, and my eyes seem as though they would start out of their sockets ?

Yes, my heart stood still, and my blood froze in my veins as I sat in speechless horror, unable to move.

And yet my desire was fulfilled ! I had received an answer to my question, and there it was, written clearly and distinctly upon the paper—seven simple words. That was all !

Ah, but those words !

' *Turn thee about—he stands behind thee !* '

There was an awful pause, like a moment of eternity. A deep silence reigned. Why did I not move, and look round ?

My head kept stiffly in the same position, my hands clung to the edge of the table, and my teeth chattered like castonets.

It was a terrible expiation of my rashness, for I dared not look upon the spirit I had conjured up—fear and horror unutterable had seized upon me.

Who and *what* was that behind me.

I do not know.

How long I sat staring at the words, and bathed in a cold perspiration I cannot tell.

Suddenly a shiver passed down my back. And something seemed to rise slowly, softly, and yet audibly behind me—an icy hand touched my throat and hair, then caught me up with superhuman strength, and flung me violently upon the hard deal floor. I felt the stinging pain of the fall, and then I seemed to be surrounded by a burning heat.

After that all was darkness. I had become unconscious.

CHAPTER XVI.

' Du wurdest ja so ernst, da sie die Leiche
  Vorüber trugen.'

KLOPSTOCK.

' Ist es wahr was mir begegnet?
  Oder Traum, der mich bethört?'

BÜRGER.

THE bold fool-hardy questioner lay senseless upon the floor. He, who in his fancied strength desired to know the secrets of the spirit-world, to raise or, if need be, tear the veil that separates it from humanity, lay prone on the ground an inanimate mass, more feeble than the little wood-louse, or death-watch, as it is called, whose tap, tap, tap, used to go on all night in the bookcase close at hand.

I do not know how long I lay there after my fall.

I did not hear my mother's knock in the morning, nor did I see her come into the room. She found me lying on the floor insensible close to the table, which was covered with books and writing materials. The lamps had gone out, and some bits of charred paper that had evidently been written on were scattered about the room. My mother's cry of grief and terror did not arouse me; but it was heard outside, and brought several of the neighbours to her assistance.

They used every effort to restore me—for a long time in vain. But at length there was a faint movement, and I was gradually brought back to life; though not to consciousness. The weeks that followed are a blank in my memory. I know nothing that went on during that time. It forms a distinct boundary line, a deep gulf, separating my earlier from my later life. I was afterwards told that I was put to bed, and that the Countess, who had two clever doctors staying at the Castle to attend Count Frank, made them look after me also, besides showing my mother many other kindnesses.

Whenever I think of that time, and of what my mother must have endured—her sorrow, and patience, her sleepless nights by the sick-bed of her unconscious son, her resignation and gentleness—I feel doubly sensible of my guilt. Before the catastrophe of my life she had been a strong, middle-aged women, with thick, soft hair, black and glossy as a raven's wing; when I came to myself again, her face was worn and sad, and her hair as white as snow.

The first day of my illness that I can remember was warm and sunny. I was sitting in a comfortable arm-chair under a blossoming elder tree, with

my mother at my side.   The flower-beds were a
blaze of tulips, auriculas, and wallflower; butter-
flies and bees were fluttering and humming all
around ; a bulfinch was singing on an apple tree
close by, and a stork was clanging somewhere
above me.   I saw that the spring was come.   But
surely it was very quickly.   Yesterday, winter; and
to-day, sunshine and flowers.   Where are we, I
enquired.   In the back-garden of Seeried Parsonage, said my mother, and then asked whether I did
not   recognise   the   sacristan's   grand-daughter,
Chrissy, who was standing behind the hedge at the
bottom of the garden with her little brother, and
looking anxiously to see how ' the Herr Pastor '
was getting on.   Yes, I recognised her.   But
where was the other girl, who had stood there once
before   at   her   side ?   I   now   remembered   that
moment distinctly.   Why was Christina dressed in
black, was my next question.   She was in mourning for her grandfather, my mother answered. · Old
Peter had died a short time before.   All his longing had been to follow his master, Count Arthur,
and serve him as faithfully in the other world as
he had done in this, and now he had gone to join
him.   Old Peter dead ?   And I had not buried
him.   I must have been ill for a long time.

And so one memory after another came back to
me as the days went on ; but of the events that
had led to the catastrophe my mother never spoke.

It was not until I was one morning walking in

the burial-ground leaning on my stick, and came to a memorial stone marking a grave, between two other mounds planted with roses, that the recollection of that time came back to me. I stood still, and gazed at the stone with its Hebrew inscription, and the blossoming elder that overshadowed it. I read the name and the date of the death of the old Jew, Rabbi Meier, who had been my guest at the Parsonage during the last days of his life. And slowly my memory awoke. I recollected the penitent, and his wanderings on the face of the earth, his talks with me, his occult knowledge, and—I repented deeply at the thought—his warnings, and his legacy. I continued to stare at the grave, and muse upon the past. I remembered having buried Rabbi Meier, all the circumstances connected with his death and his warnings were clear to my mind. I could, however, but dimly recall the events which followed that fatal night on which he had taught me his secret. Was it really true that I had put the Rabbi's legacy to so ill a use, and with such dreadful consequences, or had I merely dreamed? I could not feel sure upon this point; but the beating of my heart, and the feeling of dread that came upon me at the thought, seemed to show that it was no dream.

One bright spring day I went out into the front garden, and sat down in the sunshine, facing the road. I was still very weak, and unable for much exertion. The air was perfumed with the scent of the elder-blossom and early roses. Everything reminded me of the day on which my mother and I had arrived at Seeried, and I had made the acquaintance of Count Arthur and his lovely daughter. I wondered what had become of the Countess Helen, and why I never saw her; for my mother had told me long stories of the sympathy and kindness she had met with from the two ladies during the long anxiety of my illness, and it seemed strange to hear nothing of them now.

The church-bell began to ring, and changed the current of my thoughts, which now turned upon the old Jew and his art, and I strove to arrive at a clearer idea of that time just preceding my illness, so that I might the better separate false impressions from the true. While thus meditating, I listened unconsciously to the solemn tolling of the bell, but was soon afterwards startled out of my reverie by the sound of people coming down the road, singing. Every moment they came nearer. Who were they, I wondered, and why were they singing that mournful air?—

> ' When our heads are bowed with woe,
>   When our bitter tears o'erflow,
>   When we mourn the lost, the dear,
>   Jesu, Son of Mary, hear.'

The words came clearly to me, and at the same instant six black horses turned the corner by the nearest cottage, drawing a hearse, on which was laid a coffin decked with flowers. They came on slowly towards the church. Following the hearse were a number of servants dressed in black, each bearing a lighted candle, and in front of them, a tall, grave-looking man, with whose face I was well acquainted. It was Count Leo. Walking before the procession was Pastor Koch of Strandow in full canonicals, accompanied by another clergyman, whose hair was of the fieriest shade of red. And upon the coffin I saw a shield bearing the coat of arms with the well-known herons as supporters. The funeral train stopped at the church gate.

'Who,' I asked myself with a beating heart, 'who are they going to bury, and I not there?'

My mother came to me and her eyes were full of tears. When I asked whose funeral it was, she replied that they were burying young Count Frank, who had come home some weeks before, only to die amongst his own people.

I trembled like an aspen leaf; the recollection of how I had consulted the Kabbalistic oracle flashed into my mind, and also the answer I had received:

'His bride the grave. Dust and ashes his children!'

It was true then that I had had dealings with the supernatural. It was no dream. I had really lived through the terrors of that fearful night. I was a Kabbalist!'

I was deeply moved.

When the corpse of the son was laid in the vault beside that of his father, I hid my face in my hands and wept. The tears brought me relief. As soon as I was calm again I raised my hands in prayer. Although I did it in fear and trembling, I could not chose but do so. I returned to the God of my fathers, a humble and penitent man. Evil-doer, and obstinately self-sufficient as I had been, I felt that God would listen to my cry. I confessed my sin against Heaven, and against man also, for I knew that I had caused much suffering to my mother, my friend, and faithful old Peter. I prayed for young Count Frank, his mother and sister. I prayed for myself too, entreating that God would judge me mercifully, and have compassion upon the human weakness, which I, in my blindness, had mistaken for strength ; that He would henceforward keep me with His strong right hand, and take my arrogance away from me ; that He would keep me steadfast in the faith, until my spirit, freed from the bonds of mortality, should receive the knowledge it was forbidden to attain while here below. I prayed long and earnestly. I thanked God for having had mercy upon me, and taught me to repent the error of my ways. That I was yet alive was owing to His goodness. I thanked Him for my dear mother's sake.

Gradually a clear recollection returned to me of all that had occurred before my illness, except on one point. I could not remember the secret Rabbi

Meier had taught me.   It was gone from me completely, and for ever.   It was as thoroughly gone
as though I had never possessed the key to the
Practical Kabbalah.   I thanked God that it was
so, and never tried to regain the lost knowledge.

.   .   .   .   .

I have but little more to tell you.

The first day on which I re-entered my study I
still felt very weak.   Every thing looked much as
usual.   The bookcase was as I had left it, with
Klopstock's poems lying open on the top shelf.
My papers were scattered about the table, and
lying beside them were some volumes from the
Kabbalistic library in Count Ruttger's Tower.
But not a trace remained of the calculations I had
made, or of the papers in which I had preserved
Rabbi Meier's secret.   I was glad of it.   The
extracts I had made from the Baptismal Register
were lying on the table.   On seeing them I was
suddenly reminded of the loose sheet of paper on
which the notices of the birth and baptism of the
twins were wrongly recorded, and began to look
for it, but could find it nowhere.   When I turned
up the place in the Register where the true record
had been made, I was very much astonished to
find that Count Leo, instead of his brother
Hermann, was entered as the eldest, as in the
forged document.   It was incredible.   Whilst I
was thinking over it, and wondering when the false

entry had been substituted for the true one, Count
Leo entered the room, accompanied by my old
acquaintance, Ephraim Lebrecht.   They both
bowed stifly.   I at once embraced the opportunity
of drawing their attention to the alteration that
had been made in the Church Register.   They
looked at each other strangely, and then Count
Leo said :

'I am sorry to see that your memory has suffered
as well as your mind, Herr Pastor.   Allow me to
present your successor to you.   He will at once
enter upon his duties, as the parish has been only
too long neglected ; but in consideration of your
delicate health, you may remain at the Parsonage
for another week.'

I did not know what to say, for I was both hurt
and surprised ; so I contented myself with looking
full at Count Leo and his companion, and held my
peace.   My mother had already told me that
Ephraim Lebrecht had been acting as my proxy
during my illness, and had therefore been at the
Parsonage very often.   He obviously did not like
my silence.   I saw that he was brimming over
with malice, and determined to say nothing.
Tired of waiting, he at length began :

'Well, Bergmann, I understand that you have
succeeded in attaining the object of your ambition
in the old days at Halle.   I hear that you have
become a great Kabbalistic light.   Every one
hereabouts is tremendously excited on the subject

of your wonderful prophecies, and I foresee that I shall have a good deal of trouble in cooling them down, and making them listen to the simple doctrines of Christianity. Professor Semler wishes to be remembered to you. He congratulates you on having pushed your studies so far, which, indeed, you could not have done, had I not drawn your attention to the Book of the *Baal Teschuba* long before you found it in the Red Tower. The only thing that surprises me is, that a soothsayer like you should not have foreseen the moment when the command of Scripture should be carried out, and the wizard be no longer suffered to remain in the land.'

I saw that it was their object to rouse me, and make me speak unwisely. But I was too deeply hurt to attempt to answer. They, therefore, turned to each other, exchanged meaning glances, and began to talk about my wrong-headedness and folly as openly as though they considered that I had lost my wits during my illness, and could not understand them. With a mighty effort, I controlled myself, and made them no reply. At last they went away disappointed.

I will say no more of the impression this meeting made upon me. In spite of my weakness, and my right to remain, I hurried on our preparations for returning to Thuringia, so feverishly, that we were ready to start on the second morning after receiving notice to quit. In the midst of my labours, I often thought of the Countess and her daughter, and wondered what would become of them.

On the evening before our departure, a carriage drove up to the garden-gate, and the Countess and Helen came in to say good-bye. It was a sorrowful meeting.

The elder lady highly approved of my determination to leave the place without loss of time, and privately—I did not hear of it until long after —gave my mother a considerable sum of money to save us from pecuniary embarassment till my health was re-established, and I could get another appointment. She told us that she and her daughter were also going away, and intended to take up their abode in Holland with some of her relations. Secried was too much changed for them to care to remain. None of us mentioned Count Leo, or discussed whether he would at once constitute himself guardian to his brother's child, or whether he would first of all make enquiries as to what had become of Hermann, and endeavour to procure legal proof of his death.

It was a painful parting. The Countess told me that it comforted her to think, that should she soon be taken away, her daughter would always find friends in my mother and me. When Helen gave me her hand in farewell, she trembled, and I was no less moved than she. On drawing away her slender fingers, I found that she had left a ring in my hand.

'Keep it in remembrance of me, Herr Pastor,' she whispered, 'until we meet again ; perhaps we may, even on earth.'

And so we parted.

I was thankful that we were going away early next morning, for all the ties that bound me to Seeried were broken. By the wish of the Countess, who was taking her daughter's foster-sister Christina with her to Holland, my mother and I undertook the charge of her little brother, Peter, who, now that the good old Sacristan was dead, would otherwise have been left alone in the village. The boy went with us to the country town in Thuringia where I had been born and brought up, and where we were now received with open arms by our old friends.

Several weeks passed quietly away, and I grew daily stronger. We were not without anxiety as to the future, for I could hear of no vacant living for which I might apply. My mother's bent figure and worn face were a continual reproach to me ; but she encouraged me in every way, and told me not to be down-hearted, but trust in the Lord.

We were sitting together one evening. Little Peter had been sent to bed as usual after supper, and my mother, her horn spectacles on her nose, was busily engaged reading the 29th Psalm in a low murmur to herself; 'The Lord hear thee in the day of trouble ; the name of the God of Jacob defend thee ; send thee help from the sanctuary, and strengthen thee out of Zion.'

Suddenly, the door of our sitting room opened, and, to my intense astonishment, Bachur Benasse walked in. It was he whom I once entreated to teach me the secret of the Practical Kabbalah, and to whom I had afterwards sent the packet Rabbi Meier had left addressed to him. He now advanced towards me, greeted me as an old friend, and told me that the son he had long desired had been given him, to the great joy of himself and his people. He thanked me for the kindness I had shewn a pious man—he meant Rabbi Meier—and said it was a deed that bound his family to mine in gratitude for ever, and that when his little David was a learned Rabbi, he should requite us for what we had done for a stranger and an Israelite. He then informed me that if I would like to have a living in a beautiful part of Franconia, I had only to say so, and he would use his influence to get it for me. Little as I then trusted his power of fulfilling his promise, and only regarding it as a proof of his good-will, I have yet had reason to be grateful to him for my presentation to Hainbucken, for my home in this quiet valley, where I have lived a busy, and—I thank God—a useful life for the last forty years.

And so God helped us again out of our difficulties.

Year after year passed away uneventfully. I heard little of what was going on in the great world outside the peaceful valley in which I lived, and worked amongst my people, and still less did I know of what had happened at Seeried since I left it. Not a line reached me from the Countess or her daughter, and I was sorry, for I would have given much to hear where they were, and how they were getting on. I wondered whether they ever thought of us. I thought of them so often, of the happy hours I had spent with them at the Castle, of the first time I had seen Helen, and of the last, when she had gone away leaving the little ring in my hand, which was now my greatest treasure. I no longer nursed the hope that she might one day be my wife, I had learnt resignation—and that God knew what was best for all of us.

And so the years went on, until the long-pent revolutionary storm burst over France, carrying all before it, and spreading beyond the confines of the country of its birth, made its influence felt in Holland and the Rhineland.

In the midst of that tumultuous period a letter arrived at the Parsonage from Cologne. It was sealed with black wax, and was signed H. Vanburgh. Its purport was to ask whether we would receive two lonely women into our quiet family. Their parents were dead, and they wanted to find a secluded spot where they might live undisturbed by the dangers and difficulties of the time. I immediately despatched a letter to say how pleased I was to have it in my power to offer them the asylum they desired under my roof, and with trembling hope awaited the answer.

No letter came ; but one day when my mother and I were seated at the parlour window, a carriage drove up to the door. I started from my seat and hastened out. Two women were seated in the carriage—Christina, old Peter's grand-daughter, and beside her, a pale and beautiful lady, in whose countenance I saw the spiritualised features of the child, who once, in years gone by, had driven past me on a heath in the North Country, and who had afterwards welcomed me to Seeried from behind the churchyard fence.

How can I describe our meeting. My mother wept with joy. Christina laughed aloud as she embraced her brother Peter. And Helen, dear Helen, stood before me, looking more like an angel than ever. We clasped each other's hands, and gazed at one another, our eyes shining through tears.

That was how Helen, daughter of Count Arthur von Seeried-Strandow, came to our beautiful valley accompanied by her foster-sister. She was a blessing to us, and to the whole parish. She held no communication with her relatives in the North, but lived for us as Helen Vanburgh. It had been her mother's wish that she should do so, and it was her own. My mother lived to see, what she called the happiest day of her old age, our wedding-day.

And so Helen became my wife, as Rabbi Meier

had once foretold. The blessing of God rested on us, and we were happy.

Helen's possessions arrived later on from Cologne, packed in two large waggons. Her brother Frank had given her the portrait of Count Ruttger that had hung in the Red Tower, and the cabinet containing the Kabbalistic books, as none of them had ever been entailed. And the sight of the cabinet always kept me in lively remembrance of the lesson I had learnt on that terrible night at Seeried.

I now began to study the Kabbalah from another point of view, and derived much valuable instruction from its pages ; not only in the light thrown by its wisdom on many dark places in Holy Writ, but also as regarded what would otherwise have been incomprehensible riddles in the history of the development of early Christianity, and of certain phenomena in the civilization of diverse peoples, to say nothing of important explanations of various phases of our modern philosophy. I now learnt rightly to understand its principles, and saw that they had much in common with those contained in the Parsi-ism of Zoroaster, which is a later incorporation of the ancient myths of those races who dwelt by the Ganges and Indus, and as far west as the Euphrates. I now learnt to comprehend the Sohar, or Book of 'Splendour,' which treats of all the problems of the mind and spirit, and often rises to the sublimest heights in its

teaching. I learnt to separate the chaff from
the wheat. I was taught all this by entering
into correspondence with one of the wisest and
best men that ever lived. I mean David
Benasse, son of the poor Bachur in my native
town, and grandson of the old Jew, of whom I
had been so terrified in my childhood. Although
young in years, he was a learned man; for he was
early initiated in the mysteries of his forefathers,
and was the heir of Rabbi Meier's legacy. His
occult knowledge did him no harm. Far from
tempting him to arrogance, it only served to fill his
heart to overflowing with love to God and man.
His knowledge embraced wisdom. He might
have shone in the eyes of the world; but he has
chosen rather to lead a humble and retired life—he
is a saint in the sight of God. Even now he is not
old in years; but is ripe in experience, and in
knowledge of the true proportion of things. The
Kabbalah, which had such a ruinous effect on the
morals of all who studied it, for the sake of power,
towards the close of last century, has been a well-
spring of enlightenment to him—a beneficent and
purifying influence. When the grandfather of his
late wife, the Patriarch Jacob Frank, appeared in
Germany, everybody was disgusted with Occultism,
because of the recent discovery of the impudent
imposture practised on society by Cagliostro.
People were tired of Mysticism, and when the
French Revolution broke out soon afterwards, it—

to use a vulgar expression—made a clean sweep of the Spirits, and brought about as complete a change in philosophy as in politics. Materialism carried everything before it, and still reigns supreme. David Benasse is one of the few, who, in this time of unbelief, spend their lives in nursing and keeping alight the divine spark within themselves and others, to the unspeakable comfort of all who come in contact with them.

Once, however, when our friend, David Benasse, was staying with us, he let fall some mysterious words, to the effect that when the time should be fulfilled, the rightful heir should have his own again. He should live to see that day, he said, and so would my daughter, your wife, whose cup of happiness would then be full. Whether this was merely a guess on his part, or whether Rabbi Meier had foretold it in the sealed packet he had left to the Benasses, I do not know. But Christina at least firmly believes that his words will come true, for she declares that they are in perfect agreement with the old family traditions her grandfather used to relate.

And now, my son, I have told you the secret of my life, the history of that terrible night, when my self-sufficient arrogance was punished, and God had mercy upon me, undeserving as I was. Let my experience serve as a lesson and a warning to you long after I am laid under the sod. Have God ever before your eyes, and do not seek to know more than He has permitted to man.

Yes, my son, I know that you will take the loving advice of your old father-in-law to heart, and follow it—letting the story of my temptation and fall be a warning to you. With this conviction I can die in peace. God grant that I am right! Amen.

L'ENVOI.

Here the old clergyman's story ended. But whoever is interested in the fortune of the Seerieds, and cares to know how the forged certificate, which Rabbi Meier had hidden behind the frame of Count Ruttger's portrait, was discovered, and how the rightful heir came by his own again exactly two hundred years after the 'Black Count's' death, will find an account of this, and many other matters, in the history of Count Hermann's grandson, as preserved among the family archives in the Muniment room in the Red Tower.